With All My

Heart and Soul

Also by Jim Overturf

With All My Heart and Soul

A Swift River Valley Inspirational Romance

Jim Overturf

Three Cords Publishing

Lincoln, Nebraska

With All My Heart and Soul

A Swift River Valley Inspirational Romance

Copyright (c) 2017 by Jim Overturf

Cover by Victorine Lieske
vicki@victorinelieske.com

ISBN 978-0692926222

Three Cords Publishing, Inc.
5100 N. 27th St., Ste. A-2, PMB-306
Lincoln, Nebraska 68521

Printed in the United States of America

We dedicate this book to Him,
the One who knows our Hearts and Souls

*Thank you to my beloved Karen Lee,
my wife, my friend, my prayer-partner,
and my editor.*

*May the blessings of our Lord be
forever imprinted upon our hearts.*

CHAPTER ONE

Lucky glanced at his wristwatch. *Do I have enough time? I promised them I'd be there.* He did a double take at his watch. *Maybe I'll be okay.*

He looked up in time to see a plume of spray coming at him and jumped to one side. He moved a little farther away from the edge of the Winner's Circle. Angie's fans were having a wild time filling the air with sprays from foaming 2-liter Coca-Cola and Pepsi bottles. Lucky took the small black book out of his shirt pocket and slipped it into his pants pocket.

I don't need a sticky Bible.

The June sun was high in the sky and blazing yellow. During the race, a light breeze had stirred the air. The draft of twenty-six race cars zooming around the track had kept the air moving and comfortable. When the airflow stopped, the odor of burnt rubber, oil, and gasoline filled the air in the pit row of the racetrack. Lucky heard the dull sound of laughter and gaiety from Angie's fans, celebrating her third win of the season, and quickly dug the earplugs out of his ears.

The race was a repeat of the Kings Rapids race two weeks before, between Angie Prescotte and Jiggs Borsche—Lucky's boss. Today, however, Angie won by two car-lengths—not a layer-of-paint photo-finish.

The revelry died down as Angie climbed out of the car and took a long drink from one of the proffered Diet Coke bottles. Fans gathered around waiting to congratulate her. After a brief revelry, many blended into the throng of people at the edge of the grandstand or left for the parking lots.

Lucky glanced at his wristwatch and then watched as the TV crew moved into the circle. The cameraman focused on the blue and red, flamed hood of the number 27 race car. The producer waved for Angie to join them.

Angie was animated and radiant. Her face glistened in the sun from a

1

film of sweat mixed with oily grime. Her hair was plastered to her head where the webbing of her helmet rode. Her red, blue and gold racing outfit gave her a formless body.

Angie is a very attractive woman. Lucky nodded and smiled at the thought.

"Angie is a nice person to be around," Lucky said aloud, and quickly glanced around to make sure no one had overheard him.

After Angie had finished the interview, Lucky hung back while a long line of fellow drivers, car owners, and fans congratulated Angie on her win. He checked the length of the line and glanced at his watch again.

Maybe I'd better just leave for home. The kids are probably wondering where I am.

Lucky noted that Christina and Kurt Maxxon were the last ones in line. He moved in line behind Kurt.

Lucky fidgeted, trying to decide what to do.

Kurt turned and nudged Christina as he saw Lucky.

"Hi, Lucky," Christina said, as Lucky raised his wristwatch to eye level. "You seem nervous. Everything okay?"

"The kids are in a program at church this evening," Lucky said. "I promised them I'd be there for it."

"That's over a two-hour drive," Kurt said, looking at his wristwatch. "It's already after five o'clock."

"I know," Lucky said. "Maybe I better just go ahead and leave."

"What time does the program start?" Christina asked.

"Seven."

"You can't make it," Kurt said. "No sense—"

"I promised them," Lucky interrupted. "I—"

"I bet the kids would rather have you alive, safe and sound, rather than risking your life trying to make it home from here now," Christina said.

"The kids will be okay if you don't get to the church," Kurt said. "Kids have a way of compensating for disappointments."

"The victory party is at the Sun Setter Suites," Christina said. "Why don't you come and relax a bit?"

"Oh, I suppose you're right. It's just—it's just that I don't like breaking my word to them."

"Call them and let them know you'll stay here tonight," Christina said. "See if someone at your church will share videos of them in the program. Kurt and I love seeing videos of our grandbabies like that."

"You worked pretty hard today in the pit," Kurt said. "Come to the party, stay the night over here and go to Masonville tomorrow morning."

"I don't have a room reservation."

Christina pulled her cell phone from her fanny pack and dialed a number.

"We'll get you a room," Kurt said. "Do you know where the Sun Setter Suites are?"

Lucky wobbled his head. "No. I've just come to the track and gone back home before."

"Go out the east side of the track and turn left on River Flats Road," Kurt said, turning to gesture the direction. "The Suites are about three miles north of here. You'll see it on the left side of the road."

"I might as well," Lucky said. He'd heard about the victory parties from his boss, Jiggs Borsche. Jiggs was the one who suggested Lucky might enjoy helping in the pits during the race. He was probably talking about his own pit, but Lucky had met Kurt Maxxon first, it was Kurt who helped him get the job working for Jiggs.

This was the first-time Lucky had worked in the pit during a race. Kurt Maxxon and mechanic Maurey Kennedy had him help change the tires and gas the car during the regularly scheduled breaks in the race.

Lucky let his focus rest on Angie.

This party might be fun.

"That was a decisive win, today," Lucky said to Kurt. "Not like the last race where it was a photo finish."

"Angie did great today," Kurt said. He added, "You did a good job, too. I really appreciate your help in the pit today."

"I can't remember when I had so much fun trying something new."

"Anytime you want to help, just sing out," Kurt said.

Lucky moved aside so he could see Angie around Kurt. As Christina moved toward Angie, a small boy, wearing a scaled-down red, blue and gold, number 27 racing jacket, ran up to Angie. He whipped off his number 27 cap and handed it to her along with a black marker. In one motion Angie took the cap, signed her name on the bill, leaned down and gave the boy a hug along with a kiss on the top of his head. The startled boy looked up at Angie, and after a few seconds said, "Thank you, ma'am." He raced off toward his parents standing off to the other side.

Lucky glanced at the crowd, then at his watch. *I'll call Granny. Tell her I lost track of time.*

He tapped Kurt on the shoulder and moved up between Kurt and Christina to talk to both. "I'm going to call Granny Watson, and let her know. I'll be back in two seconds."

They nodded, and he walked away.

After finding a quiet corner away from the track, behind the grandstand, Lucky pulled his cell phone from his pocket.

Granny Watson answered on the third ring. "Hello, Kyle."

Lucky smiled every time Granny Watson insisted on using his christened name. "I'm going to stay in Evandale tonight."

"Where at?"

"I'll be at the Sun Setter Suites. They're here in Evandale, two, three miles north of the racetrack. There's going to be a victory party since Kurt Maxxon's car won the race—"

"I listened to the race on the radio," Granny Watson said, "The driver is a girl."

"Yes, and a very attractive girl," Lucky said. "I want to get to know her better."

"Is she married?"

"No. Her boyfriend was killed in a car wreck a couple of years ago."

"That's too bad. Is she looking for a man?"

"I don't think so, Granny. She is one whale of a race driver. She could probably have any one of a dozen young single drivers in the league."

"Never hurts to ask."

"How is Sophia doing with her math homework?" Lucky asked.

"I think she got it. She seemed satisfied that she was ready for the exam tomorrow."

Lucky felt guilty about Sophia having to take a remedial summer school course in math. "I wish I could have helped her more," Lucky said. "Unfortunately, I was never very good at math."

"Me neither," Granny Watson said. "It runs in the family."

Lucky glanced at his wristwatch and realized the time. "Are the kids there?"

"Nah! They got antsy to get to church. So they left a few minutes ago."

Lucky felt another shiver of guilt constrict his chest. Even though it was only eight blocks, Lucky always drove the children to church. "I'm sorry I wasn't there to drive them."

"It didn't bother them," Granny Watson said. "Kids have a way of getting through and over things that bother us. They would have left early anyway."

"Thank goodness," Lucky said. "Good night, Granny. Thank you for all you do for us."

After he ended the call, Lucky stood for a minute praying, "Please, Lord. Watch over the kids tonight and help them perform to the best of their abilities. And, please, help them understand that I didn't mean to desert them. Thank you, Lord."

Lucky rejoined Kurt and Christina in line, just as Angie was greeting the last two people ahead of them.

* * *

Angie watched Christina walk toward her and stepped into her embrace. Behind Christina, she saw Kurt Maxxon, and behind Kurt, Angie could see the coal black, wavy hair of the guy who had helped in the pit all day.

"Congratulations," Christina said. "There was no question about who won today's race."

Angie grinned and bobbed her head. "Yeah. Jiggs was two car lengths behind me today. Not nose-to-nose like two weeks ago, at Kings Rapids."

Christina stood aside to let Kurt approach Angie. "You did great today," Kurt said as he hugged Angie. "I'm proud of you."

A thrill rippled down Angie's spine.

To have Kurt Maxxon say, "I'm proud of you" is the highest praise I can get.

At the back of her diary, Angie kept a folded sheet of paper with Kurt Maxxon's historical racing records: Wins, seconds, thirds, fourths, fifths, top ten wins, and DNFs. On the same sheet, Angie kept a running matrix of her own racing records. She never compared her short career with Kurt's, but she secretly hoped to someday equal and eventually, do better than Kurt.

"Maybe Jiggs will take me seriously, not," Angie said to Kurt.

"Oh, Jiggs takes you seriously," Kurt said. "But he can't let you see the fear in his eyes." Kurt grinned and moved aside to let Lucky move toward Angie.

"You are really a great driver," Lucky said.

Angie beamed brightly. "Thank you," she said. "I don't really know your name. Uh, other than Lucky?"

"Yes ma'am," Lucky said, slowly. "My Christian name is Kyle Tipton O'Rourke. I've always been known as Lucky."

"How come?"

"My pa started it when I was still toddling around. I guess each time I survived another scrape, he'd say: 'Boy, you are lucky to still be alive.'"

They both laughed.

"I think I saw you at the first two races. Right?"

Lucky dipped his head. "Yes, ma'am. I was there. I sat in the first row of the grandstand."

"Well, Mr. Lucky, you must be my good luck charm. I think you're the reason I've won the first three races of the season, and I thank you very much for that."

"You're, uh, you're very welcome," Lucky stammered. "And you're going to win a bunch more this year."

"I hope you're right," Angie said. "I really appreciate your help in the pit during rest breaks. You make me feel like a special lady while I'm climbing in and out of Nikki." Angie chuckled audibly.

"Thank you," Lucky said. "You *are* a special lady, and you deserve as much attention as your car." Lucky moved aside, but there were no others in line waiting to see Angie. The Winner's Circle celebration had lost all but a handful of people. The noise level had diminished considerably.

They watched as Maurey Kennedy drove up with Nikki's enclosed transporter behind his pickup. Maurey deftly backed the trailer in front of Angie's car and got out of his truck. Even though she had been the best car today, Angie's car—Nikki—looked forlorn sitting alone in the middle of the Winner's Circle. Kurt helped Maurey open the double doors of the trailer and pulled one ramp out while Maurey pulled the second ramp into position.

Angie walked beside Nikki, steering, while Kurt, Lucky, and Maurey pushed Nikki up the ramps and into the transporter. Then Kurt and Maurey climbed into the trailer to secure Nikki for the ride home. Lucky watched how they did it so he could help the next time.

"Thanks for hauling Nikki home for me," Kurt yelled as Maurey climbed into his pickup.

"Have fun at the party," Maurey called as he waved and drove off.

Other people around the Winner's Circle watched the winning car leaving the track. A few shouted kudos to Angie as they walked away.

With Nikki safely on her way to her garage in Centralia, Angie looked toward her red Porsche Carrera sitting in the driver's parking lot.

"I'm going to the hotel," Angie said to Christina.

As she lowered herself into her car, the chill from her wet racing suit made her shiver. She studied her face in the rearview mirror—streaked with sweat and grime. Her hair was mussed from the helmet lining.

Time for a hot shower and then kick back and relax.

* * *

Lucky watched Angie walk toward her car. *Not only is Angie very attractive, but, she's also smart, witty, and terribly athletic.*

"We're leaving for the party," Kurt yelled to Lucky. "You want to follow us?"

"No. I'm parked way out in the far parking lot. Go ahead. I'll find it somehow." Lucky glanced at his wristwatch. Another shiver of guilt gripped his chest.

Lucky walked to his service truck, sitting at the edge of the nearly empty parking lot.

He swung his legs into the cab and settled into the driver's seat, Lucky raised his eyes upward. He took a deep breath. "Thank You, Lord, for giving me such a good life."

CHAPTER TWO

As she drove across the huge racetrack parking lot, Angie dug out her cell phone from the console between seats. She used her thumb to punch the buttons to call home on the speaker phone. "Hi, Mom. How are you guys doing?"

"We listened to the race on the radio. We're both *really happy* you won again."

Angie knew her mother and Auronia would listen to the race. "Yeah. It was great. How is Auronia?"

"She's fine. You want to talk to her? She's playing in her room watching TV."

"I hope she's not watching one of those stupid cartoony electronic games you keep playing just to keep her occupied."

"There's nothing wrong with the cartoons," her mother chided. "She's only two years old. It'll be years before she's ready for college."

"I want her taking part in the Early Childhood Education stuff that I bought for her," Angie said. "Learning about animals, foreign peoples, science, math, so she will grow up to be a useful human being. Kids who just sit and watch cartoons all day long grow up to be the kids you see on the TV every night—in trouble with the police."

Angie could tell her mother was walking down the hall, while she fumbled with the buttons on her cell phone to put it on speaker. "Your Mommy is on the phone."

"Hi, Mommy," she heard Auronia yell. "You won the race, huh? The man said it looked easy."

Angie chuckled. "Yes, Baby, I won. Are you happy for me?"

"I'm always happy for you, Mommy. Even more when you win."

"What were you playing with?"

"I'm learning my numbers on the computer."

"That's a good girl. You need numbers so you can learn to count. And, you need the alphabet so you can learn to read all those books you have in your bookcase."

"Nana took me to Sunday school this morning, and they showed us how to read a story about Jesus. I want to read more stories about Jesus. Is that okay, Mommy?"

"That's great," Angie said. "The more you know about Jesus, the better off you will be. You already have several books on your bookshelf about Jesus and other religious stuff."

"How soon can I read them?"

"You're learning to read now. Those books will just become part of your reading list."

"What's a reading list?"

"It's a list of books you want to read."

"Oh, yeah. Can I start making a reading list now?'

"Yes, you can. Do you have some books in mind?"

"The teacher talked about number twenty-three in the Book of Sal— uh, what was that book, Nana?"

"The Book of Psalms," Angie heard her mother say from a distance.

"Oh, okay," Angie said. "Well, Baby, the Book of Psalms is in the Old Testament of the Holy Bible. It might be awhile before you can tackle that book but we'll get you some children's books about the Twenty-third Psalm."

"Are you coming home now, Mommy?"

"No, Baby. I'm going to stay over here tonight. But, I'll be home about noon tomorrow."

"Is noon when we eat lunch?"

"Yes, that's the same. I'll be home about lunch time, tomorrow. You have Nana fix you your favorite sandwich for lunch, okay?"

"Okay. My favorite sandwich is Tuna Salad."

"Do you have tuna, mother?"

"After raising you, I always have plenty of tuna on hand," her mother said. "I think you weaned this little girl off the bottle and onto tuna salad sandwiches."

"Tuna is nutritious," Angie said, "As long as you use light mayonnaise and whole wheat bread."

"Yes, dear. This house is the model of nutrition."

"I know mother, I appreciate how well you manage the house and meals."

"Thank you, dear."

"Okay. I've got to go," Angie said, not really wanting to end her conversation with her little girl, but needing to pay attention to traffic so she could cross over the highway to turn left and go north.

"I love you, Mommy."

"I love you, too, Auronia. I'll see you tomorrow noon."

Angie slipped the cell phone into her pocket and drove to the Sun Setter Hotel.

At the front desk, the clerk welcomed her and gave her the key to her suite. A bellhop with a cart followed her out to her car and took charge of her small suitcase and clothes bag. Angie gave her car key to the parking lot valet and accepted the parking tag.

The bellhop led Angie back into the hotel and to the elevators.

Once in her suite, Angie surveyed the amenities. The suite smelled fresh and was spotlessly clean. A tall bottle of Chardonnay was in a chiller. Potato chips, popcorn, cookies, and snack crackers with a variety of patés filled a basket next to the chiller. She smiled. *Kurt takes good care of his drivers. Correction: Driver. ME!*

Angie moved to open the refrigerator door. A beautifully arranged tray of cold cuts and vegetables sat on the top shelf. There were also two cans each of three well-known beers.

After I shower, I may try the cold cuts.

She swiped a taste from the bowl of salad dip in the center of the plate. *Spicy Ranch. Just what I like.*

Angie unpacked her small suitcase, arranging a set of underwear neatly on the end of the bed and putting the rest into the dresser drawer. After smoothing a pair of jeans and a yellow tank top next to her undies, she hung the other clothes in the closet.

She unpacked her pink and yellow jogging suit and spread it on the easy chair, and placed her hot pink jogging shoes on the floor next to the nightstand. Even though she was physically and mentally worn out from today's race, she made a mental note about tomorrow morning's early trip to the fitness room on the first floor where she would get in her daily two-mile jog, plus work out using weights. Kurt Maxxon had convinced her early in her racing career to get into good physical condition and then maintain it.

Angie stripped out of her red and gold racing suit and, after grabbing the plastic bag for laundry, stuffed her suit in it. When she closed the closet door, she stood studying her body in the full-length door mirror.

Wear and tear. Stretch marks. You're not a spring chicken anymore, lady.

After a long, hot shower, Angie walked into the bedroom toweling off. She looked at her undies, lying on the bed, along with the jeans and tank top, and went into the living room nude. She fought the cork out of the bottle and poured half a glass. She sat down on the sofa with her leg under her and leaned back to relax.

As she sipped on the wine, she looked around the suite. The gleaming stainless steel kitchen. The living room. The two bedroom doors off to the side, each with separate baths.

All this space for one person? A family of four could live comfortably in this suite.

The low-income family that she and Auronia had sponsored last Christmas came to mind. The family consisted of a single mother and her four children, ages one through six. They lived in a small flat in the projects—one bedroom, one bath, and a kitchen/living room combination—about half the size of this suite.

Angie had wrestled with the dichotomy between the *Haves* and the *Have-nots* in society and decided she was thankful to be on the *Haves* side of the equation. She also decided that she would do what she could to help the *Have-nots*. That included raising Auronia to respect them and instill a sense of generosity toward those less fortunate.

As her mind wandered through several other subjects, one of the TV interviewer's questions popped into her mind: "Are you planning to win all the races in the SRVSCRA this season?"

"Well, of course, sure," Angie remembered replying without pause.

That would be an accomplishment. Angie mused. *I wonder if any driver in the history of the SRVSCRA has ever won every race during the season.*

I'll have to ask Kurt Maxxon. He'll know.

She let her mind wander into the fuzzy world of imagination.

In rapid succession, *she saw herself in the Winner's Circle at Maplewood in two weeks. Then two weeks after that in Centralia. Then Ford Junction. And the other racetracks blurred by until she was standing in the Winner's Circle at the Grand Finale, the Centralia Shoot Out again next October.*

The Centralia Shootout was the last race of the year; a by-invitation-only event featuring the top ten points winners from the season. Angie had already been invited to participate in two Shootouts. *Pretty decent.*

"And now, Ladies and Gentlemen," she imagined the loudspeaker blaring, "The only driver ever to win every single race in the SRVSCRA season, Ms. Angie Prescotte."

As the crowd roar became deafening, Angie saw herself dancing around the circle, her hands held high. "Yes. Yes." She said over and over. "Life is so good."

As the fantasy faded from her mind, she hugged her chest, curled up, and raised her eyes to the ceiling.

Life is good. Except—Tugs isn't here to share it.

"Why did you have to take Tugs away from me?" she asked the ceiling. "From Auronia?" Her thoughts turned to the same questions she had pondered over and over.

She replayed the telephone call from the Memphis Police Department on New Year's Day two years before.

"Hercules Matthews has been injured in an automobile accident and has been transported to Baptist Memorial Hospital."

"Is he hurt bad?"

"We don't know, ma'am. You'll have to contact the hospital."

The frantic call to the hospital. "Are you family?"

"I'm his girlfriend."

"Are you married?"

"No. Dammit. I love him."

Then the more frantic drive to Memphis and finally finding Baptist Memorial Hospital. Running into the ER almost knocking a little old lady on her butt. Then the same run-around at the emergency room. "Are you family?"

And then the coup de grace. "Ms. Prescotte, Mr. Hercules Matthews passed away about an hour ago. We're sorry."

She remembered calling Christina from the hospital. And then Christina and Kurt were there at her side. They didn't leave her alone all during the ordeal of getting Tug's body back to Ford Junction; planning and scheduling the funeral, and all the follow-up of getting Tugs' name off contracts, deeds, stock certificates, and important papers.

She bit her lower lip and visualized them lowering Tug's casket into the ground. The tractor pushing the dirt in onto Tugs' casket. The hollow sound of dirt clods falling on the casket in the grave.

And all the while, Auronia, Tugs' daughter, was growing inside her. Then Auronia's birth just nineteen days after her daddy was buried in the ground.

She remembered pressing Christina and Kurt Maxxon, both of them born-again Christians for answers to her questions.

God's motives?

Why did he take Tugs from me?

What did I do?

What about Auronia's future?

Angie had become a little cloyed with Christina's most frequent reply to her complaint: "God works in mysterious ways."

Suddenly, as if a fuse had blown, the visions went black. Angie blinked her eyes and looked around the suite. What's that noise?

The room phone was ringing. Angie pushed the speaker phone.

"The party is getting underway," Christina said. "Everyone's wondering where you are?"

"I really enjoyed that hot shower," Angie said. "I was just relaxing." She squinted to read the clock radio on the nightstand. "Did you guys invite Lucky to the party?" she asked Christina.

"Yes, we did. He's here. He's talking to Jiggs right now. They're probably discussing you, the race, and how you beat him."

"I'll be right down," Angie said as she walked toward the bedroom to dress.

As she went out of the room into the hallway, she hoped she was presentable. She made a survey of her appearance as she waited for the elevator.

Nothing spectacular. Just little ole me—warts, stretch marks and all.

CHAPTER THREE

Kurt set the glass of wine in front of Christina and pulled out his chair.

"Did they have to send to the kitchen for iced tea?" Christina said.

"That's why you're drinking white wine, my dear." Kurt gazed around the huge ballroom. "The bartender said it would probably take about forty-five minutes to get an iced tea from the kitchen."

"Even though I'm in no hurry, wine will work. Thank you."

"He made it. That's good," Kurt said.

Christina swung her head to look where Kurt had been looking. "What's good?"

"Lucky made it. He's over there talking to Jiggs." Kurt pointed with his chin to a group of men standing near the bar.

Christina bobbed her head. "Oh. Yes, I saw him arrive. I told Angie he was here when I called her."

"Angie seemed happier today," Kurt said.

Christina nodded her head. "Yes, she did."

Kurt smiled. "Winning the first three races of the season has had a good effect on her. She was a lot more animated this afternoon. She was actually bubbly during the TV interview."

Christina smiled and said, "Lucky might have something to do with that."

"You think so?"

Christina nodded. "I'm sure he's part of it."

"Lucky was very helpful today," Kurt said. "Besides helping with the tires and gas, he helped Angie climb in out of the car at the breaks, just like the gentleman that he is."

"He definitely is a gentleman," Christina said. "His only problem, if it is one, is he's totally devoted to his kids."

"That's not a bad problem to have," Kurt said and looked to see Angie come into the hotel ballroom through the lobby door. He watched her as she made her way around tables, shaking hands, patting shoulders, waving and speaking to people along the way. Christina swung around in her chair to watch Angie's approach.

Angie was radiant in her bright yellow tank top that accented her deep bronze suntan and blue jeans. Her black hair had a reddish tint in the fluorescent lighting.

As Angie approached the table Kurt moved to assist her with her chair. "Chardonnay?" Kurt asked as he helped Angie scoot her chair in under the table.

"That'll be fine."

Kurt walked toward the bar. While he waited for the wine, Lucky and Jiggs moved beside him. "Am I invited to your table?" Lucky asked.

"Naturally," Kurt replied. "Both of you. Where's Katy?" he asked Jiggs.

"She's out in the motorhome talking to her sister. Their mother is in the hospital again, and they're handling that. She'll be in in a minute."

"Did you get your room?" Kurt asked Lucky.

"Yes, sir. I did. Thank you. I'm all settled in."

"Good thing you keep that bundle of clean clothes stored in your truck," Jiggs said, with a glint of humor in his eyes. "I told you it would pay off someday."

"Yes, sir. I planned to be ready if I got caught away from home. Tonight will be the first time 'someday' happened."

Jiggs and Lucky followed Kurt back to a large round table in the corner.

"At least it wasn't a photo finish," Jiggs said as he sat down in the chair next to Angie. "I decided to let you win it by a comfortable margin."

"Thank you for that," Angie said with a broad grin. "But, you couldn't have beat me today anyway; because I had my good luck charm with me."

"Your good luck charm?" Jiggs asked, raising his eyebrows.

Angie pointed to Lucky. "Him! He's my good luck charm."

Christina stood and forced Kurt to move to the next chair, sat down and waved for Lucky to sit down between her and Angie.

"Hello, Mr. Lucky," Angie said as Lucky sat down next to her. "I'm glad you came to the party."

"I—I'm happy to be here," Lucky said, then lapsed into shyness. *I wish*

I knew how to talk to people as easily as Kurt and Jiggs do. Especially to Angie.

Charley Anderson and his wife came through the door. Both of them stopped to let their eyes adjust and then looked around. Jiggs stood and waved. Charley spotted Jiggs and walked to the large round table.

Charley introduced his wife, Megan, to the table and pulled a chair for her. "Man, that is starch-wilting weather outside," Charley said.

"Starch-wilting?" Jiggs asked and frowned.

"That heat and humidity will wilt all the starch out of your collars," Charley said. "If you put starch in your collars to start with."

"Hey, Charley," Lucky said, standing to shake hands across the table.

Jiggs said, "Kurt, have you met Charley Anderson? He's my superintendent on the Hangman's Creek Dam Project north of here."

"Yes. We met at a Kiwanis Club Convention several years ago."

"I'm a fan of Kurt Maxxon's," Charley said to Jiggs. "But, he's always been second to you, boss."

Jiggs chuckled audibly. "That'll get you a chair at this table every time."

The newcomers took the seats nearly opposite of Kurt and Christina. "Congratulations Angie," Charley said. "That was a close race, today."

Jiggs nodded agreement.

"When are you coming out to the site?" Charley asked Lucky.

"I'm tied up Tuesday," Lucky said, looking at Jiggs. "The members of the Racing Club from Vo-Tech are coming to visit the Borsche shops. They want me to talk to them about tools used in the field. I can run out to your site on Wednesday or Thursday. I'll see what's happening in the shops."

"Do you need something special?" Jiggs asked.

"No," Charley said. "I just like having Lucky checking the equipment. This guy has a special touch."

Lucky dipped his head.

Jiggs laughed. "Yeah. I know. He's also the good luck charm for my nemesis there."

Charley frowned. "Good luck charm?"

Everyone at the table was so absorbed in the conversation that no one saw Katy Borsche coming toward the table. When she arrived, Jiggs jumped up to help her scoot to the table.

"How's your mother doing?" Jiggs asked.

"Not well, I'm afraid."

Everyone at the table suddenly realized the gravity of Katy's mood.

Kurt stood and offered to go to the bar for Megan, Charley, and Katy.

"Sit down, old man," Jiggs said. "I'll go to the bar. What does everyone want?"

While Jiggs was at the bar, Sheriff Cletus Weinberger came strolling into the ballroom through the parking lot door. He took his sunglasses off and made a survey of the room. Several drivers stopped what they were doing and watched the sheriff wander toward the big round table of honor, where he stopped and looked at each person sitting there. "I guess I won't need to check IDs of most of you. But you miss," He looked at Angie. "I might have to check yours."

"Thank you, Sheriff," Angie said, "but my ID is up in my room."

"A likely story," the sheriff said. "I'll let you slide today. Mind if I sit down?"

"Please do," Christina said. "We've been waiting for you."

"I'll bet you have," the sheriff said and smiled.

Lucky watched the exchange and then turned his attention to Angie. He glanced at her wine glass and noted it had gone down only a fraction of an inch.

She's a sipper.

* * *

Angie said, "You've been around Masonville a couple of years now, haven't you?" "I remember seeing you sitting in the stands with Christina during some of the races over the last couple of years. But I never knew exactly what the connection was."

"Yes. I came to Masonville two years ago. In fact, it was the first race of that season. I was thumbing my way to Masonville in a monsoon rainstorm. Kurt picked me up and carried me the last eighty miles into town."

"What made you go to Masonville?" Angie asked.

Lucky paused. "My sister, Darby was dying from stomach cancer. I came to visit her."

"Oh, yeah, I heard Kurt talking about Darby," Angie said. "Then you adopted her two children."

"I took legal guardianship over them," Lucky said. "That way they kept their given last names."

Angie nodded her head. "That's nice. And the kids made you decide to settle down in Masonville?"

"Well, they influenced that decision." Lucky swung to look toward Jiggs Borsch. "The tie-breaker was that Kurt hooked me up with Jiggs, who gave me a dream job. I am truly blessed. I also took custody of my own daughter, Olivia Maye, after my ex-wife was stabbed to death in a barroom brawl in Tupelo, Mississippi."

"So, you have three children?"

"Yes, ma'am. Two girls and a boy," Lucky said, then paused. "Thank the Lord, all of them are healthy and thriving."

"How old are your kids?"

"The two girls are thirteen. Jason is fifteen."

"Both girls are the same age?"

"Yes, ma'am, they're the same age, same grade in school."

"Do they fight with each other over clothes?"

"Not really," Lucky said. They wear different sizes."

"Do the girls share a bedroom?"

"They do since Granny Watson came to live with us. Before that, they each had their own rooms."

"Who's Granny Watson?"

"She's my mother's mother. In reality, she is a sweet little old lady who loves kids and helping other people. She's another one of my blessings. She came to Masonville to get treatments for her chronic sciatica. I told her she could stay with us while she was here for that. She moved in and liked it so well, she stayed. Now she's one of the family. The kids love her. She cooks. She does laundry. She watches the kids when I'm not there. She's trained the kids to keep their rooms clean. That was a major accomplishment."

"I guess," Angie chuckled. "My little sister and I shared a bedroom while we were growing up. It was always a mess. I used to blame Nicole for it. But in truth, I was just as sloppy."

"With Granny Watson's help, the kids have learned it's easier to be neat."

"So, you're happy in Masonville," Angie said.

"Oh, yes ma'am. The house is probably too small, but we're cozy in it. We all keep busy and on the move. After work, school, school events, Church life pretty well takes up the time."

"You all go to church every Sunday?" Angie asked.

"Well, generally we do." Lucky looked at the ceiling and smiled. "Granny Watson goes to The Way of Holiness Church. It's a Pentecostal

Church, which some people call the Holy Rollers. Olivia Maye is the only one of the kids who'll go to church with her because of the noisy service. But, Sophia and Jason go to our church, the United Lutheran Church by themselves if I'm not around. Both the churches are only about six blocks from the house."

"Does Granny Watson walk to church?"

"Yes, ma'am. That's her preferred means of transportation in the big city."

"I've also been blessed—sort of," Angie said. "My mother moved in with me after I bought my place near Copperville. She helps take care of Auronia. She takes Auronia to Sunday school each Sunday."

"That's wonderful," Lucky said. "It's good to get children interested in church when they are young."

"I want Auronia to grow up right," Angie said.

"I don't think I've ever heard a name so beautiful. Do you have a picture of her?" Lucky asked.

"Naturally," Angie said as she pulled out a thin wallet from the hip pocket of her jeans. She opened it to show Lucky five different pictures of Auronia that she had caught at the milestones of Auronia's growth.

"She's a very pretty little girl," Lucky said and smiled. "She takes after her mother, except, well, I love that golden head of hair."

"Yeah. That's why I named her Auronia," Angie said. "I saw that head of hair a few minutes after she was born and I knew she was my golden-haired baby. My baby pictures show me with the same yellow gold hair. I wanted a descriptive name for her, so I put the Latin for 'gold' together with the Latin for 'one and only,' and she seems to love the name as much as I do."

Lucky leaned back to look at Angie's black hair. "You grew up with black hair after starting with golden locks?"

"I got tired of the name *Blondie*," Angie said. "So, I started dying my hair black when I was in high school."

"You're a natural blonde?"

"If I don't dye it, I'm a dishwater blonde," Angie said with a deep frown. "Some people call it an ash blond, but to me, it's just a dirty dishwater color that I don't like."

"What's wrong with that?"

"Nothing in particular. But, since I would have to dye it anyway, dying it black is easier than bleaching it to a pretty blond."

* * *

The noise echoing in the ballroom was so loud, Lucky was having difficulty hearing the discussion around the big table.

Christina and Angie excused themselves saying they needed to visit the powder room. Megan Anderson stood and said, "I'll join you." The three women left through the lobby door.

"Anything new on the Brittany Garfield case?" Lucky asked Sheriff Weinberger.

The sheriff wobbled his head. "Same old dead ends. We keep investigating, though."

Jiggs offered the narrative to the others at the table. "Lucky was out at the dam site a while back to fix one of the large earth movers we're using up there. He found a young girl's body stuffed under one of the storage trailers. Then when he took the big rig for a test drive, lo and behold—he discovered pieces of evidence around the site."

"It's crucial evidence, but we haven't unraveled it yet," Weinberger picked up the story. "Lucky spotted some unique tire tread marks in the dirt near the culvert being poured. Then Lucky noticed the same tire treads in the driveway of the largest farmer in Herman County, and we tracked them to his oldest son's pickup truck. But the kid appears to have an airtight alibi."

"What about the condom?" Lucky asked.

Everybody around the table stopped and looked at Lucky.

"Not the best subject for a party," Weinberger said. "Lucky found a used condom inside the culvert. DNA on the inside belonged to the farmer's kid. But, the DNA on the outside was not from the victim. So that piece of evidence linked the suspect to the site but did not link the suspect to the victim. At the same time, the victim had also had sex just before her death. But we don't know with whom. The lab said her sex also involved a condom. We searched every inch of that site, looking for another used condom. But, no luck."

Charley Anderson nodded agreement. "I lost two days of schedule while they did that."

"You're the only one who has ever been able to find any evidence in the case," the sheriff said to Lucky. "Are you coming back to the site soon?"

"This coming week, probably Wednesday," Lucky said.

"That's good," the sheriff said. "I'll get up with you out there. Give me a call."

A lull settled over the group at the table. Angie, Christina, and Megan returned to the table and sat down. Angie had just scooted her chair under the table when she pointed toward the parking lot door and said, "There's the Greek."

Eugenios Christofides stopped just inside the door as his eyes adjusted to the darkness. Then he made his way to the bar for his usual snifter full of ouzo. Waving to other drivers as he walked, he made his way to the big round table in the corner. He walked around, hugged and congratulated Angie where she sat. Then he moved to hug Christina, then sat down in the chair the other side of Kurt. "This only empty chair in the place," he said.

"It had your name on it," Kurt said.

Christofides looked around the table. Jiggs gave him a two finger salute. Christofides let his focus stop on Sheriff Weinberger. "You invite the local sheriff to this party?" He asked Kurt.

"I had to," Kurt said. "If I don't, then the neighbors call and complain about the noise, and he has to make the trip out here anyhow. That irritates him. If I invite him, he doesn't seem to mind so much."

"Good thinking," Christofides said.

The band members began tuning and testing their instruments and equipment. That brought a momentary stillness around the ballroom. When the band started playing a slow ballad, several couples moved onto the dancefloor and began various gyrations.

Angie leaned close to Lucky and whispered: "Do you dance?"

Lucky wobbled his head. "No. Your feet would never recover if I tried."

"That's good," Angie said. "I don't care for dancing, either."

Motion drew Lucky's attention, and he turned to look that way. He saw a tall, burly African-American man standing just inside the lobby door. The man focused on the group around the big round table and then made his way to the bar on the other side of the room, having to detour around the dance floor and band area. The man got a drink—a tall highball glass full—and walked back to them, where he skirted the table and congratulated Angie. He nodded at Lucky, then moved to hug Christina and shake hands with Kurt. He took the chair on the other side of

Christofides without saying a word.

Lucky leaned close to Angie's ear and whispered. "Who is that guy? He looks familiar, but, I can't place where I've seen him before."

"That's Don Epperley," Angie replied. "He's an old, old friend of Kurt's. You probably saw him at one of the other races."

Lucky nodded. He looked at the man again.

Don said, "It's a good thing the sheriff is here. If the Greek here gets out of line, Cletus can just haul his sorry butt to jail and throw the key away." Lucky jerked back, afraid a fight was brewing.

Sheriff Weinberger turned at the sound of his name. "Oh, hello, Lieutenant. How've you been?" he said.

Lucky leaned closer to Angie's ear. "Lieutenant?" He whispered.

"That was Don's rank in the Kings Rapids Police Department. He had to retire early because of a gunshot wound that tore up his left shoulder. Over the years since he retired he's helped neighboring law enforcement agencies, including Sheriff Weinberger's, with training and writing procedures," Angie whispered back.

"Where do you live now?" Weinberger asked Angie.

"I bought a small acreage north of Masonville, near Copperville," Angie said. "I was living in Ford Junction, and Kurt suggested I might be happier living someplace more centrally located to all the racetracks in the SRVSCRA. I actually looked at a couple of places outside of Masonville. I'd gone to a real estate agent in Ford Junction, and she set up a virtual tour on her computer. When I saw my place, I said, 'I want that place, I don't care where it is.' I bought it that day. My longest drive is to Carpentier Falls, which is just over three-hundred miles. But, I love the place."

"I drive to each track Friday morning. Kurt and Christina usually are already there with the car. I practice Friday afternoon and Saturday mornings. I drive the race Sunday afternoon, and then I drive back to Copperville Monday morning."

"Yes," Lucky said. "The distances are a problem. I can only get to the nearby races: Masonville, Kings Rapids, Evandale, Maplewood, and Centralia. But I can't travel to the other racetracks—they're too far away."

"You're going to have to now, Mr. Lucky," Angie said nodding her head for emphasis. "Because you are my now my official good luck charm, and I want to keep winning all the races."

Lucky grinned as he shrugged his shoulders.

Christina leaned toward Angie's and said, "You'll have to talk to Kurt about getting Lucky a travel account."

"That's a good idea," Angie said.

At the sound of his name, Kurt turned to look at the faces staring at him. "What?"

"Lucky needs a travel allowance from Kurt Maxxon Racing," Angie said.

"A travel allowance?" Kurt asked.

"Angie wants Lucky to be at all the rest of the races this year," Christina said.

Kurt leveled his gaze on Angie.

"Lucky is officially my good luck charm," Angie said. "He's the reason I'm winning races. So, I want him to travel to all the remaining races."

Lucky said, "Well. It's a little more than just *travel money*. It also involves me getting off work. I work just about every Saturday, at least Saturday mornings. To go to the races, I drive to the tracks Sunday morning, before the races start. But, goodness gracious, from Masonville to Carpentier Falls has to be three-hundred-fifty miles, maybe more. That's more than a morning's drive. And then I'd have to drive back Sunday afternoon after the race is over to be at work Monday morning."

"Ahhh, geez," Angie feigned a whiny voice.

Kurt glanced over at Jiggs and waited for a lull in the conversation on that side of the table. Raising his voice, he said, "Hey, Jiggs, do you still have your Beech Bonanza?"

"Yeah. You want to borrow it?"

"No. Thank you. Do you still fly to the races in Carpentier Falls, Ford Junction, and Tawnytown?"

Jiggs bobbed his head. "Yeah. And also Jamesboro."

"Lucky needs to catch a ride with you on those trips."

Jiggs leaned back and looked directly at Lucky. "You want to go to those races, too?"

Lucky looked blankly at Jiggs and leaned back, gesturing toward Angie and the Maxxons. He grimaced and shrugged his shoulders.

"He has to come to those races because he's my good luck charm," Angie said innocently. "I want to win all the rest of the races,"

"You want me to fly your good luck charm to those races so you can beat me?" Jiggs frowned severely. "What's wrong with this picture?"

"Ah, be a good sport," Kurt said.

"A good sport?" Jiggs laughed. He looked at Katy. "Should I be a good sport and fly Angie's good luck charm to the races?"

"You certainly should," Katy said and winked at Angie. "If you don't, you'll have to give Lucky Saturday afternoons and Monday mornings off so he can drive to the races."

"Sounds like a lose-lose situation," Jiggs groaned.

"Get Lucky qualified in that airplane," Kurt said. "Then he could handle some of the piloting,"

"He's already qualified," Jiggs said. "He's used the plane to get up to the Horneby Project north of Tawnytown several times."

"Well then, what's the problem?" Kurt countered.

"Probably none," Jiggs conceded. "The next two races are Maplewood and then Centralia One. So, we have some time to work it all out. I usually fly to the tracks Saturday mornings so I can get a few practice laps in before the qualification runs. Katy or one of my kids, drives the motor home pulling the car carrier to the track Friday, during the day, and back home on Mondays."

"Lucky could fly out and back with you," Kurt said.

"I suppose," Jiggs conceded. "He can bunk on the sofa bed in the motorhome. We'll talk about it."

Lucky drained his beer and stood up. "Anyone else need a refill?"

As he looked around the table, each face shook a head, and some added "Thank you, no," except Don Epperley, who said, "I'll go with you."

Angie took a long draught from her glass and held it up for Lucky to see. Lucky nodded acceptance and led Don toward the bar.

When Lucky returned to the table, Angie said, "If you're gone overnight on the weekend, are your kids okay staying with Granny Watson?"

"Oh, sure," Lucky said. "But, I still worry about them."

"It might all work out for good," Angie said. She sampled her new glass of wine and set it aside.

Kurt stood and clanged a knife against a glass. Slowly the conversation around the ballroom died down. "A toast," Kurt shouted. He held up his glass of Diet Coke. "To the winningest driver in the SRVSCRA this season, Ms. Angie Prescotte. Salud."

Cheers, whistles, and clapping went around the room.

"You gonna let the rest of us win some?" a voice asked from somewhere.

Angie stood and turning to the direction of the question, she laughed and called out. "NO!" Then she held her glass high and said, "Thanks to each of you. It's nice to compete with a bunch of men who don't mind a woman beating them."

A loud chorus of boos rang throughout the room.

Angie noticed several women slugging their mates in the arm.

"Okay, then. Just thank you."

CHAPTER FOUR

Lucky watched Angie leave through the lobby door and stared after her until the closing door blocked his view.

A very attractive lady.

"What room are you in?" Christina asked Lucky.

"Oh, uh, let me look." Lucky dug out his plastic key card in its paper slipcase. "Uh, I'm in room four-oh-six."

"Kurt and I are at the opposite end of the hall in room four-seventy-four."

"That was quite a party," Lucky said to Kurt. "Jiggs has told me about them, but he could never describe them like they really are. Very enjoyable."

"I might break down and have a nightcap," Kurt said. He looked at Christina. "Do you want an after-dinner liqueur?"

"I could go for a Grasshopper," Christina said. "What did you have in mind?"

Kurt wrinkled his mouth. "I was thinking Dram Bouie, or maybe something with amaretto."

Christina wobbled her head. "You get whatever you like, but, I want a Grasshopper."

Kurt looked at Lucky. "You want an after-dinner drink?"

"What is a Grasshopper?" Lucky asked.

Christina said, "It's made with a shot of green crème de menthe, a shot of white crème de cacao, vanilla ice cream, and garnished with a sprig of mint."

"The only ingredient I recognize is the vanilla ice cream," Lucky said, grinning. "I've not been out in the big world very much."

"It tastes a lot like a minty malt," Kurt said. "You want to try one?"

"Why not?" Lucky said. "If I'm to become a man of the world, I might as well get started, right?"

"I'll go across the hall to the regular bar," Kurt said as he stood. "This little satellite bar may not have the recipe, nor the ice cream." He left through the lobby door.

"A minty malt?" Lucky said to Christina.

"That's Kurt's interpretation," Christina said. "I guess it's accurate enough."

Lucky looked around the ballroom which was emptying steadily. Only a half-dozen couples sat around the room chatting.

Kurt returned with a large tray bearing three huge glasses of green drinks. He set one in front of Christina and one in front of Lucky.

"You decided to have one, too?" Christina said.

"Yes, ma'am," Kurt said. "It was easier to order that way."

"This is good," Lucky blurted after sampling his drink. "I like this stuff."

"It grows on you," Kurt said and grinned at Christina.

"Very tasty," Christina responded.

"It's nine-thirty already," Lucky said looking at his wristwatch.

"Is that your bedtime?" Kurt asked.

"Oh, no. I was just wondering how the kids did with their program tonight. I feel guilty for not being there for them. I'll be up until about eleven or so. I plan on reading the Bible some yet tonight." He pulled out a well-worn miniature Bible from his shirt pocket. "But I'm hoping there's a Gideon Bible in my room, so I can read it without squinting through the words."

"Where's the big Bible Christina got you?" Kurt asked.

"It's at home. The kids use it as much as I do, so I just leave it at home and carry this little thing around."

Christina said, "If there isn't a Bible in your room, just call the front desk. They'll send one up."

Several of the lingering celebrants came by the table to thank Kurt on their way to the door.

Lucky emptied his drink and said, "Thank you for the party, and the drink," raising the empty glass. "I'm heading to my room; have a wonderful evening."

"You do the same," Kurt said.

As he passed through the lobby door, Lucky decided to go out to his truck for his cell phone charger.

I think I'll call home to see if they're still up and how things went. I can leave a message if they're sleeping and don't answer.

* * *

Angie had brought her baby doll pajamas. She didn't wear them at home anymore because Auronia was at that stage where she emulated everything her mother did. But, when she traveled, like tonight, Angie put them on and let memories of Tugs Matthews waft through her mind. She'd turned on the TV, muted it and located the news channel. She often just sat reading the news streaming in a banner at the bottom of the screen.

She glanced at the wine bottle sitting in the chiller. "I've had enough," She told herself.

A few minutes later, she decided to fill a wine glass and sip on it.

Memories of a trip she and Tugs took to New Orleans flooded her mind. That trip had been shortly after she started driving Kurt's race car—about a year after she moved into Tugs' apartment on a permanent basis. She'd never been to New Orleans before, but she quickly became quite fond of The Big Easy. The food. The music. The ambiance. They had stayed at the Hotel St. Pierre in the French Quarter, on Burgundy Street, two blocks from Bourbon Street.

She remembered the leisurely strolls she and Tugs took from their hotel along Burgundy Street to Canal Street, the southwestern edge of the French Quarter. Then along Bourbon Street from Canal Street to Esplanade Avenue—the northeastern border of the French Quarter.

She remembered the people; both locals and tourists. The bars. The restaurants. The cafés. The Bistros. The souvenir shops. The merchant stores. A city that was vibrantly alive any time of the day or night.

Angie looked around her suite. Suddenly it became suffocatingly small.

I need to go outside and walk around the building, or something. But first, I'd better put some clothes on!

She went into the bedroom and looked at her jeans, tank top, and undies on the bed, while she considered her options and the lateness of the hour. She glanced at the jogging suit on the back of the chair. She rubbed her face.

Do I feel like going down to the treadmill for a short jog—maybe a half mile?

Nah. I don't think so. Just dress and walk around the outside of the building a couple of times.

She put on her blue jeans and the bright yellow tank top. As she swung the door open, she stopped and went back to get her wine glass and filled it to the brim. She left the suite and decided to use the elevator rather than the stairwell.

When the elevator doors opened on the ground floor, Angie noticed the swimming pool across the alcove. She pushed through the double doors into the pool area and stopped to look around. Two couples were sitting at the end of the pool chatting over drinks. Angie saw a table off to the side and went to sit down.

She sipped on her wine. *Life is good. Except … except … Tugs is gone.*

She raised her eyes to the ceiling. *Why did you take Tugs away from me? What is Auronia going to do without a Daddy? How is she going to grow up?*

* * *

Lucky strolled around the room looking it over. Over the years he had stayed in several motels, but they had always been cheap ones.

This is incredible. I've never had such luxury.

A king-size bed with nightstands on each side. A telephone on one nightstand and another phone on the desk across the room. A sofa and an easy chair. A huge flat screen TV, bigger than any TV Lucky had seen before.

"Wow," he said to himself. "Wow, wow, wow."

He walked to the nightstand with the telephone and pulled the drawer open. It contained a green Gideon Bible. He picked up the book and leafed through it.

I need to study John again.

Lucky carried the green Bible to the easy chair, sat down, reclined it, and began to read.

The room phone jangled.

Curious, Lucky picked up the receiver.

* * *

Lucky exited the elevator, crossed the wide alcove, and pushed through the double doors into the pool area. His mind whirled through his concerns, the most prominent being: *Is this meeting proper? Especially if she is wearing a swimsuit. And more especially, if that swimsuit is a bikini.*

The warm, humid air made him pause, and breathe through his mouth. The teal green color of the pool was highlighted by submerged lights around the edge. The water lay calm; only the recirculation system giving the water a slight ripple. A low murmur of voices reached him from two couples chatting at the far end of the pool.

Lucky saw Angie sitting at one of the round tables with a multi-colored umbrella above her. The table was off to the side in the shadows and the umbrella added to the darkness. If not for the bright yellow tank top she was wearing, Lucky might not have spotted her. Her short black hair framed her face in the darkness.

Lucky walked to the table. "Hey, Miss Angie."

"Hey, to you, Mr. Lucky." Angie smiled. "Please sit down."

Lucky straddled a chair across the table from Angie. His natural shyness around women kicked in. *What do I say next?*

"The room kind of closed in on me," Angie said. "So, I thought about walking around the building in the fresh air. Then I saw the swimming pool. I like the warm, humid air in here. It reminds me of New Orleans."

Lucky pursed his lips. "It does feel like Louisiana in here."

"I felt like I needed to be with people tonight. I decided to call you and ask you to come talk to me."

"About what?"

"Oh, I don't know. Nothing in particular. I guess … I guess I'm just lonely. When I'm away from home, I miss Auronia a lot."

"Auronia is a beautiful little girl. I can understand why."

"Yes. She's my pride and joy. It's been an incredible journey watching her grow from a totally helpless little bundle of flesh into a rambunctious two-year-old; going on three. When she started crawling, I had to keep everything up off the floor. When she started walking, I had to move all the stuff to higher places so she couldn't pull them over on top of herself."

"I missed the crawling stage with Olivia Maye," Lucky said. "I rotated overseas to Japan when Olivia Maye was three months old. She was seventeen months old when I returned. I remember the 'learning to walk' phase, however."

"So, your wife took Olivia Maye and left you?"

"Yes, ma'am."

"How old was Olivia Maye when your wife left?"

"Six—"

At the sound of a commotion, Lucky paused and looked around. He and Angie sat silently as the two couples walked past them and out the door, wrapped in each other's arms.

"Do you want another Bud?" Angie asked. "The bar is just around the corner through that door," she said, pointing toward a nearby side door.

"No. I've had enough."

"Do you drink Budweiser all the time?"

"That's what I drink on special occasions."

"My victory parties are special occasions?"

"Yes, ma'am. And, you are a very special lady," Lucky said quickly.

"Thank you," Angie said and smiled.

"That was quite a race today."

"Yes, a lot better than the last race where I beat Jiggs by only a hair. Today I beat him by a couple of car lengths."

"I think you led every lap in the final heat."

"No. Jiggs took me coming off turn two and then he led for four laps. Other than that, though, I led them all. I've never done that before."

"Well, forty-six laps out of fifty is pretty much *all* of them, I'd say," Lucky said smiled broadly.

"Today's race was a lot of fun for me," Angie said, and her eyes focused on something above and behind Lucky. "I'm not sure what it was—"

"I really enjoyed working in the pit with Kurt and Maurey today," Lucky said. "That was a lot of fun for me."

"Maybe that's what it was," Angie said and frowned. "Maybe having you in the pit was why it was so much better."

"I need to learn about the racing game."

"I can teach you that. I'll teach you everything that Kurt Maxxon has taught me. That'll make you a pro for sure."

"How long did it take him to do that?"

"He's still working on it," Angie said and giggled.

"Okay. I'm not planning on going anywhere."

Angie sipped on her wine glass. "Both Christina and Kurt like you a lot—they're big fans of yours," she said.

"They've been a blessing to me ever since I met Kurt."

"They raised my interest in you when they told me that you had had a unique 'born again' experience. They both described their own experiences when they started walking with Jesus. Umm, I've been hearing 'born again' from a couple of other people, too. It makes me want to be 'born again.' People who describe their faith that way seem so self-assured. That was one of the reasons I called you to come talk to me, I guess. I'm missing Auronia's Daddy."

Lucky paused, remembering his feelings of emptiness during his tours overseas, and especially after Bobbi Jo took Olivia Maye and went back to her home in Tupelo, Mississippi. "Well, needless to say, my calling to Jesus was rather unexpected," Lucky said. "We were deployed in Iraq, just north of Baghdad. Another unit in the area was supposed to leave Iraq in a couple of weeks. That unit got hit by a suicide bomber, who was a local they all knew. One of the two guys killed was a gearbox mechanic, like me. My outfit was scheduled to rotate out of Iraq three months later. I got so nervous. I started praying that I'd make it back stateside. I prayed every morning and night. Then, one night I saw my unit get hit, just like the other one. In the aftermath, I saw Jesus walking among the dead and wounded. He selected certain people, prayed over them, then lifted them up and sent them floating up into heaven. Others, he prayed over, touched them on the forehead and they floated over to the area where the medics were working on the wounded. Still others, he prayed over, touched them, and they got up to walk away like nothing had happened. Eventually, there was only me and Jesus. He looked at me. His eyes were so friendly, so peaceful. As I looked into his eyes, I felt so in tune with the world. After a few seconds, Jesus slowly wobbled his head, made the sign of the cross at me, turned and vanished into thin air."

"Thank God you made it," Angie said.

"It turns out," Lucky said slowly, staring at the table, "It was all a dream—a nightmare in reality. But, it made me sit up and think about life and my future. I made it back from Iraq. And I thank my Lord, Jesus Christ, for that."

"It was a dream?"

"Yes, but so realistic, it scared the living daylights out of me." Lucky slid his chair a little closer to the table. "You want to share your story with me?" Lucky asked.

"I don't have one yet," Angie said. "I'm still searching."

Lucky studied Angie for a long beat and smiled with gentle eyes. "You're searching. You have more to tell about your experiences at church," he paused, "and life."

Angie sipped on her wine, breaking eye contact. "I don't understand what it's all about," Angie said slowly. "I—I uh, I've never really understood what being a Christian is all about. I talk to Christina, who tells me about her life now. Same thing with Kurt. But, what does it mean? What does it do for me?"

"Do you go to church?"

"Yes, of course, we do, when I'm home. Once in awhile, I attend church with Kurt & Christina when we're in town together on Sunday mornings, but I usually reserve that time for preparations, and of course, there's always a prayer during the drivers' meetings," Angie responded.

"You're halfway there, then. What do you know about sin?" Lucky asked.

"Sin?" Angie said, confused.

"Yes, ma'am, sin. What is sin?"

"Sin is bad," Angie said, with a low, soft voice.

"Right," Lucky said. "But, *what is* sin?"

She stared at the ceiling as she responded. "Sin is doing bad things."

"Doing bad things to whom? And who decides they are bad?"

Angie brought her stare to Lucky's face.

Lucky kept his expression neutral.

"I guess God is the one who decides they are bad things," Angie said.

"You're approaching this from the negative view," Lucky said and smiled. "Doing things that God decides are bad is the opposite of what God really does. It's easy to think of God's commands as all being negative, after all, the Ten Commandments are all chiseled in stone in the negative, *thou shalt not,* what, kill, bear false witness, covet thy neighbor's wife, etc. But, the truth of the matter is that throughout His Holy Book God gives us a very complete script of how to live our lives righteously—from a positive standpoint."

Lucky reached into his shirt pocket and dug out the small black book.

"That book is so small—tiny."

"Yeah. It's tough to read, but it's very handy. I found this in a used bookstore in Nashville a couple of years before I separated from the Army. It's the *New Living Translation,* and I normally study the *King James Version.* But any Bible is still a Bible—the Good Book."

He dug a pair of reading glasses from his shirt pocket. "These magnifying glasses help." He stood and wrestled the umbrella closed so that the rows of fluorescent lighting above made reading a little easier. He glanced at Angie over the rim of his glasses. Strands of red were sparkling in her hair. He opened the tiny book and flipped the pages. "It says here in First John Five, Seventeen; 'All wicked actions are sin.' The 'wicked actions' of this version are translated as *unrighteousness* in the King James Version of the Bible."

"Sin is unrighteousness?" Angie said.

"That passage from First John helps us define *sin*," Lucky said and leafed through the book. "In Romans Six, Twenty-three, we read that 'The wages of sin is death; but the gift of God is eternal life through Jesus Christ our Lord.' This means that committing sin has consequences—it's deadly. We can logically say that the wages of unrighteousness is death. But what kind of death is this?"

Angie sat up straight and stared at Lucky. "What kind of death?"

"We all eventually die. Our earthly lives come to an end," Lucky said. "It's a question we all wrestle with. Where am I going after death? Man has been asking that question ever since man developed the ability to reason, and distinguished the soul from the body. The human animal is the only animal who knows he is going to die someday. And so, the human animal is the only animal that worries about life after death. Where does my soul go?"

"Are you talking about heaven versus hell?" Angie said.

"Partly. There's more Jesus teaches about sin, and about how people should care about one another. The thought of death is what brought me to my experience, of course. Each person has that emptiness inside that only Jesus fills, and each person has their moment of realization."

"Is it loneliness?" Angie asked.

"I can't describe the feeling. Jesus is there when you are alone. I can't imagine being separated from God. Other people read their Bible, and pray, and go to church regularly. But, for them, something or someone else stands in that place they can't imagine being separated from. For you to be aware of his presence allows you to ask him to walk with you."

"So, lots of people hear about him, or read about him, but I have to realize that he is a person here and now instead of someone in a book?"

"There you go," Lucky said and smiled at Angie. "That's what this is *all* about. When I breathe my last breath, I know my body will remain here. It was made from dust, and it will return to dust. But, where does my soul go—my spirit? My spirit will exist forever—but, where? The options are heaven or hell."

"I've never thought about it like that before," Angie said. "I understand the separation of the body and the soul. Whenever I think about dying and going to heaven, I visualize me, in my body, standing before the Pearly Gates, waiting for Saint Peter to accept me into heaven. But, in reality, it'll just be my spirit standing there, huh?"

"That's right," Lucky said. He flipped pages in his little book. "In First Corinthians-Fifteen we read: 'For when the last trumpet sounds, those who have died will be raised to live forever. And we who are living will also be transformed. 'For our dying bodies must be transformed into immortal bodies.'"

Lucky closed the tiny book.

"And it all depends on how we live our individual lives. If I live my life righteously, I can hope for eternal life in heaven. If I live unrighteously, refusing to know him and listen to him, even though I've heard of his grace, I can expect eternal death in hell. It's that simple."

So how do I guarantee my spirit will go to heaven and not hell?" Angie asked.

"That's the question, isn't it? God expects us to obey all his laws and commands. There are thirty-nine books in the Old Testament and twenty-seven books in the New Testament all available to us to help us read and understand God's laws—how we show our love for God and our love for all of God's creation. In Matthew twenty-two, the Pharisees asked Jesus, 'What is the most important commandment in the law of Moses?'" Lucky paused to let his question sink in as he looked at Angie.

Angie realized he made the question personal and shrugged.

Lucky flipped pages. "In verse thirty-seven, Jesus answers: *'You must love the Lord your God with all your heart, all your soul, and all your mind. This is the first and greatest commandment. A second is equally important 'Love your neighbor as yourself. The entire law and all the demands of the prophets are based on these two commandments.'*"

"That's it?" Angie said.

"That's it," Lucky said as he closed his tiny book and pushed it into his shirt pocket. Then he did the same with his reading glasses. "That's enough for tonight," he said. "You have to decide when and how you want to accept Jesus into your life."

"Do I have to do that in church?" Angie asked.

"Not unless you want to. You can do it publicly or privately. Jesus was constantly chiding the Pharisees for the pomp and circumstance they demanded in showing off their religion; always praying and reading the law in public. But, Jesus basically advised, 'Go into your closet and pray.' It's totally up to you how and when you want to do it. You'll eventually realize that there is a benefit to meeting with other like-minded people. Christian fellowship has always been a great help to individuals. The group helps us understand life and stimulate us to live even better lives. The only thing we are expected to do publicly, as Christians, is acknowledge him."

"That's good to know," Angie said. "Thanks for sharing. I hope I get my experience soon."

"God never turns down his children. All you need to do is read the Bible and ask him."

Lucky changed the subject. "How long have you been driving Kurt's race car?"

"This is my eighth season," Angie said. "God, it doesn't seem possible it's been that long."

"How did you get involved with Kurt Maxxon Racing?"

"One of my friend's brothers was a race driver up in Carpentier Falls and was asked to consider driving for Kurt, since Kurt wanted to retire from racing. Her brother said he wasn't interested. A classmate of mine from Centralia College saw Kurt Maxxon shopping for groceries and on a lark, told him I was available and would make a damn good driver."

Angie went quiet, remembering the past.

"Christina called me, and we talked. They invited me over to Albertstown for an interview. The rest is history."

"Did you do any racing before Kurt hired you?"

"No. Just on the streets and roads around town."

"I'll bet the cops didn't like that," Lucky said and grinned.

"No, as a matter of fact, they frowned on that." Angie looked away and smiled at the memories flooding her mind. "The cops gave me so many speeding tickets I lost count. The straw that broke the camel's back was when they caught me doing ninety-seven miles-per-hour on the highway west of town. That led to my mother forbidding me to drive her car."

"Ninety-seven miles-per-hour?"

"That's as fast as the car would go. I had the foot feed floored."

"Wow. That's fast." Lucky chuckled. "What is your average speed during a race like today's?"

"About eighty to eighty-five miles-per-hour."

"It's a good thing you're doing it on a racetrack."

"You're right. Did you have problems with cops when you were growing up?" Angie asked.

"Well, yes I did," Lucky said slowly. "I never had a car. My folks were dry-land farmers just making ends meet. My dad had an old 1937 Ford pickup that barely ran. I drove it into town occasionally. I graduated high school, and the local John Deere Dealer gave me a scholarship to Vo-Tech up in Centralia. I was doing okay at Vo-Tech, but, then I picked up one bad habit. I started smoking pot. I got hooked on pot. So, when the summer break came, and I was going back to Sinclaire to work for the John Deere Dealer all summer, I stocked up on pot before I left Centralia. Then, I got busted. And they found my stash of pot. The sheriff said I must be selling it since I had so much of it, and he whispered in the judge's ear. The judge gave me the option of doing five to seven years in the penitentiary or going into the military. I chose the Army. Three years in the Army seemed a whole lot better than five to seven in the pen."

"You weren't actually selling drugs, though, right?"

"Right. I was only using then. *But I was not selling.*" Lucky paused. "Someone had to take the fall so the sheriff and judge could get re-elected that fall. Anyway, it wasn't the worst thing that's ever happened to me. The Army turned out to be my cup of tea. They trained me in mechanics and made me a gearbox mechanic on helicopters. I was assigned to a helicopter airborne unit. I liked it so well, I stayed fifteen years."

"Why'd you leave the Army?"

"My sister, Darby. I thought about visiting her on leave. But I could only get a three-week leave. I figured if it took me a week to hitchhike here, and a week back, that wouldn't leave a lot of time to spend with her— hardly worth the effort. So I just decided I was tired of the Army."

"You didn't have a car?"

"No. I've never have been car-oriented," Lucky said and grinned. "When I was married, my wife had a car and drove me everywhere. After I had left the Army, I didn't have enough money to buy a car."

"Didn't you save any money?"

"Oh, a little bit. When my wife left me, she took our daughter and most of my savings and went back to Tupelo, Mississippi. After the Army, I put my separation pay and savings into a pile and split it four ways. One part I sent to my parents. One part I sent to my ex-wife, one part I sent to my sister in Masonville, and I kept the last part for myself."

"You need to stop worrying about other people and start worrying about yourself," Angie said, and hoped she didn't sound preachy.

"Oh, I do that now. I've got three teenage kids dependent on me."

"They can't be that hard to manage," Angie said, absently. "They don't need a babysitter do they?"

"No. They're no problem at all. Granny Watson looks after them. It's great."

"As I told you, my mother moved in with me," Angie said. "She sold her little house in Ford Junction and gave me half the profit she made. She told my brothers and sisters they would just have to wait for her estate."

"How many are there?"

"Two older brothers and one younger sister. But they're all pretty well off. Nobody needs the money. Do you have brothers and sisters?"

"A bunch," Lucky said and smiled. "One older brother, three younger brothers and five younger sisters."

"*That is a bunch*," Angie said. "Is your family close?"

"Not all of us. My older brother and all my sisters moved to Texas years ago. Three of my brothers still live down in the Sinclaire area. Darby, my youngest sister, moved to Masonville about five years ago and passed away two years ago."

A woman came through the door, walked to the corner of the pool near where they sat, and walked down the steps into the pool. She sat down on one of the steps.

Angie glanced at her wristwatch. "I need to let you go to bed."

Lucky said, "I've got a busy day tomorrow. Got to get up and drive back to Masonville and go to work. So, you're right. I need to be hitting the sack."

"Thank you for talking to me," Angie said. "I'd like to do this again, soon. Are you coming to the race in Maplewood in two weeks?"

"I'm certainly going to try."

"Good. I'll win the race so Kurt can throw another victory party, and then you and I can get together after the party and talk, like tonight."

"Sounds good to me," Lucky said. He stood and offered Angie his hand to help her up.

"You are such a gentleman. Not many men like you around anymore."

Lucky dipped his head and said: "Thank you."

They walked together to the elevator and got on when the car arrived. Lucky punched the second floor. "What floor are you on?"

"Punch the 'P.' It'll stop at the fourth floor, and I have to use my keycard to continue up."

"The 'P' stands for Penthouse?" Lucky said.

"Yes. Kurt takes very good care of me."

The door opened, and Lucky said, "Good night. Sleep tight."

"You do the same," Angie said as the doors closed.

CHAPTER FIVE

Lucky looked through the menu selections a second time, even though he had quickly decided on the Hungry Man's Platter during the first pass through, just in case something more appealing caught his eye. He saw the *Huevos Rancheros* and paused. Then he saw the Eggs Benedict. *I've never had Eggs Benedict,* he thought to himself. *Maybe I should try them.*

"Good morning, Mr. Lucky," he heard a voice say and looked up to see Angie.

"Good morning," Lucky said. In the bright daylight, Angie looked radiant; her smile was infectious.

"Have you ordered yet?"

"No ma'am."

"Mind if I join you?"

"Not at all. Please do." He started to get up to hold the chair for her, but Angie scooted it out and sat down opposite him. "Do you always get up this early?" He asked.

"I've been up for a couple of hours. Went to the fitness room already, jogged two miles and worked out with the weights."

"You sound like Kurt Maxxon."

"Well, *he is the one* who convinced me that to be a successful race car driver you have to be in top physical condition." Angie paused as if to let a fond memory float through her mind. "I've been jogging at least two miles every day for over five, six, years now. I work out with the weights every third day."

"You were up pretty late last night," Lucky said.

"I slept pretty soundly," Angie said. "Once I finally got to sleep."

"That's good. I slept very well, too," Lucky said, and grinned. "But, I never have any trouble getting to sleep, or staying asleep."

"Never?" Angie teased.

"Not ever," Lucky said with emphasis.

"After a particularly tiring race, I sometimes can't relax and go to sleep," Angie said. "And yesterday's race was really tiring."

"Was it worse than normal?"

"Yes, it was. Not only was it the hottest day yet, but then one of the cockpit air blowers quit working about half-way through the second heat. You heard Maurey say there was nothing he could do about it then. So, I ran the rest of the race with the temperature in the cockpit running close to one-hundred and thirty degrees. I was drinking water like crazy."

"Can they fix that before the next race?"

"Oh, sure," Angie said. "It's just a twenty-dollar electric motor up under the hood. Maurey is a wizard when it comes to making the car run well—and keeping me comfortable in it."

"Just so you're comfortable during the next race."

"The weather is getting warmer all the time," Angie said, tilting her head. "There's not much I can do about that."

A waitress arrived. Angie ordered a Diet Coke and a spinach and bacon omelet. Lucky ordered coffee and the Hungry Man's Breakfast Platter.

"Are you as big an eater as Kurt?" Angie asked, spreading a wide grin.

"Probably even bigger."

"Wow. That means a lot of breakfast." Angie sat back in her chair. "All night I kept thinking about our discussion about sin," she said. "I guess I've got to make a decision—and soon."

"As I mentioned last night, you need to start reading the Bible," Lucky offered.

"I need to get myself a good Bible," Angie said. "Any suggestions which one to buy?"

"Don't get a little one like this," Lucky said holding up the tiny book in his hand. "I don't remember the publisher names. I recommend you buy a good quality Bible. And, I'd buy one with large print. That way you can use it into your old age. Oh, and since you're studying, you might want a Study Bible, with plenty of room to write notes."

"I guess we need to think about old age, don't we?" Angie smiled.

"It's coming," Lucky said. "Whether we want it to, or are ready for it, it's coming. I'm getting new bifocals next week so I can read better."

"There's a Bible bookstore in a shopping mall near where we live,"

Angie said. "I'll run over there tomorrow and buy one. You've mentioned several different versions. Which version do you think I should buy?"

"The King James Version is the original Bible in the English language. But, it's written in seventeenth century Old English, which is difficult to understand at times. One of the modern versions would probably work better for you. This book I'm using here is the *New Living Translation*. It's easy to read and makes sense to me most of the time. There's also the *New American Standard Version* and the *New English Bible, and the New Jerusalem Bible."* Lucky chuckled. "Whew, that's quite a list. I read all of them at different times, to compare verses, which helps me understand what is being said."

"You have copies of all those Bibles?"

"No. I go to the library. They have a very nice assortment of Bibles. Kurt and Christina gave me a new King James Version shortly after I met them. My kids use it more than I do."

"I'll see what versions the Bible store has," Angie said.

"If they don't have what you want, they can always order it for you. So, don't buy something just because they have it on the shelf."

"Where does it talk about the camel going through the eye of a needle and rich men going to heaven?" Angie asked.

"You have someone in mind?"

"No," Angie said and laughed. "I remember it from my Sunday school days when I was small."

Lucky leafed through the pages of the tiny book. "In Matthew 19:23 Jesus says 'I tell you the truth, it is very hard for a rich person to enter the Kingdom of Heaven. I'll say it again—it is easier for a camel to go through the eye of a needle than for a rich person to enter the Kingdom of God."

Lucky flipped pages of the tiny book. "Something that's interesting to me, as I've read this passage before, is that Matthew used first the Kingdom of Heaven and then the Kingdom of God. But, later, in Mark 10:23, Jesus says, "How hard is it for the rich to enter into the Kingdom of God! *This amazed them. But Jesus said again,* Dear children, it is very hard to enter into the Kingdom of God. In fact, it is easier for a camel to go through the eye of a needle than for a rich person to enter the Kingdom of God." Lucky paused at looked at Angie, then smiled at the bewildered look on her face.

"In both places in Mark, the writer used the term *Kingdom of God.* I've not found an explanation for the deviation anywhere. But, it's not a major issue, so, I just accept it."

"How often do you *just accept* things without proof or explanation?"

"Oh, I do that every once in a while," Lucky admitted. "I accept things as they are. That doesn't mean, however, that I won't look at it again, later, and try to understand it fully."

"So, how does the camel get through the eye of the needle?" Angie asked, laughing. "I just remember looking at a needle and wondering about that."

"I've read a couple of things. For a long time, people were told there was a gate in Jerusalem where camel riders had to remove baggage to get their camel through, and some suggest that it could have been an egregious mistranslation of the Aramaic meaning 'rope,' instead of camel. Either way, it points out how people think they're going to heaven simply because they do good things and call him Lord."

"Really? People can call themselves Christians and not know him?"

"Yes. Jesus talks about that. That's why you need to read it yourself. It's not just going through the motions."

"Wow. Talking to you has made me interested in studying the Bible," Angie said. "Maybe I'll stop at that Bible store today, on my way home."

"That makes me happy," Lucky said, "You'll never regret getting into the Bible."

Lucky's phone jangled. He looked at the caller ID and said, "This is my youngest girl, this won't take long. He punched the button to answer on speaker. "Hello, Sophie. How are you this morning?"

"Hi, Daddy. I'm going shopping with Emily and her mother. We're going to the antique mall down in Fairfield. Can I borrow some money if I need it?"

"Sure," Lucky said quickly. "Take it from the family petty cash fund. You know the rules."

"Okay, Daddy. Thank you. I love you."

"I love you too, Sophie. Have fun shopping."

He watched the waitress coming toward them with a tray loaded with plates.

* * *

Angie unwrapped her napkin and dumped the silverware onto the table. As she reached for the salt shaker, she noted that Lucky was sitting with his head bowed and whispering something.

Angie stopped her actions and waited. When Lucky looked up, she said, "You say Grace in public?"

"Yes, ma'am. I always thank the Lord for providing me with another meal, whether it's at home or in an eatery."

"I'm sorry I didn't wait. Is saying Grace in the Bible?"

"Not specifically," Lucky said. "In the Sermon on the Mount, Jesus teaches us the Lord's Prayer, in which he says, *Give us this day our daily bread.* In the last supper, talked about in all the gospels and First Corinthians, it says, essentially, Jesus *took the bread,* and after blessing it, *broke it and gave it to his disciples,* and Luke nine mentions he blessed the five loaves and two fishes. There are several references throughout the Bible about blessing bread and meals. So, in a sense, I'm copying Jesus by just offering thanks for my own personal situation. If you feel blessed also, then you'll offer your own thanks."

"Those are the things I'm going to have to think about so I can do what's right," Angie said. "That's part of what we talked about last night, isn't it? Learning to live righteously. I need to learn how to do that."

"The Bible is available to us to help us read and understand God's laws—how we show our love for God and our love for all of God's creation, and when you come to your moment, you'll have Jesus in your heart, helping you."

"I'm going to try," Angie said.

Lucky laid his tiny black Bible on the table next to his water glass. The waitress came up and filled Lucky's cup.

"That coffee has a very pleasant aroma," Angie said. "I don't drink much coffee, but being around Kurt Maxxon, I smell a lot of coffee. Most of what he consumes is pretty good stuff, but occasionally, he gets some smelly stuff. That coffee you're drinking smells like it's a good blend."

"I agree with you. And it does have a great taste. Whenever I find a place like this with great coffee, I come back as often as I can."

"Do you get over here to Evandale very often?"

"No, ma'am. The two times I've been in Evandale, before, were both to come to the race."

"Well, if you do get over here, I'm sure you can run in, and they'll get you a cup of coffee."

"I'm going to have one of the kids create a database on the computer for places with good coffee." Lucky smiled broadly and bobbed his head. "I already know all the convenience stores with good coffee in the three-county area. Now, I need to branch out into diners, restaurants, and other places."

"I might even have a cup after breakfast," Angie said. She looked at Lucky. "I'm curious," she said. "On the phone with—was it Sophie?—you mentioned a family petty cash fund. What is that all about? How does that work?"

"Yes, that was Sophie—uh, Sophia Lynn—she's my youngest girl, by about nine months. She collects antique doily designs for end tables. She saves her allowance money and what she earns doing odd jobs around the house and babysitting. When she gets a chance to do some serious shopping for doilies, she likes to have the money to buy something if she really wants it. We keep a petty cash box in the kitchen. There's usually around one hundred dollars in it. If any one of us wants extra money, we can borrow up to fifty bucks from the box without family approval. Anything over fifty dollars you have to get a majority vote from the rest of the family by explaining what you want the money for."

Lucky sipped his coffee. "The rules are that it has to be paid back within three months," he continued, "which usually means the borrower must negotiate with the others to help with the repayment."

"That's interesting," Angie said. "I like that idea. You're teaching the kids responsible spending as well as responsible debt management."

"It seems to work pretty well," Lucky admitted with a smile. "I even borrow from the fund once in a while."

"I've never heard of anyone collecting doily designs," Angie said. "It sounds interesting, though."

"Most of her collection is from the colonial period. It's quite intricate and very ornate."

"Is it expensive?" Angie asked.

"A couple of the pieces she has cost more than a hundred dollars. They're usually large pieces that fit on a coffee table. Average price for what she has is probably somewhere between twelve and fifteen dollars. I suspect you could find pieces out there that cost thousands of dollars. Fortunately, she hasn't run into them yet."

"Or she ran across them, but, was smart enough to know they'd have to wait until after she marries her prince charming and can afford them."

"That's part of my plan, too." Lucky bobbed his head and chuckled.

"How did she get into doilies?"

"I mentioned, I think, that Sophia and Jason were my sister's kids. When my sister got sick, one of the church members, Grandma Abbey, took the kids down to stay with her son and daughter-in-law on their farm just south of Masonville. Grandma Abbey gave Sophia three doilies from her apartment. That got Sophie interested. Since then, she's gathered about thirty doilies from antique malls around the area."

"Do the other kids have collections?"

"Oh, yes. Jason is probably the only down-to-earth collector. He collects baseball cards. He has nearly three hundred cards since he's been collecting them for about ten years. He has a couple of cards that may be worth twenty-five or thirty dollars."

"My older brother collected baseball cards for years," Angie said. "He got them out of bubble gum packages, as I remember. He stored them in old shoe boxes. I don't know how many he wound up with, but it had to be thousands. I think he may still have them. I guess I've not asked him about them for many years. Did you collect anything?"

"No. I never had any spare money growing up. My folks were dry-land farmers barely making ends meet. How about you?"

Angie looked away. "I collected matchbook covers for years. Then, after I became a race car driver for Kurt, I started collecting die-cast model race cars of the famous NASCAR drivers. I've got about thirty of them now. Does Olivia Maye collect anything?"

"Oh, yes. She collects Raggedy Ann and Raggedy Andy dolls," Lucky said, and smiled. "That's because Christina Maxxon gave her a Raggedy Ann doll for Christmas the first year we moved her up here to live with me."

"From Kurt's collection?"

"Yes. And, probably the most expensive one he had." Lucky sipped on his coffee. "Ollie has seven dolls now; five Raggedy Ann and two Raggedy Andy. She can spend some big bucks at the antique malls also."

"I'll bet." Angie finished her diet Coke. "Won't be too many years until your petty cash fund will need to be a thousand dollars." She laughed softly.

Lucky nodded agreement.

After the waitress had bussed the empty plates, Lucky accepted a coffee refill while Angie waved off a Coke refill.

"What is this murder case you're involved with?" Angie asked.

"Oh, I'm not really that involved," Lucky said. "I went to the site to repair the transmission on one of the big earthmover machines. I spotted a girl's body stuffed under one of the storage trailers. Naturally they—uh, Charlie Armstrong and his assistant, Gregg, called the sheriff."

"That's the sheriff that was at the party last night?"

"Yes."

"I didn't hear his name."

"It's Cletus Weinberger, the Justinian County Sheriff."

"Where is this construction site?"

"Northeast of here on Hangman Creek. It's right on the county line between Justinian County and Herman County to the north."

"Not close to Copperville?"

"No. A couple hundred miles away."

"That's good, Angie said. "I hate it when there are murders close to where I live. You mentioned the evidence you found includes a used condom. Good Lord, do the cops analyze used condoms?"

"The Crime Lab does. There's DNA material on the inside and the outside. They can tell a lot from that analysis."

"Nothing surprises me these days."

"I also spotted a unique tire tread pattern in the dirt near the crime scene," Lucky said. "The sheriff may have identified who the tire treads belong to."

"You need to be careful," Angie said. "If the killer is still on the loose, he or she might not like you poking around trying to identify them."

"You're probably right. I guess Kurt has had some close calls in the past. One time he even got Christina in serious jeopardy. I'll try to be careful."

"Well, you've got me interested in this religious quest, so I don't want you getting hurt or worse before I get where I want to go. I'll need your help down the road."

"I agree wholeheartedly," Lucky said and grinned. "What's on your agenda for today?"

"All I'm planning to do today is; drive to Copperville, stop at the Bible store, and go home. I always look forward to playing with Auronia." She emptied her Coke glass. "What are you doing today?"

"I've got to drive to Masonville, stop at home and then go to the shops and go to work."

"The Borsche shops?"

"Yes. They're southeast of town—"

"Yes, I know where they are. I've been there several times."

"Oh, that's right. You and Jiggs are old enemies."

"Enemies on the track. Good friends off the track."

"There you go," Lucky said with a chuckle. "You're practicing what the Jesus told us to do." He picked up his tiny book and leafed through it. "Yes, here it is. In Luke Jesus says, 'But to you who are willing to listen, I say, love your enemies! Do good to those who hate you. Bless those who curse you. Pray for those who hurt you. If someone slaps you on one cheek, offer the other cheek also.'"

Angie wrinkled her face. "Jiggs isn't that bad of an enemy. You know him, you *work* for him. So, you know he'd give you the shirt off his back if you asked for it, or he thought you needed it."

"Jiggs is an exceptionally good person," Lucky agreed. "Especially since he races against you, but I'm going to work in your pit, and then he's to let me take time. That's being nice."

"My point exactly, Mr. Lucky. My good luck charm."

Lucky reached for the check, but Angie grabbed it before he could reach it. "I'll get it," Angie said. "It's the least I can do for all the guidance you've shared with me."

"It has been my extreme pleasure," Lucky said as he stuffed his tiny book back into his shirt pocket. "If you have questions, about any part of it, just give me a call. I may not be able to give you an answer right then, but I can research it, or ask someone else to help us and get you an answer."

"When I get my Bible, where should I start reading?" Angie asked.

"That's a good question," Lucky said. "I suggest you start with the Gospel of John. It's an amazingly informative book and an excellent place to start getting to know Jesus."

"The Gospel of John, huh?" Angie said, "You're such a big help. I'm blessed, just for being surrounded by wonderful men. You, Kurt Maxxon, and Jiggs Borsche."

"Don't forget the most wonderful man of them all," Lucky said. "Remember our Lord, Jesus Christ. He gave his life on the cross so that you and I may have salvation—eternal life with him in heaven."

"I'm still learning," Angie said. "Isn't John the fourth gospel?"

"It's the fourth, but to me, it's the one that helps me understand Jesus best. Who he is. What he is. It honors Jesus' deity—his status as the Son of God."

"I'll stop on the way home and buy a new Bible. Any place in particular where I should start reading in John?"

"Chapter One, Verse One. Go from there. You won't be disappointed."

CHAPTER SIX

When Lucky turned off State Route 60 to go north on Justinian County Road 57 the sun was just peeking over the horizon. He glanced at the clock in the truck's radio. Six-forty-five.

I timed that just right; I was smart to leave Masonville for the site at five o'clock so I wouldn't be driving into the sun.

I wonder how the kids are doing this morning? I've been putting in some long hours hoping Jiggs won't mind me taking time off to go to the races and work with Angie. I wonder what Angie is planning for today?

Please Lord, help me to honor you and the blessings you have given me. Thank you for everything.

He watched a road sign as he went by—*Ralston 11 miles.*

His cell phone jangled, and he looked at the caller ID. He answered, "Hello Ollie, what's up?"

"Good morning, Daddy," he heard Olivia Maye say. "I just wanted to check to make sure you remembered that today is the Junior Achievement convention downtown. None of us will be here when you get home tonight. It's all day, and then there's an awards banquet from five o'clock until seven."

"I remember you telling me about it," Lucky said. "But it slipped my mind. Is Jason going to be with you and Sophie?"

"No. He's in a separate program. He'll be with us for the banquet."

"How are you guys getting to and from downtown?"

"Pastor Judith, from church. Her daughter, Ellen, is in one of the younger groups."

"I'm glad you called me to remind me about this."

"I didn't see you last night," Olivia Maye said. "You didn't get home until late—after I'd gone to bed."

"I'm sorry about that—"

"Not a problem, Daddy. Where are you?"

"I'm about ten miles south of Ralston, I'm going to stop in Ralston for breakfast. There's a pretty good little diner on the north side of town."

"We'll probably just nuke breakfast sandwiches and get ready for the day."

"Is Granny Watson up yet?"

"Yes, But, she doesn't feel too well. She's sipping herbal tea right now."

"I hope she's going to be okay."

"She will be. She's just having a bad start. I gotta go. I love you, Daddy."

"I love you, too. Have a great day."

By the time he parked in the parking lot of Maple's Diner, the day had turned to early morning brightness. Lucky grabbed the newspaper from the car seat and went inside the diner. All the booths and half the tables were occupied, so he walked to a table at the back of the room. A waitress followed him with a menu.

Lucky sat down, and before the waitress laid the menu in front of him, he said, "Coffee, wheat toast, hash browns, sausage, and three eggs over easy."

The waitress said, "Thank you," picked up the menu and walked toward the kitchen.

Lucky opened the newspaper and scanned the headlines on the first page; then scanned the headlines on the following pages.

The waitress brought him a mug of steaming hot coffee. Lucky savored the aroma for a long time before he took a sip. He went back to scanning headlines in the newspaper. Eventually, he came to the comic page, and he read his favorites—older comics that somehow just keep going, *Hi and Lois, Family Circus, Dennis the Menace, Blondie, Hagar the Horrible,* and *Pickles.* The page behind the funnies contained the daily crossword puzzle, which Lucky separated and carefully folded to a quarter-page size. He pulled a pen from his pocket and started working the crossword puzzle.

The waitress delivered his breakfast order and asked if he wanted more coffee.

Lucky nodded the affirmative and carefully arranged his crossword puzzle next to his plate, entered a word, and then salted and peppered his breakfast plate. He ate while studying the puzzle clues, taking bites of breakfast, and entering letters in boxes.

Lucky heard the squeak of leather and looked up to see Sheriff Cletus Weinberger sitting down in the chair across from him. The waitress arrived with a mug of steaming coffee for the sheriff and fled back to her station.

"You didn't wait for me," the sheriff said.

"I, uh… I didn't know you were coming," Lucky said and chuckled. "Good morning, sheriff."

"I saw you drive past the station. I was in the middle of the daily briefing, so it was a few minutes before I could leave. I figured at this time of the morning, I'd find you here at Maples."

Lucky looked toward the waitress trying to get her attention. "She didn't leave you a menu."

"Oh, I ate breakfast at home at three-thirty this morning," the sheriff said, and smiled. "About all I consume at Maples before lunch is coffee. Anyway, I won't be able to make it out to the site today; just too many irons in the fire. You weren't able to grill me about this information at the victory party, but I thought you should know the details. We've tied that tire tread design you spotted to a truck owned by Arthur Tanderford—Benjamin Tanderford's son. Ben Tanderford owns the biggest farm in Herman County; five thousand acres and counting. Their farm is just north of the county line, about two miles west of the northwest corner of the site."

Lucky thought about the one-hundred-sixty-acre farm he grew up on, and that his parents still owned and lived on. It occupied one-quarter of a square mile.

Since a section of farm land is one square mile, it contains six-hundred-forty acres, Five thousand acres would be nearly eight square miles of land. Wow!

"They probably raise every crop imaginable," Lucky said from thought.

"Yeah. They grow corn, soybeans, oats, some cotton, and they have a big cattle feedlot. Ben breeds Gelbvieh cattle. Damn good beef."

Lucky nodded understanding. "If this kid was driving on the site, how did he get there? The site is fenced off. Locked gates and so forth."

"There's a water-gap in the northwest corner of the site where Hangman's Creek comes onto the property. Charley didn't think fencing it was a high priority until this happened. They're working to finish the water gap; building a barrier fence across it now."

"I'm going on up to the site. I'll see what they're doing."

"Tell them I said *hello*," the sheriff said and stood up to leave. He walked over to the waitress and handed her something.

Lucky finished working the crossword puzzle. He sipped on his coffee and stared off into space. "I wonder what Angie is doing," he said aloud.

What does she do during the weeks between races? I'll have to ask her. The next time I see her.

Lucky emptied his coffee mug and waved for the waitress. "I'll take my check, and the sheriff's, too," he said.

"Sheriff Cletus paid for you and himself," she said. "He even gave me a tip. So, you're free to go."

"Thanks," Lucky said and walked out to his truck.

* * *

Angie pushed through the mudroom door and carried her gym bag into the laundry room where she took out her jogging suit and underwear and threw them into the washer. She set the gym bag with her hot pink jogging shoes on the floor and went into the kitchen. She listened for noise from Auronia's room, and when she didn't hear anything, she walked to peek in.

Auronia was sitting in front of her big screen TV holding a controller, and wearing a headset obviously meant for an adult. She manipulated the controller lever and giggled at the screen. Angie's mother was sitting on the bed with a magazine and glanced up. Angie quickly brought a finger to her lips and smiled.

Angie quietly moved so she could see what was on the screen. The program was an arithmetic education program, with large numbers in different colors. Red and blue polka-dotted mice carried the numbers around the screen, occasionally bumping into one another.

That's good! I'm glad she's enjoying the Early Childhood programs Christina suggested.

Angie walked down the hall into her office and sat down. Blinking lights indicated she had a voice mail. She punched the buttons to listen to them.

The message she had been waiting for was there. "Hello, Ms. Prescotte. This is Randall at Family Christian Book Store. We have your Bibles ready for you to pick up."

Angie glanced at the clock. Nine-forty-five.

I'll just run over and get them and come right back.

Auronia is engrossed in that educational program.

Angie walked back and sat down on Auronia's bed "Aurie, Mommy has to run over and pick up a couple of Bibles I ordered," she said. Auronia had been so engrossed in her program, she didn't see her mother come into the room. She jumped.

"That's okay mommy. Nana and I will stay here and watch the TV."

Angie smiled. "You're learning about numbers?"

"Yes. I like numbers," Auronia said.

"That's wonderful," Angie said. "I'm so proud of you, and how smart you are."

"She's getting really good at counting," Angie's mother said.

Angie nodded and stood to leave.

"How many Bibles did you order?"

"Two. I ordered one for myself, and another one for Lucky."

"Lucky doesn't have a Bible?"

"Oh, he has a Bible. But, the one he keeps with him is a tiny little copy of the New Testament that's impossible even for me to read. He has a big family Bible that Kurt and Christina gave him, but he leaves it at the house, for his kids to use. I decided to get myself the *Updated New American Standard Study Bible* with giant print and everything Jesus says in red letters. Then, I decided to get Lucky one just like mine that he can keep with him as he travels around. And for an extra five bucks, they personalized each Bible with our names in gold on the cover. I had mine engraved with *Angie Prescotte*. I had his engraved with *Kyle O'Rourke*. I know he's going to like it."

"He better—there's not much you can do with a Bible with the name Kyle O'Rourke engraved on it."

"I'm sure he'll like it, mother."

Angie walked down the hall and stopped for a glass of water in the kitchen.

"How are you going to get Lucky's Bible to him?" her mother called after her.

"I'm going to drive down to Masonville later this afternoon, and then I'll come back here after supper," Angie answered.

"Will you eat supper alone?"

"Mother!" Angie growled. "What the hell are you talking about? Do you think I've got something going with Lucky? Well, I don't. Lucky is a very nice man. We're just good friends, that's all. He's very helpful to me in the pit. That's why I bought him the new Bible."

"You are still a young woman," her mother countered. "You shouldn't be living alone."

"I'm not living alone. I have Auronia. I have you. That's all I need."

"Yes, dear," her mother said.

"I'll leave for Masonville after Auronia gets up from her nap this afternoon."

"It's not that long a drive, but the timing seems odd," her mother said.

"If I leave here at three, I'll be down there about four. Go see Lucky at work, and give him his new Bible and then come home. Be back here by about seven."

"Can you do that? See Lucky at work?"

"Lucky works for Jiggs Borsche, you know, the driver I race against. I'll just go to the Borsche Excavating yards to see Lucky. I've been to Borsche's yards several times in years past. Jiggs won't mind."

"What does he do there?" Angie's mother asked.

"He's a transmission mechanic, Mother. He repaired helicopter transmissions in the Army."

"Oh. That's a decent income."

Angie scowled at her mother and raised an eyebrow, but decided against further confrontation.

When Angie returned from the bookstore, she walked down the hall toward her office. She stopped to look into Auronia's room and saw Auronia and Nana sitting at the table engrossed in reading a book. Angie carried the two Bibles into her office and sat down at her desk. She took her Bible out of the box and studied it. *Angie Prescotte* in gold letters caught her attention.

She glanced at the box with Lucky's Bible in it. "What does Lucky do?" she said under her breath. *He's a Transmission Mechanic! Except, the transmissions he works on are ten times bigger than anything I've ever seen.*

* * *

As Lucky walked into Charley Anderson's office in the site trailer, Charley said, "Am I glad to see you."

Lucky eased into one of the guest chairs in front of Charley's desk. "What's up?"

"They've got a dozer down—in the middle of the creek. I need you to go see if you can fix it."

"Where's it at?" Lucky said. He waved a "no," to Charley's secretary offering to bring him a cup of coffee.

"In the water gap up in the northwest corner of the site. Just follow the creek road, and you'll get there."

Lucky got up to leave.

"Grab one of the site radios," Charley said. "Leave it on channel six. If you need anything, just give me a call."

Lucky drove to the water gap. As he approached, he saw the disabled dozer sitting in the middle of the creek, water flowing around and through its metal tracks. The water gap had been dredged deeper and graded so that there were steep slopes on both sides of the creek flow. An eight-foot high chain-link fence ran to within about twenty yards on each side of the water gap slope. Lucky drove up the slight incline to the end of the fence line.

An eight-foot wide swath of brush, weeds, and tangle had been cleared to allow construction of the fence. The wild growth had already started reclaiming the cleared space.

Lucky got out of his truck and walked around to the right-side tool boxes where he kept his hard hat and safety glasses. Both were required everywhere on the site. As he put on his hard hat, Lucky spotted a piece of clothesline rope about four feet long, lying in the nearby thicket of briars. He picked it up and inspected it. Then he coiled it into a small ball and threw it into the open area of the truck bed.

Been through some rains, but still in pretty good shape. Might come in handy someday.

"We're bringing one of the behemoths over to pull the rig out of the water," the foreman of the crew yelled to Lucky from the other side of the water gap.

"That's good," Lucky yelled back. "I need to get to the gearbox from the right side."

"Give us about twenty to thirty minutes."

"I'll start loosening the nuts on the cover," Lucky said. "I can do that from above."

Lucky dug the wrenches he needed out of his tool box and then walked to the bank opposite the stranded dozer. He leaped across the small water swirl under him and landed on one of the metal tracks. He went to work at taking the cover nuts off while the crew hooked chains onto the dozer to drag it out of the water up onto the bank. During the move, Lucky sat on the operator's seat and hung on. Once the dozer was up on the dry bank, Lucky finished removing all the nuts and took the cover off. When he looked inside the transmission, he saw the problem.

The main ring gear is missing some teeth. The pinion gear is probably about as bad.

"What's the matter with it?" the foreman yelled, noticing Lucky's somber appearance.

"It ate some gears. Chewed up the rack and pinion gear set, for sure."

"Is that bad?" the foreman asked.

"It's not going to move anywhere until those gears are replaced," Lucky yelled back. "And, those are gears I don't have in my truck. We'll have to order them and have them overnighted in."

"At least it's out of the water."

"That's the only good news," Lucky said.

His radio crackled, and he heard Charley Anderson say, "Come up, Lucky."

Over the radio, Lucky gave Charley an overview of what he found.

"I'll get the serial number from this rig and call Roselyn at the shops and have her look up the part numbers for both the ring gear and the pinion gear for the model D-6 Caterpillar dozer and order them for overnight delivery to site."

"I wanted you to check a couple of the big rigs," Charley said. "The operators are complaining about them not working as good as they should."

"I can do that," Lucky answered. "It works out fine. It'll give me a reason to stay overnight, and fix the dozer when the gears get here tomorrow."

Except, I'm going to let the kids down again, having to stay out here. I won't be there when they get home to share their big day at Junior Achievement.

Lucky climbed into his truck and drove across the site to find the other equipment. Once again, thoughts of Angie came to mind. "I wonder what's she's doing right now?"

* * *

Angie sat at her desk, leafing through her new Bible. Then she stopped, closed the book, held it out at arm's length, and studied the cover. *Angie Prescotte* was emblazoned in gold on the cover. *I like that. Too cool.*

She opened the box with Lucky's Bible in it, careful not to damage the box. She looked at Lucky's Bible. *Kyle O'Rourke* in gold leaf on the cover made her smile.

The name Kyle *sounds important. I'll have to look up what the name means.*

She walked to the kitchen to get a Diet Coke from the refrigerator. The house phone rang, and she reached to answer it. She saw her mother come into the kitchen.

"Hi, Jiggs, thanks for calling me back," Angie said. "How come you called me on this phone? Uh-huh, okay. Anyway, I'm coming down to Masonville this afternoon so I can see Lucky. I have a surprise for him."

She listened, watching as her mother fussed with things on the kitchen counter, but always focused on the conversation.

I know she wishes she could hear the other side of the conversation. That's why I didn't put it on speaker phone like I usually do.

"Oh, goodness. You don't think Lucky will be there today. Uh-huh. Uh-huh. He has to wait for a gear set to arrive. Uh-huh. He might not be there until Saturday morning? Wow! Yeah. Let me know. Man, it's a good thing I decided to call you."

She listened to the phone.

"Okay. Well, maybe it would be best if I drive down Saturday morning. If Lucky has a meeting Saturday afternoon at the church, I might get with him before that."

"The surprise? Oh, I bought him a fancy new Bible. I'm sure he'll like it and start using it all the time."

After she had hung up, Angie sat down in the breakfast nook and opened the can of Diet Coke.

"You're not going to Masonville this evening?" Her mother asked.

"Oh! Hi, mother. I didn't notice you," Angie said. She continued leafing through her Bible. "No. Lucky is hung up out at the dam site where that girl was murdered. Jiggs said he had to wait for a new set of gears to be shipped in from Saint Louis. Lucky may not be done at the site until late Friday. So, I guess I'll wait and run down there Saturday morning. Maybe, I'll just stay overnight and drive back up here Sunday morning."

"Can't you just send the Bible to him by UPS?" Her mother asked.

"No!" Angie said quickly and laughed. "I want to see his face when I give it to him. I want to be there when he sees his name on the cover."

"Okay, dear," her mother said as she walked through the arch into the dining room. "It seems like a lot of driving to me."

"It'll be worth it," Angie called after her. "I'll miss being with Auronia. But, you know I love to drive, and it will still be worth it."

* * *

Lucky dug the soft brown-paper-wrapped bundle out from the space behind the truck seat. It contained a clean uniform, including skivvies and socks. He'd prepared the emergency outfit shortly after he started working for Borsche and traveling around to the different sites. Lucky was glad he'd replaced it after his stay at the Sun Setter Suites a few days before in Evandale.

Lucky was in the middle of Ralston, a small town of five thousand people. He glanced up at the long narrow vertical sign jutting out from the corner of the ancient brick building that read, *Ralston House.* Across the bottom, it read HOTEL.

Billed as a unique experience, it was the only place he could stay without going twenty-three miles to an equally ancient motel out on the highway.

At the front desk, he filled out the Registration Form and accepted the key to room 419. The antiquated elevator lurched and ground its way to the fourth floor. Lucky found his room and pushed through the door.

He walked around the small room surveying the Spartan amenities.

Back to the old cheap rooms.

He glanced at the black rotary phone sitting on the nightstand next to the bed.

Good thing I have my cell phone.

He removed his cell phone from the holster, speed dialed his home number and punched the *speakerphone* button.

Granny Watson answered the phone on the third ring. "Hello, Kyle," she said.

"Hi, Granny. How are you guys?"

"We're all fine," she said. "I'm the only one here right now."

"I knew the kids would be at the Junior Achievement convention today."

"They said they'd be home late," Granny Watson said. "They're at the banquet. What time are you going to be home? It'll just be the two of us for supper."

"It'll just be you, Granny. I'm tied up out at the dam site. I won't be home until tomorrow evening, if then."

"I'll fix myself a bowl of chili," Granny Watson said. "You sound tired."

"I am tired," Lucky admitted. "I got up so I could leave at five A.M. this morning. Anyway, I'm at the Ralston House in Ralston. I couldn't finish the job today because I didn't have the replacement gears I need to fix the rig. Hopefully, the gears will be here tomorrow about noon, and I'll be able to get the rig running by late Friday. I have a meeting Saturday afternoon at church about the new roof they need. I have to be there for that."

"Anything you need me to do here?"

"No. Just take care of the kids. I suppose I could have driven home tonight and drive back over here tomorrow afternoon. But I was completely worn out."

"Is there some place to eat close by?"

"Yes, ma'am. There's a pretty decent restaurant in the lobby of this hotel. The locals love it. I'll let you know if the reputation fits tomorrow."

After Lucky showered and donned his clean uniform, he went down to the restaurant. On the way, he stowed his bundle of dirty clothes in the truck. The pork chop dinner was better than average, and Lucky returned to his room satisfied. Once he got settled for the evening, he looked through the drawers of the chest and nightstand. No Gideon Bible. He called the front desk, who assured him they would have a Bible delivered. Lucky turned on the TV and found the news channel streaming a news banner muted it.

At least they have cable news.

At the knock on his door, Lucky got up and opened the door. A young man handed him a black Bible and quickly turned and walked away. Lucky said, "Here, I'll give you a tip for delivering it."

"Not necessary," the man said as he got onto the open elevator.

Lucky looked at the Bible. It was not a Gideon Bible; just a well-used black leather King James Version of the Bible.

Lucky realized the only chair in the room was an antique wooden straight chair at the small desk in the corner. He sat down on the bed, swung his feet up, and leaned back against the headboard. He opened the Bible to the Gospel of John, Chapter five.

Marvel not at this: for the hour is coming in which all that are in the graves shall hear his voice. And shall come forth; they that have done good, unto the resurrection of life; and they that have done evil, unto the resurrection of damnation. I can of mine own self do nothing: as I hear, I judge: and my judgment is just; because I seek not mine own will, but the will of the Father which sent me. If I bear witness of myself, my witness is not true. There is another that beareth witness of me; and I know that the witness of me is true.

Lucky stopped reading and gazed at the faded forest scene on the wall.

I've got to figure out how to explain these things to Angie so she can understand them. I gotta do that. But how?

I wonder what Angie is doing right now.

He glanced at his wristwatch. *Nine-twenty-five.*

I wonder what time Angie goes to bed? No, wait. Mom raised me to never call after nine. People can be asleep, or they are watching favorite shows on TV.

CHAPTER SEVEN

When Lucky's cell phone jangled, he glanced at the caller ID and quickly reached for it. "Hey, Jason, what's up?" He continued to work with one hand as best he could, holding the phone with the other. He wondered how some people could wedge their cell phones between cheek and shoulder to talk without holding the phone.

"Oh, goodness, that is tonight, isn't it?" He glanced at his wristwatch. "Yes, I told you I would take you and Gwendolyn. To tell you the truth, Jason, I doubt I'll make it back to Masonville this evening. So, I'll have to make some other arrangements. I'll—"

He listened.

"No. No, don't cancel anything," Lucky said quickly. "I said I'd get you guys there and I'll get someone to take you to that concert. Just sit tight, okay? I'll take care of it, even if I have to hire a taxi."

Lucky laid his phone back on the tool box lid. He needed two hands to finish wrestling the pinion gear onto the splined shaft.

Lucky glanced sideways and watched as a co-worker deftly climbed up onto the dozer and sat down in the operator's seat. Lucky remembered his name was Ralph and returned his attention to fighting the two mating parts together.

"Is it hot enough for you?" Ralph asked absently.

"I've been in hotter places."

"Iraq?" Ralph asked.

"No. Kandahar, Afghanistan. Southern Afghanistan was hotter than Hades when I was there."

"So, you were in Afghanistan, too," Ralph said. "I'd heard you talking about Iraq."

"Yes, sir. I did a tour in Afghanistan before I went to Iraq."

"How's the job coming?" Ralph asked, nodding toward the gearbox opening.

"It's going okay. I'm glad those gears were delivered a little earlier than we planned. But, it's still going to be another four or five hours before I get it all buttoned back up."

"That'll be after quitting time. Can I do anything to help?" Ralph asked.

"No, there's barely room for my hands in this gearbox. Can you stay over?"

"Yeah. I can stay over. My wife went up to Centralia for a meeting. She won't be home until tomorrow evening."

"Good. After I get this rig back up and running, I'll need you to take it for a test spin—run it around a little to check it out."

"Like I said, if there's anything I can do, just sing out. I've got nothing else to do."

"You can grease the rack gear," Lucky said, pointing with his chin. "The grease is in that can on the floor there in front of your seat. The putty knife is over on top of the gear."

"How much grease do you want on it?"

"Just fill the gaps, a putty-knife wide around the outside edge of the gear. Soon as I get this pinion gear secured, I've got to call the office to see if Jiggs can get someone to take Jason and his date to the Live Rock Concert out at the fairgrounds tonight. I promised him last week I'd take him and come get him after."

"Jason is your oldest child."

"Yes, sir."

"My sister lives in Masonville," Ralph offered. "You want me to call her and see if she'll chauffeur them? She lives out there in Northwest Masonville, about the same area you do, I think."

"That would be great if she would."

Ralph pulled his cell phone from its holster and dialed.

Lucky continued working as he listened to the conversation.

"What's your address?" Ralph asked, holding his phone away from his mouth.

Lucky told him and then listened as Ralph repeated it to his sister.

"Yeah, she'll go get them," Ralph said. "She'll pick them up about six. Tell your kids she'll be driving a red Chevy Suburban."

"Wow. That's great," Lucky said. "I sure do thank you."

"Her twins are going to that same concert, so she'll just have a couple more in the car."

"She's got twins?"

"Yeah. Robert and Roberta. They're fourteen years old."

"Is that why she drives a Suburban?"

"She has two sets of twins and three singles. She can fill up the Suburban pretty fast by herself."

They both laughed.

"Just as soon as I get this pinion gear secured, I'll call home and tell them," Lucky said as he felt the gear seat on the shaft. "How many kids do you have, Ralph?"

"None, yet. I've got two older sisters. One has seven kids, and the other one has six. My wife and I are in no hurry. There are a lot of kids in the family."

"But none of them are Abernathy's."

"Good point," Ralph said. "I'll talk to my wife and see if that is important enough."

They both chuckled again.

Lucky grabbed a shop rag to wipe his hands clean. He dialed Jason's cell phone number.

Lucky told Jason about his chauffeur arriving at six. Jason asked Lucky what her name was. "What's your sister's name?" Lucky asked Ralph.

"Pamela Westerfield," Ralph answered.

"I know the Westerfield kids from school," Jason said. "There's several of them."

"These are twins—" Lucky started to say.

"Oh, yeah. Robert and Roberta," Jason interrupted. "They're a year behind me, but they're in the same class as Gwendolyn. We'll enjoy going with them."

"I told you I'd get you there," Lucky said.

How many blessings can I get? Thank you, Lord!

Lucky decided to relax for a few minutes. He still had a lot of work to get the gear box back together and working. He glanced at Ralph, who was dozing while he sat in the operator's seat of the dozer.

I'll bet he doesn't do much dozing while the rig is running. I don't blame him, though. I feel like napping myself with this hot day. I don't have time for that. He shook his head and squared his shoulders to wake up. He reached for a cup hung on the picnic thermos of cold water the office had sent out to him. He lifted the thermos. It was still about half-full.

I wonder where Angie is right now? What's she doing?

* * *

Angie ignored her self-induced guilt for not jogging this morning and drove to Maxxon's Auto Parts store where she parked behind the building near the door into the private garage. The noon sun was blazing hot, and she was glad Kurt had Nikki's specially built garage air-conditioned. *Very thoughtful!*

Angie cradled her new Bible in her arm and laid it on the seat inside Nikki while she and Maurey Kennedy did a walk-around inspection of the number 27 Ford Fusion race car. The blue race car with flames engulfing the hood and lower body sat in the center of the gleamingly clean work area. Her hood was up, and there were wires and tubes hooked to a test console.

"I replaced the motors of both the cockpit fans," Maurey said. "I bought heavy duty motors, so they better not quit working again. You don't need another hot ride like last race."

"It's just going to get hotter each race," Angie said. She leaned in, moved her Bible up onto the dash and climbed into the driver's seat through the door window.

Where is Lucky when I need him?

On Maurey's signal, Angie started Nikki's engine. A special exhaust system muted the otherwise deafening racket and carried the noxious gasses outside. Maurey slowly scanned the gauges and meters on a huge panel he could roll around. Angie looked at the black Bible sitting on the dash. She wondered if she could read it while helping Maurey with the regular post-race inspection and test. She smiled at all the green and pink sticky notes sticking out from the book.

She'd used pink sticky notes for things she needed Lucky's help to understand, while the green sticky notes denoted things she had researched on her own, thought she understood, and only wanted Lucky to confirm her understanding.

But how and when am I going to get up with Lucky to talk about these things? Maybe we can set up a schedule to meet for Bible study.

She heard Maurey shout "four thousand."

Angie brought the engine up to four thousand RPM on the tachometer.

Through the gap between the raised hood and the car body, she saw Maurey reading data and making notes on his clipboard.

After a few minutes, Maurey shouted "six thousand."

Angie raised the RPMs to six thousand. She watched Maurey again.

And finally, the "seventy-five hundred" test.

Angie saw Maurey move so she could see him and slice his first two fingers across his throat. She shut the engine down. She knew she would have about ten minutes before they did a repeat of the engine runs. She reached for her Bible and opened it to the place she had marked with the ribbon marker.

She was reading John, Chapter Eight. "*So Jesus was saying to those Jews who believed Him, If you continue in My word, then you are truly disciples of Mine; and you will know the truth, and the truth will make you free." They answered Him, "We are Abraham's descendants and have never been enslaved to anyone; how is it that you say, 'You will become free?' Jesus answered them, "Truly, truly, I say to you, everyone who commits sin is the slave of sin.*

Angie looked around to see if Maurey was ready. She saw him fussing with something at his workbench and continued reading.

The slave does not remain in the house forever; the son does remain forever. So if the Son makes you free, you will be free forever.

She heard Maurey yell "Okay!" and then he gestured for her to start the engine up again.

Angie made the adjustments as Maurey directed, reading whenever she could. Eventually, the tests ended, and Maurey had her shut Nikki's engine down. He walked to the window next to her. "Since when are you reading the Bible?" Maurey asked.

"Since I talked to Lucky after the last race."

Maurey nodded. "I've heard it's good reading."

"It certainly is. I'm learning a lot."

"That Lucky fella, he's a born-again Christina like Christina and Kurt, right?"

"Yeah. He reads the Bible all the time. In fact, he actually *studies* the Bible."

"What are all the green and pink stickers for?"

"The pink ones are things I need Lucky to explain to me."

"Is Lucky a good teacher?"

"The best," Angie said and smiled. "I'm really enjoying having him tutor me."

* * *

Lucky stood at the back of his truck filling out the three-page service report required. He glanced at his wristwatch, *six-forty-five*. He jotted the time on the form and glanced at the starting time. *Six-thirty. Over twelve hours. I am going to sleep well tonight.*

What time did Ralph say his sister was going to pick up Jason and Gwendolyn? Six or seven? He shook his head. *I need to drink more water on hot days. It's a good thing that Gwendolyn lives just across the street. Not a lot of trouble.*

At the intense roar of an engine, Lucky looked out at the dozer being test driven by Ralph. He was doing figure eights on the creek bank. Black smoke belched out of the exhaust occasionally as Ralph put the dozer through its paces.

Lucky needed to record the serial numbers of the gear-set he had installed. He stepped up on the bumper so he could reach the boxes he threw into the back of his truck. He saw the coil of clothesline rope laying on the bed and scooted it into a corner. With the boxes in hand, he got back down on the ground. He copied the serial numbers onto the form along with the part number. He heard the dozer approaching, and he looked around to see it parking close to his truck.

Ralph stopped the dozer, set the brakes, shut down the engine, stood, stretched, and climbed down the ladder off the dozer. "You need anything else?"

"How's it running?"

"Better than ever."

Lucky grinned, "Good."

"I'm going to the house," Ralph announced and walked toward his blue Ford F-250 parked a little way off. "Thank you," Ralph shouted over his shoulder. "I'll be able to get some work done tomorrow. See you next time."

Lucky watched Ralph get into his truck and drive down the Creek road toward the office complex. He climbed into his truck and started the engine to let the air conditioner cool the cab down. He lowered the driver's side window, while he balanced the clipboard on the steering wheel and started writing the Description of Repair.

He heard a loud thud in the door next to him, and he automatically jerked back against the seat.

Then the passenger's side window exploded and flew away from him. The windshield spider-webbed around two holes on the driver's side.

Somebody is shooting at me.

Lucky's breath caught in his chest. Bending low, he slid down in the seat and then scooted across the seat and slowly, carefully, opened the passenger side door. He lowered himself to the ground. Shattered glass covered the ground, so he didn't want to lay down and crawl through it. Bending at the waist, he moved to the rear of the truck and peeked around the corner of the tool box. *Nothing!*

Then he heard someone thrashing through the underbrush along the creek bank. Lucky bent low and ran toward the commotion, using the creek bank as cover. He ran along the water's edge toward the noise. Lucky could make better time running along the relatively clear creek bed than the person running through the bramble. At one point, Lucky stopped and looked at the creek as it bent around in an exaggerated S-shape. He stopped dead and watched a man in a red shirt fighting his way through the brush, holding a rifle high in his hand. Lucky was too far away to get a good view of the man. Then Lucky heard a door slam and an engine start. He struggled up an erosion rut to the top of the creek bank in time to see a black Ram pickup spinning dirt and dust as it sped away.

Lucky ran to the area. It looked to be a party area on the creek bank, probably created by, and frequented by, local kids. A well-worn cow path angled north. Lucky knew there was a gravel county road about a half-mile in that direction, and he made a mental note of the relative location. Then he made his way back to his truck. He leaned in and picked up the site radio. "Are you still there, Charley?"

After a half minute, Charley Anderson responded, "Go ahead, Lucky."

"Somebody just shot at me," Lucky said loudly. "Call the—"

"Shot at you! Oh, good Lord, are you okay?"

"I'm fine," Lucky said. "Get the sheriff out here. He hit my truck and shot out the windshield and the passenger side window."

"You're okay, though? Can you drive the truck?"

"I don't think I should move the truck until after the sheriff's people get a chance to look it all over. And even then, it's probably not safe to drive the way it is."

"Oh, yeah. Right. Good thinking," Charley stammered. "I'll send Gregg out to get you. Bring you back into the office."

"I'll be right here," Lucky said. He walked over to look at the two bullet holes in the driver's side door. *At least a 30-06 rifle.*

He walked around to the other side of the truck so that he was on the opposite side from the shooter's position, in case the guy returned.

What if he comes back on this side?

He heard the noisy muffler of the site runabout truck coming up the Creek Road.

Gregg leaped out of the truck and walked quickly toward Lucky. "Did you see who did this?"

"Yes, I did. From about two-hundred yards away. I'd never be able to pick him out of a line-up, though."

Gregg stood looking at the hole in the driver's side door and shook his head. "That looks like a cannon shot," he said.

"Pretty big caliber," Lucky said, nodding.

The radio crackled. Charley Anderson said, "The sheriff is on his way. There should be a car here in about five minutes."

"If they're that close, I'll just hang around out here and tell them all I know."

"Okay. Ask Gregg if he wants me to come get him. He may want to go home."

"Do you want to go home?" Lucky asked Gregg.

"Hell, no," Gregg said. "I love this mystery stuff."

Lucky stowed his clipboard in the site truck. Then he locked all the boxes and access doors in the back of his truck. Out of sight of Gregg, he shook his head, then bowed it. *Thank You, Lord, again, for seeing me through.*

As he walked past the driver's side door and saw the bullet holes, he suddenly remembered how close they were to hitting him. And the bullet that went through the truck and took out the passenger side window—that one had to literally fly past his nose. His eyes watered as he realized how blessed he was.

Maybe Lucky is a good name, after all.

* * *

Angie pushed through the kitchen door and hung her key ring on the hook next to the door. She saw her mother sitting in the breakfast nook, clipping recipes from a magazine.

"I'm home, mother. Has Auronia gone to bed?"

Her mother looked at her over her bifocal glasses. "Yes, she's down for the night. Are you still carrying that Bible everywhere you go?"

"Yeah. I read it every chance I get. And I'm enjoying it very much."

"That Jiggs fellow called. He said to have you call him back."

Angie glanced at the clock on the wall. *Nine o'clock.* "What time did he call?"

"Just a few minutes ago."

She walked down the hall to her office, cradling her new Bible. She sat down in her chair and dug her cell phone from her pocket. She looked through her contacts list to find Jiggs Borsche and punched the dial button calling Jiggs.

"Hey, Angie," Jiggs said. "I thought you might like to know that someone shot at Lucky out on the dam site. He's—"

"Is he hurt?"

"No. They missed him, thank God. Anyway, he's probably going to be tied up out at the site for most of the night. I told him to just get another room at that hotel in Ralston and stay out there. He'll probably be in the office here sometime tomorrow, probably about noon, or so. You said you wanted to come see him tomorrow morning."

"He's not hurt, though, huh?"

"No. He sounded okay on the phone."

"Just frightened, probably," Angie said.

"I don't think there's much scares Lucky," Jiggs said, "He did a tour of duty in Afghanistan and then one in Iraq. So, he's seen some dangerous places. If that'd been me got shot at, I'd have to change my shorts and take a bottle of anti-depressants."

"He is very confident with life," Angie said. "I think it's his faith in God that makes him that way."

"I sometimes wish I had faith like his."

"I'm working on mine," Angie said.

"That's great," Jiggs said.

"Lucky is helping me. I've started reading my Bible, at John, where he told me to start."

"Lucky knows his Bible," Jiggs said. "He reads his little book every chance he gets."

"I think I'll drive down tomorrow morning anyway, probably get there about twelve o'clock. Hopefully, Lucky will get there shortly after that. I'm anxious to see him, make sure he's okay."

"He sounded okay to me on the phone. Come on down. You can hang out here in the offices until he gets here. There will be people around, the offices are open seven days a week from daylight till dark. My secretary works Saturday mornings."

"Does he pick up his paycheck every week?"

"No. He has it direct deposited to his bank."

"So, the shooting wasn't an armed robbery?"

"No. Lucky rarely has more than a few bucks in his pockets," Jiggs said. "I've never seen a guy who is so unconcerned about money. I guess he just believes that God will take care of his needs."

"Did he go to the hospital to get checked out?" Angie asked.

"No. When he called me, he said he'd wait next to his truck for the sheriff."

"But he said he hadn't been hit, right?"

"Yeah, right. That's what he said."

"So, it sounds to me like God *did take care* of him," Angie said. "We have a lot to be thankful for."

"Yes, we do. Have a good night," Jiggs said.

After she ended the call, she sat a moment and began to cry.

Lord, why? Why did you take Tugs? And now why did you let Lucky nearly get killed? Why? How can anyone see the good in this?

CHAPTER EIGHT

Angie parked her car in a Visitor space in front of Borsche Excavating Offices and leaned back to let the tension recede. She glanced at the clock on the radio. 11:45.

Exactly forty-five minutes. You made darn good time, lady—especially after doing that three-mile jog around the neighborhood first. You are ready for the day.

She studied the box on the passenger's seat—silver with blue letters that read HOLY BIBLE. It held Lucky's new Bible, and she was anxious to give to him.

He's going to love it. I'm sure.

Next to the box with Lucky's Bible lay her own version of the same Bible. Coal black with gold lettering on the cover. HOLY BIBLE. And down in the lower right corner: *Angie Prescotte* in gold lettering. She picked up her Bible and looked at the green and pink sticky notes jutting out of the pages.

The sun was about midway in its climb to its zenith, casting shadows at a slight angle. Angie slid out of the car and cradling her Bible in her arm walked to the office's front door.

I've never been here on Saturday. I wonder if the doors are locked.

She tried the door which swung open and pushed through it and stood in the open atrium with the glassed ceiling three stories above her. The receptionist's desk was unoccupied, but a woman in an office a few feet away stood and came out to meet her.

"Good morning, Ms. Prescotte," the woman said. "You're looking bright and cheerful."

"Hello, Juanita," Angie answered. "How have you been?"

Juanita Suarez had been Jiggs Borsche's secretary for as long as Angie had known Jiggs—this being the ninth or tenth time Angie had visited the

Borsche Excavating office over the five years they had been racing against each other.

"Has anyone heard from Lucky this morning?" Angie asked.

"Not yet," Juanita said. "He may have called Jiggs on his cell phone. Jiggs should be here any minute now." She looked at her wristwatch and nodded positively.

"That's terrible that someone shot at Lucky out at the site."

"I know Jiggs was a little more than just upset about it." Juanita led Angie to a waiting area in the corner of the atrium area. Several sofas and comfortable overstuffed chairs were grouped around a large square coffee table.

An assortment of magazines, including several that featured auto racing, littered the table.

"You drink Diet Coke, right? Jiggs keeps some in his refrigerator. Would you like me to get you one?"

"No, thank you. I'm fine. I'll just sit here and read my book until one of them arrives."

"Did you bring Auronia with you this trip?"

"No. She's at home with her Nana. This is going to be a fast trip."

"I'll bet she's growing like a weed," Juanita persisted. "My youngest grandbaby is the same age, and every time I see her, she has grown three sizes."

"Auronia is growing. You're right, I'm amazed at how fast they grow."

"Devante and I had four children. Keeping them in clothes was a full-time job." Juanita nodded with memories. "I had to work full-time here to help pay for it all." She gave a small laugh.

Angie realized how fortunate she was in not having to worry about money, and smiled.

"My little Francisca is starting to read," Juanita said. "They get her books and then teach her to read them."

"That's great," Angie said. "Auronia is reading and learning her numbers. She's my little bookworm and very bright."

"Yes. So is Francisca." Juanita looked toward her office. "I need to get some filing done. If you need anything, just ask." Juanita looked down at the Bible and shook her finger at it. "That's a very good book you're reading," Juanita said and walked back to her office.

Bragging about Auronia reminded Angie of Tugs' death in Memphis on

New Year's Day and then Auronia's birth on January 26th. In rapid succession, Angie replayed the series of events in her mind as she had done so many times before.

The frantic rush to the hospital in Memphis. *But, Tugs was already dead— killed by a drunk driver who only had a few cuts and bruises and only got a measly sixty days in jail for it.*

Then Tugs' funeral. The pain of loneliness afterward. The agonizing of what to do about Auronia growing inside her. Then Auronia was born, and Christina and Kurt Maxxon supported me through it all.

"And it was all worth it," Angie said aloud, and then looked around quickly to see if anyone had heard her. The empty building remained mute, the only noise came from the air moving through the ceiling vents.

Why didn't I bring Auronia with me this trip? It's going to be such a happy trip. Lucky will love his new Bible. I can't wait to give it to him. I can't wait to see his face when he opens the box.

Angie opened her Bible to the section of the Gospel of John she was reading. Nearly every page had at least one pink sticky note sticking out from it, and several had a few green notes. She read a few pages, pausing when she heard a sound from the back of the building. She looked around and her breath caught in her throat. Lucky came walking into the atrium from the rear of the building.

He was so tall. So poised. Angie jumped up.

Lucky stopped and looked at her.

"What are you doing here?"

"Waiting for you."

"Waiting for me. Why?"

"I—uh, I have some questions about the Book of John." She held the heavy book as high as she could to show him.

Lucky smiled and then unexpectedly, he leaned in and gave Angie a kiss on the cheek. "I'm really glad to see you," he said.

"I'm glad to see you, too. Glad to see that you're all in one piece."

"They told you about the shooting?"

"Jiggs called me last night. I worried about you—"

Jiggs Borsche walked through the front office doors. He stopped and studied Angie and Lucky. "You found him, huh?" Jiggs said to Angie.

"He found me," she said, fighting down a huge sigh.

"You two are welcome to use my conference room," Jiggs said, pointing with his chin to the room next to Juanita's office.

"Thank you," Angie said.

"I came in here for coffee," Lucky said. "Do you want a Diet Coke?"

"Not right now," Angie said.

"I'll be in my office," Jiggs said and walked to the office next to the conference room.

"I've got something for you out in my car," Angie said to Lucky. "Let me go get it. I'll meet you in the conference room."

Angie walked quickly out to her car and retrieved Lucky's Bible. When she came back into the building, she saw Jiggs standing in Juanita's office talking to her. Their voices didn't carry too far, so Angie was satisfied that she and Lucky could be confidential talking in the conference room. She went in and sat down in a chair at the end of the huge conference table. Lucky came strolling in with a large mug of coffee.

He set the coffee down on the table and wrestled a chair closer.

"Okay. What've you got?"

* * *

Lucky frowned as he looked at the boxed Bible being proffered by Angie.

Lucky took the box, reacted to how heavy it was, and set it on the table. He opened the lid and sat looking at the book before him. When he saw the gold embossed *Kyle O'Rourke* on the book, he took it out of the box and studied it for several beats. "My own personalized Bible," he said slowly and looked at Angie.

"It's yours. It has your name on it."

"I see that. Goodness gracious, it's—" Lucky ran his finger over the embossed name.

Angie thought she detected tears in Lucky's eyes.

"Golly," Lucky said in sing-song fashion stretching it out. "I've never had a Bible this fancy. And it's a Study Bible. A red-letter edition. And in giant print. Golly, this is just great. Just fabulous."

Angie thought she detected a glow about Lucky's face.

Lucky opened the Bible and scanned a few pages. "You shouldn't have spent so much money on me."

"Why not? You're worth every penny of it, Mr. Lucky. You've already been a gigantic help to me. It's just a small *thank you*."

Lucky flipped pages through the Bible. "This is wonderful." He opened the back of the book and studied the full-color map for a minute. Then he flipped pages back. "Look at the size of this Dictionary, Concordance, and Thesaurus. He moved pages looking at the context. "Wow, this is great," he said. "This Concordance is where you start any search of the Bible. Find the keyword or phrase of the subject in this Concordance and then go read the references. I do that sometimes just to pass the time."

Lucky smiled and looked at Angie. Then he noticed her Bible laying on the table near her. "Is your Bible just like mine?"

"Identical, except for my name on the cover. Angie Prescotte."

"That's neat," Lucky said. "We have matching Bibles." Then he paused and focused on Angie's book. "What are all the green and pink tabs?"

"Green tabs are the things I researched myself and think I've got it figured out," Angie said slowly. "But, I need you to say I'm right. The pink tabs are things I need you to explain to me. At least, some part of it."

Lucky leaned his head to one side and did an exaggerated look at Angie's Bible. "That looks like a year's worth of explaining. How far have you read?"

"I'm just now reading chapter three."

"Uh-huh. Do you have plenty of sticky notes?"

Angie giggled a little. "I hope you don't think I'm a slow learner. It's just—well, it's just, I want to learn this stuff really well."

"Like your life depends on it?"

"Something like that, yeah."

"Your life probably does depend on you learning this stuff well," Lucky said and smiled. "Your eternal life, that is."

"Eternal life in heaven is something I never really thought about before I met you. But, now, it has become very important to me," Angie said, as she gestured with her hand on her heart.

"That's wonderful," Lucky said, nodding. "You are well on your way toward salvation."

Jiggs stuck his head in the door. "Excuse me, Lucky. What's the number of the truck you're driving?"

"Five-three-eight," Lucky said.

Jiggs stopped and thought for a minute. "That's the oldest pickup in our fleet," he said. "It's been beat all to hell. How did you get stuck with it?"

"It was sitting there with the key in it, so I decided to use it temporarily."

"Is Pleasant Valley Ford towing your service truck in for repair today?"

"Yes. They picked it up about eight this morning. I left to come here after that."

"Any idea how long it's going to take to fix it?"

"The service manager said if it was just replacing windows and plugging a couple of bullet holes, it should be done by next Wednesday."

"What did your kids think about your getting shot at?" Angie asked Lucky.

"Haven't told them," Lucky said. "Probably won't either. It's already old news. No need burdening them with it."

"You were able to secure all your tools in that service truck, weren't you?" Jiggs said.

"Yes, sir. Each box is locked with both an installed lock and a padlock. The swinging doors are secured with padlocks. Then there's a cover that locks in place over the open area. She's all buttoned up. Nobody going to get anything out of that truck except maybe the street map of Masonville I left in the glove box."

"That's good. I guess if they need that, I can afford another one," Jiggs said gesturing at the advertising maps laying on the conference room credenza and walked to his office next door.

Lucky sipped on his coffee.

"Where are the Coca-Colas?" Angie asked.

Lucky stood up and walked to a cabinet in the corner of the conference room. He opened a cabinet door to reveal a small refrigerator. He opened the refrigerator door and took out a Diet Coke and carried it back to Angie.

"Juanita offered me one earlier," Angie said. "I've never seen Jiggs drinking Diet Coke."

"He doesn't touch the stuff. He keeps those for Kurt Maxxon, whenever he comes to visit Jiggs."

"How often is that?"

"Two or three times since I've been around," Lucky said.

"These are just for Kurt?"

"Yes, ma'am. And Kurt's favorite racecar driver."

Angie dipped her head and smiled widely.

"Can you stay for supper at my place?"

Angie paused. "Sure. I'll call my mother and tell her I won't be home for supper."

"Good. You can meet the gang," Lucky said. "Granny Watson always cooks enough for the family plus any company that happens by."

"That sounds like a great idea. I'm looking forward to meeting *your gang.*"

"If we're going to be studying the Bible together, we need to figure out a way to get together more often. Maybe Lucy's would be a good spot. Except we'd have to pick a good time. She gets busy at times."

"There's a yummy place in Copperville," Angie said eagerly. "*The Farmer's Platter.* It's the restaurant in the Twilight Motel on the north side of Copperville."

"That's what we need," Lucky said. "How long would it take me to drive up there?"

"Probably about forty-five minutes."

"Hey, that's not bad. We could meet there Saturday afternoons. I usually work Saturday morning."

"Saturday afternoon works fine with me, too," Angie said. "After we put Auronia down for her nap, I could leave and meet you there. What do you think, about two, two-thirty? We could study the Bible for a couple of hours and still get home in time for supper."

"Or we could have supper at the ... what did you call it?"

"The Farmer's Platter."

"That sounds interesting," Lucky said. "Is the food any good?"

"It's better than most. If we get there before about four o'clock, we should be able to get a parking space close in. After four, you'll have to walk three or four blocks to the door and stand in line for about thirty to forty minutes to be seated."

"That's Saturday, a week from today," Lucky said as he pulled his pocket notebook out.

Angie smiled. "Unless you want to make it Monday, Tuesday, Wednesday, Thursday, and Friday, also."

"Probably can't do that," Lucky said grinning. He glanced at his wristwatch. "We've got an hour or so right now. Let's see what you got in questions."

"I don't want you laughing at me. Some of my questions may seem kinda stupid."

"In Bible study, there are no stupid questions. Keep that in mind."

"Good. In that case, let's look at the first one." She opened her Bible at one of the pink tabs sticking out.

Lucky laughed out loud. "How come there are four or five green tabs and thirty or forty pink ones?"

"Are you laughing at me?"

"No. I'm laughing at your pink tabs."

Lucky noticed that Angie's breathing quickened.

"What time is your meeting at church?" Angie asked.

"Four o'clock. Why?"

"I was just wondering if I was holding you up from that."

"You're reading the Gospel according to John, right?"

"Yes. I'm up to chapter eight. But a lot of my tabs are in chapter three."

"Three's a good one," Lucky said. "John has a lot of information needed for understanding the entire New Testament and Jesus' life. And it contains the most quoted Bible verse of all."

"Which one is that? Angie asked with a slight frown.

"John three, verse sixteen," Lucky said and opened his new Bible to the page. "For God so loved the world, that He gave His only begotten Son, that whoever believes in Him shall not perish, but have eternal life."

"Oh, yeah. I remembered that verse from Sunday school many years ago," Angie said.

"Actually—" Lucky started, then paused, running his finger down the page, "the whole paragraph, verses sixteen through twenty-one, contains the basis of Christianity. In verse seventeen, it says 'For God did not send the Son into the world to judge the world, but that the world might be saved through him.' A little further down it says, 'This is the judgment, that the Light has come into the world, and men loved the darkness rather than the Light, for their deeds were evil. But he who practices the truth comes to the Light, so that his deeds may be manifested as having been wrought in God.'"

Angie stared at Lucky for a long time. "Pretty heavy stuff, huh?"

"Very heavy stuff," Lucky said.

Angie opened her Bible to John three. She looked at all the pink tabs sticking out. "This chapter started out rather bland, with the guy named Nicodemus asking how to be born again. I thought it was interesting."

"The key to being born again is first you are given life with water in the amniotic sac," Lucky said and looked at Angie. "That's what Jesus meant by 'water and the Spirit' referencing our birth in water. Then to be born again, you must be baptized by the Holy Spirit, where He says Spirit gives birth to Spirit."

"Is that why there was a John the Baptist before Jesus came?"

"John the Baptist led the way, baptizing converts with the water of the River Jordon. But, John the Baptist consistently said, even in the latter parts of this chapter, that another one was coming who would baptize with the Spirit. So, yes there is an analogy there."

"All my questions in this section were centered around the being born again. That's what I'm trying to understand."

"You're doing great studying the Bible. You're an excellent student."

"Not dense?"

"Not dense," Lucky repeated and smiled.

"I want to understand it completely," Angie said. "I can't just accept anything that I don't understand completely."

"That's the best attitude to have," Lucky said. He glanced at the clock on the wall. "It's lunchtime, and I'm hungry. Let's go down the street and get a sandwich."

"I'm hungry, too," Angie said. She closed her Bible and stood up. "We can take my car."

Both picked up their Bibles, cradling them.

Lucky walked to the door to Jigg's office. "We're going for a sandwich. Do you want to join us?"

"No, thanks. I had a big breakfast. Are you guys coming back here after?"

"Probably for a couple of hours."

"Juanita and I will be leaving shortly. We'll lock the front doors. So when you come back, you'll have to come in through the shop. You have your key to that door, right?"

"Yes, sir." Lucky glanced toward Angie standing a few feet away and noticed the red and green tabs sticking from her Bible. "It looks like we have quite a bit of studying to do."

* * *

Angie accepted Granny Watson's handshake with only a little trepidation. Angie's mother was also not given to hugs and embracing other people. Angie had learned that from Christina more than anyone else.

After a short tour of the house, Lucky pulled a chair out at the kitchen dinette table, and Angie sat down. Granny Watson continued flitting around the kitchen cooking supper.

"The kids will be here any minute," she assured Lucky and Angie. "It gets to be five-thirty or six o'clock, and they're hungry." She smiled broadly.

"What are you fixing, Granny?" Lucky asked. "It sure smells good."

"Baked beef stew."

"One of my favorites," Lucky said.

"It does smell good," Angie agreed.

The three children arrived separately, but within five minutes of each other—banging through the kitchen door and putting backpacks and valuables on racks near the door.

When each of them saw Angie sitting at the dinette, they stopped and let Lucky introduce her as the race car driver sensation of the SRVSCRA.

"Wow, that's a cool job." Olivia and Sophia said in unison. They turned to each other and laughed.

Jason, who arrived last, said, "I need you to teach me how to drive. Dad doesn't have the time."

Lucky smiled and said, "When you need to learn, I'll teach you."

"Yeah, but I'd rather have her do it," Jason persisted. "When the other guys see me being taught by a racing star, I'll be the envy of them all."

Lucky chuckled, and Angie blushed slightly. "I'll think about it," Lucky said. "Do you want to teach him how to drive?" he asked as he nodded sideways at Jason.

"How could I refuse?" Angie said and laughed.

After supper, they sat at the dinette table and got to know each other. Sophia brought out three of her prized doilies for display. Olivia Maye brought a Raggedy Ann and a Raggedy Andy doll to show Angie.

Jason said, "My baseball card collection is pretty Plain Jane. Not very interesting."

"Sure they are," Angie said with gusto. "My brother collected baseball cards for years and had quite a collection that he was very proud of."

"Well, then you've seen a baseball card collection," Jason said.

"What if you show me the prized ones? I love to hear about treasure hunts."

Granny Watson changed the subject. "Does anyone want pie for dessert?"

Everyone, except Angie, said "Yes," even though no one knew what kind it was. Angie nodded only after everyone else had acquiesced. It turned out that Granny Watson's homemade flaky crust would have made any filling delicious. But the fresh rhubarb and strawberries made this pie exceptionally good.

"That was fabulous!" Angie exclaimed after they'd finished off the pie.

Jason excused himself and went to his room, and the two girls chatted with Angie about what was involved with driving a race car and about Auronia. Lucky contributed occasionally.

At one point Angie said, "I better head north toward home."

"How far is it?" Olivia Maye asked.

"It's only thirty miles from here."

"Wow. We can go up and play with Auronia," Sophia said. "Will you take us up there, dad?"

"I can do that," Lucky said. He grinned at Angie. "If Angie wants us to come."

"Anytime," Angie said. "You're all welcome anytime."

CHAPTER NINE

The service manager for Pleasant Valley Ford led Lucky through the service bay to the lot behind, where Lucky saw his service truck sitting by itself towards the back of the lot. They walked to the back of the truck, and the service manager pointed with his index finger.

"Those are the marks I was talking about. We don't think they were there when we locked up last night," He said and looked at Lucky.

"Those weren't there when he towed the truck," Lucky said.

"You're sure?"

"Positive," Lucky said and bobbed his head for emphasis. "I locked all the tool boxes and that cover in place. Then I checked them again while the guy was loading the truck onto the wrecker. Those marks look like someone tried to jimmy the padlocks on the cover."

"That's what we were wondering. We called the sheriff, and he's on his way. He should be here any minute since he's just on the north side of town,"

Lucky walked around the truck surveying the repaired bullet holes in the door.

"Have you got coffee?" Lucky asked.

"Sure do," the service manager said leading Lucky back into the service bay. He pointed to a sign that read WAITING ROOM. "It's in there, just around that corner. There are donuts, too."

Lucky walked around the corner into the waiting room, poured himself a cup of coffee, picked out a chocolate-coated éclair, and moved to the table where the local newspaper was scattered. He dug through the paper and found the crossword puzzle. It was different from the one he had worked earlier in the Masonville paper.

Lucky carefully folded the newspaper sheet to quarter page size and studied the puzzle. He quickly filled in a dozen boxes; stopping when he heard the service manager coming toward him talking to someone. Lucky stood up.

The service manager said, "Lucky, this is Lester Whittington, the Herman County Sheriff."

Lucky shook the sheriff's hand.

"I've wanted to meet you for a while," the sheriff said. "I've been working with Cletus Weinberger over in Justinian County on the Garfield homicide."

"Oh. Yes, sir. I found her body."

"Yeah, I know," the sheriff said as the three men sat down at the table. "And, you found a lot of other evidence, too. Most, if not all, of the people involved, or thought to be involved, in the case, live up here in my county. I've been up to my eyeballs interviewing them and investigating the case from here." The sheriff took out a small notebook and laid it on the table. "So, those marks were not on your truck when you left it here?"

"I didn't bring it over here," Lucky corrected him. "They came and towed the truck in from the construction site."

"You couldn't drive the truck?"

"No, sir. The windshield was shot up."

"Oh. Okay. Did you check the tool boxes and that cover when you left the truck?"

"I made sure they were all locked," Lucky said. "In doing that I'm pretty sure I would have seen those pry marks if they had been there."

"Was it dark when you did that?"

"No, sir. It was just after sunup, Saturday morning."

"Your tow driver wouldn't have looked for anything like that would he?" the sheriff asked the service manager.

"No."

"Was there anything of value in the back of your truck?" the sheriff asked Lucky.

Lucky shrugged. "The toolboxes are full of valuable tools and such. But under that cover where the pry marks are, not much value to anyone other than myself I wouldn't think. If someone was trying to pry the locks off to get in there, they had to be hoping to find something of value."

"Can we open it up and look?" the sheriff asked.

"Sure," Lucky said and stood up. The other two men followed him out to his service truck. As he neared the truck, Lucky pulled out his key ring from his hip belt loop. He climbed up on the rear bumper and leaned in to unlock the padlocks holding the cover down. He scooted the cover over on top of the tool box and folded it at the seams with hinges welded on. He jumped down off the bumper.

The open space contained a five-gallon pail of 90 WT axle grease, three quarts of motor oil, a roll of paper towels, a small coil of copper tubing snuggled into the corner, along with a dozen cardboard coffee containers bearing the logos of various convenience store logos on them.

"The most valuable thing in there is that copper tubing," Lucky said. "It's probably worth twenty-five, thirty bucks. The grease and motor oil, I suppose they cost another twenty-five, thirty bucks." As he spoke, he noticed the coil of clothesline rope he'd thrown into the truck in the far corner of the open space. "And the rope, no value."

"We were hoping there was something in your truck that would lure someone to break into our shop trying to get to your truck," the service manager said. "Nothing was missing from our shop."

"There weren't any tools missing from your shop?" The sheriff said to the service manager.

"No, there weren't."

"What about car parts missing?" the sheriff persisted. "Like radios, GPS gizmos, electronic things. Anything like that missing?"

"No. Besides Lucky's service truck, we had Mrs. Bradford's Lincoln Continental and Cal Hickey's Ford Fusion in the shop overnight. Cal picked his car up earlier, and we had him look it over. Nothing gone from it, and no damage to any other vehicles. We're having someone look at the cars on the lot."

"What about Wilma's Lincoln?"

"Mitch, Ronny, and I went over it with a fine-tooth comb. It doesn't look like there's anything missing from her car."

"She keeps her thirty-two-caliber handgun in the glovebox," the sheriff said. "Did she leave it in there?"

"No. Mitch always makes sure she takes it with her when she leaves the car, for that very reason. We don't want someone breaking into our shop to get her pistol. Her grand-daughter always follows her over here and carries her home. Mitch always makes sure the grand-daughter knows Mrs. Bradford is carrying." He smiled and winked. "You need to tell her she can't carry a firearm within the city limits, sheriff."

"You tell her that," the sheriff retorted. "I don't want to go through it again. She damned near cost me the election the last time I told her to leave her weapon at home."

Lucky looked at the sheriff and raised his eyebrows.

The sheriff grinned. "She's ninety-four years old and tough as nails. She's been carrying all her life. She thinks she has a constitutional right to do it. The last sheriff told me: 'She's harmless. But, you best not mess with her.'"

"Is the weapon loaded?" Lucky asked.

"Hell, yes, it's loaded," the sheriff yelped. "Anyhow, we'll have to dust your truck for fingerprints. That'll take a couple of hours. "

"I'll just have to cool my heels in the waiting room," Lucky said.

"You know," the service manager said slowly. "Some kid was nosing around your truck while it was parked out front last Sunday. We saw him on the security cameras."

"You still got those tapes?" the sheriff asked.

"Sure. I can have Ronny email copies to you."

"Do that," the sheriff said.

The service manager led them back into the service bay. As they entered a white van drove past them and parked just behind the rear door. The sheriff walked to the van and spoke to the driver, pointing to Lucky's service truck. Then he returned to go into the waiting room for a cup of coffee and a donut.

"That's pretty good coffee," the sheriff said as he sat down at the table.

"I agree," Lucky said. "I'm going to put this place on my list of good coffee stops."

"You do that," the service manager said. "A lot of our customers stop by for no other reason than to say hello and have a cup of coffee."

"I'm glad I found this place," the sheriff said. He grinned at the service manager.

"I'll buy an extra can of coffee each week," the service manager said.

"Where do you buy your coffee?" Lucky asked.

"Sam's Club. It's their store brand."

Lucky recalled his conversation with Angie at breakfast a few days before. "I need to have one of the kids build me a database of places with good coffee." He said out loud. He took his notebook from his pocket and jotted himself a note about it.

* * *

"Are we still solvent?" Angie's mother asked her as she hung her car keys on the hook near the door and walked to the refrigerator to get a Diet Coke.

"Yes. The portfolio is growing nicely. We just made a few adjustments to it."

"You like that advisor, don't you?" her mother said.

"He's been excellent for us, Mother, " Angie said. "He's managing my money a lot better than the woman I had doing it before. I'm happy with the results."

"What's his name?"

"Christopher Swanson."

"Is he married?"

"No. He's single and dating one of the girls at the library."

"Does the girl at the library have as much money as you do?"

"What difference does that make, mother?"

"I'm just talking."

"Talking nonsense. Stop trying to get me married off," Angie said and took a long draft of soda. Angie's eyes twinkled. "Mother, what happens if I get married, and my new husband doesn't want a nagging old mother-in-law living with him?"

"I can't imagine that happening, dear."

"In the meantime, has Auronia had lunch?"

"Oh. Sure. We eat lunch about noon around here. It's already two o'clock."

"I'll be in my office," Angie said and walked down the hall.

She sat down at her desk and opened the Bible lying on it. The green and pink sticky notes jutting out from the pages drew her attention. There were three times as many pink tabs as green.

I wonder what Lucky is doing now. I wish there was a way we could get together more often for Bible study.

Angie dug her cell phone out from its holster and speed dialed a number. "Hey, Angie. What're you doing?" she heard Lucky say.

"Talking to you," she said and smiled. "What are you up to?"

"Right now, I'm cooling my heels."

"Are you on your way back to Masonville from getting your truck?"

"No. Not yet. I'm sitting in the service waiting area of Pleasant Valley Ford. The sheriff wanted it dusted for fingerprints of whoever tried to break into it."

"Somebody tried to break into your truck?"

"Yes, ma'am. The back part."

"Did they get anything?"

"No. I had it all locked up. Nothing is missing that I can see."

"What is going on? First, someone shoots at you. And now they're trying to get into your truck. Do you have something in the truck you should be telling the sheriff about?"

"If I do, I don't know what it is."

"Are you going to have to spend the night over there?"

"I sure hope not. I've got an end loader in the shop that needs to be fixed. UPS should have delivered the gear set before noon. I promised I'd have it done and ready to go by quitting time. So, it looks like quitting time might be anytime between now and tomorrow morning when they come to haul it back to the site so they can get some work done."

"You might have to work all night?"

"I do, sometimes. The sheriff is coming to talk to me. Did you need something?"

"No. I was just starting to read John Eight, and I got to wondering what you were doing. I'll talk to you later."

"Okay, Angie," Lucky said and rang off.

"You're really hung up on that Lucky fellow, aren't you?" Angie's mother said, standing in the office doorway.

"I'm not hung up on anyone or anything, mother," Angie said sharply. "Give it up."

"Okay, dear. I just wanted to tell you we're going to have baked chicken for supper, with broccoli and onions."

"I've never said anything about having to approve the menu. Chicken and Broccoli sound fine to me."

"Auronia loves broccoli."

"That's great," Angie said. "I'm glad she's getting a nutritious diet."

"Auronia will be getting up from her nap in a little while. Do you want to play with her for a little before supper?"

"Yes. Let me finish reading this chapter."

"You're still reading the Bible?" her mother said.

"I'm still reading the Bible, mother, and I'm going to keep reading the Bible. Lucky is helping me understand it."

"You got a lot of Bible reading at church growing up."

Exasperated, Angie spoke with an edge to her voice, "Mother, I'm thinking there's more than just growing up in the 'going to church' habit, and that's why I'm reading the Bible!"

"Okay, dear. I'll let you know when Auronia wakes up."

"Just let her come romping in here."

"She won't bother you?"

"Auronia has never *bothered me*, mother. I can't imagine a time when she would."

* * *

Lucky got home and into bed about twelve-thirty after a long night in the shop. He slept soundly until he heard the kids banging around getting ready for their day. He knew the three of them were very involved in building a float the church was sponsoring for the upcoming Independence Day Parade through downtown Masonville. They had been chattering about the project for several days.

Lucky rolled over and looked at the clock radio. *Six-fifty.* He considered trying to get more sleep but decided that would never happen with three teenagers rummaging around in the house. Then he heard Granny Watson's voice yell "The pancakes are ready!"

Pancakes sound great. Potato chips and cupcakes from the vending machine in the break area of the shop don't hold one over very well.

Lucky sat up on the edge of the bed and glanced toward the bathroom he shared with Jason.

There was no light shining under the door. Lucky stood and moved to test the doorknob into the bathroom. It twisted, and he peeked around.

Empty. Thank you, Lord.

Lucky walked into the kitchen just as the kids were exiting it. Granny Watson eyed him as he moved to his stove-top percolator and poured a cup of fresh coffee. The pungent oils reached his nose.

Wow, that is great smelling coffee.

"What brand of coffee do we use?" Lucky asked Granny Watson.

"Oh, it's Folgers something," She walked over and swung a cabinet door open.

Lucky followed her gaze to a red plastic can of coffee. *Folger's Black*

Silk.

"You want some pancakes?" Granny Watson asked.

"Yes, ma'am, please. They smell awfully good."

Lucky sat down at the table. The morning newspaper was refolded and lying next to his place at the table. Lucky scanned the pages of the paper, reading headlines. Eventually, he came to the comics and read each of his favorites. Then he turned the page over for the crossword puzzle and folded the paper to a quarter of the full size. He reached for one of the pens in a cup on the shelf behind him and started filling in the puzzle boxes.

Granny Watson swung a plate full of pancakes in front of him and then went to get her homemade blueberry syrup out of the refrigerator. She also brought a tub of margarine. Lucky moved the folded newspaper next to his plate and worked the crossword puzzle as he ate.

Granny Watson busied herself cleaning the kitchen, putting dishes in the dishwasher.

Lucky had polished off the plate of pancakes and had nearly finished the puzzle when he heard his cell phone jangling in the bedroom.

"I'll bring it to you," Granny Watson said, and she walked down the hall.

Lucky pulled up the recent calls. He didn't recognize the last number, but it was the same area code as the dam site. Lucky punched the speakerphone on and punched the redial button.

"Justinian County Sheriff's Office," a voice said.

Lucky jerked back and studied the number.

"This is Lucky O'Rourke," he said. "Did someone there just try to call me?"

"What's the number on your caller ID?"

Lucky read the number.

"That's Sheriff Weinberger's cell phone. Hang on, let me patch you through."

Lucky listened as the line buzzed, beeped, and went to static, and then he heard.

"Weinberger," the sheriff answered.

"O'Rourke."

"Hey Lucky, how are you?"

"I'm fine. Did you call me?"

"Yeah, I did," Weinberger said. "I was talking to Sheriff Whittington last night at a meeting. He told me about someone trying to break into your tool boxes over there at the repair shop. It's not bad enough that they're shooting at you; now someone is trying to steal your stuff. We're wondering if they're connected somehow. But to the point. Whitt told me he saw a roll of clothesline rope in the back of your truck."

Lucky glanced at Granny Watson, whose face turned sour with a frown. *I need to be more diligent with using my speaker phone.*

"Uh, yes, sir. There is a short piece of clothesline rope coiled up in the back of my truck."

"Has it been in there for a while? If not, where did you get it?"

"I found it laying in the brush up near the water gap last week while I was fixing the dozer."

"This is not for general publication," Weinberger said. "The Garfield girl was strangled using clothesline rope. The lab has fibers from the wound."

"Well, someone had thrown it into the brush. I put it in the back of my truck. If you want it, you're welcome to it."

Good thing Granny Watson is good at keeping things secret.

"I'd like to get it and have the lab test it."

"I can run it over to you."

"I can have a deputy meet you at the County Line Truck Stop. That's only a forty-five-minute drive for you."

"What time?"

"You tell me when you can be there, and I'll have a deputy there to get the rope."

"Ten o'clock," Lucky said.

"Ten o'clock," Weinberger confirmed. "He'll be there. I think it might be young Benjamin Dickens. You met him the day you found the body."

"I'll be there," Lucky promised. "Let me know the lab results."

"Do you want the rope back?"

"No. It just looked like a handy thing to keep."

"Are you a pack rat?"

"I've been accused of that," Lucky smiled as he caught Granny Watson bobbing her head. She turned away at his glare.

"Somebody shot at you?" Granny Watson said after Lucky rang off talking to Sheriff Weinberger.

"Yes, they did. But they obviously missed. So, it's a closed subject. I don't want the kids to know about it."

"I'm not going to tell the kids," Granny Watson said as she picked up his empty plate from the table. "But you could have told me."

"What good would that have done?"

Granny opened a cabinet door and started to put the plate into the cupboard as she said, "It would have worried me."

"That dish needs to be washed," Lucky said.

Granny Watson stopped. She looked at the dish. "Oh yeah. You're right," she said and leaned down to put it into the open dishwasher.

* * *

Lucky walked to his work area in Borsche Excavating shops. The end loader he'd worked late into the night to repair was being loaded onto a huge flatbed trailer to be taken back to a site.

One of the operators will be glad to have it back so they can work today.

Lucky set the large cup of coffee on his tool box, and he noticed an old crossword puzzle he had folded and stuck behind his tool box. He sat down on the bench he kept in the area and sipped his coffee while he studied the crossword puzzle.

His cell phone jangled. He answered it on speaker phone. "You found the murder weapon," Sheriff Weinberger said.

"I did?"

"Yeah. The clothesline rope."

"Good golly," Lucky said. "It was the clothesline rope I found up in the brush?"

"Yeah. There were latent fingerprints on the rope. Not good enough to convict, but good enough to corroborate. They also matched the ones we found on the girl's purse. And the fibers match those they found in the wound on her neck."

"So, you can identify the killer?"

"Well. Not really. We don't have a match in the IAFIS system."

"What is IA—"

"IAFIS is the FBI's old Integrated Automated Fingerprint Identification System. It's been replaced by a newer system called the NGI system. NGI stands for Next Generation Identification. The prints of the killer don't match anything in the files. We need a name. So, we're no closer to IDing the killer than before."

"Why aren't the fingerprints in the system?"

"Probably because the person wearing them has never been fingerprinted for anything. That means he or she has never been in the military, never been arrested, never applied for weapons permits or anything like that."

"A young person?"

"Yeah. Probably a friend of Ms. Garfield's. Probably early- to mid-twenties."

"Did the girl have a boyfriend?"

"Yeah, she did," Weinberger said. "We've talked to him several times. He passed a polygraph test a couple of days after you found her under that trailer. He's been more upset about the girl's murder than the girl's mother."

"Did Sheriff Whittington tell you about the kid spotted on surveillance tapes nosing around my service truck Sunday night?"

"No. What's that all about?"

"I have no idea. The service manager at Pleasant Valley Ford mentioned it while we were talking. He told Sheriff Whittington that he would have somebody email the surveillance tapes to the sheriff. I assume they did that."

"I'll have to check that out," Weinberger said. "You're turning into one hell of a detective. But, I guess you understudied Kurt Maxxon, didn't you?"

"Why certainly! It started the same day I arrived in Masonville; in Kurt Maxxon's truck, I might add."

CHAPTER TEN

Lucky glanced at the clock on his dash as he approached Copperville.

Whew. That didn't take long.

The main street through the three-block downtown area was made of fired bricks and broad enough for four lanes of traffic plus angle parking on either side. At the north end of downtown, a huge sign on the west side of the road heralded the Twilight Motel and, on top of it, an even bigger sign read: *The Farmer's Platter.*

Lucky drove slowly south through town looking for a parking space, and then made a U-turn to drive back north, eventually finding a parking space two blocks away from the motel/restaurant. He looked at the Bible laying on the passenger seat but decided to leave it while he explored the area. He didn't think he had seen Angie's red Porsche parked anywhere, but he made a thorough check as he walked to the restaurant.

As he read the menu posted in the window, he heard a horn honk. He turned to see Angie neatly U-turn into a space across the street.

Lucky stood watching Angie, as she exited her car and strolled across the street. She was wearing her signature yellow tank top and form-fitting blue jeans and wearing bright pink sneakers. The breeze ruffled her short hairdo. She smiled broadly as she approached.

"You found it, huh?" Angie said.

Lucky looked up at the sign above them. "How could I miss it? The smell of great food fills the air for miles around here."

"How long did it take you get here?" Angie asked.

"Only about twenty minutes," Lucky said.

"That's because you're north of Masonville."

Lucky smiled and pulled the door open for Angie, following her into the restaurant.

The buzz of conversation and the clanking of silverware and plates greeted them along with even more intense aromas of food cooking in the kitchen. The restaurant held about four dozen tables in an open area, with two dozen booths along three of the walls. Every booth was occupied, and most of the tables had at least one person.

"This place is still busy," Angie said to the waitress.

"We had a late lunch bunch today because of the Boy Scout get together this morning at the park. Most of these people have eaten and will be leaving."

The waitress led them to a table at the back of the room and laid menus in front of them. "You want something to drink?"

Angie ordered a diet Coke. Lucky ordered coffee.

"I'd say, from the size of this crowd, your assessment of the food quality is right on point," Lucky said.

"It sure is. There aren't many restaurants this big in a town this size around here," Angie said as she swung her gaze around the room.

Lucky's eyes followed hers. "This is a big restaurant."

"In a town where downtown is all of four blocks long. It's a farmer's gathering hole on rainy days."

"I noticed you just whipped a U-turn to get into the parking space across the street. You best not try that in downtown Masonville."

"Everyone does it all the time here in Copperville. You see a parking space, you go get it," Angie said. "What is this about someone trying to break into your truck?"

"Well," Lucky started, and then paused as he glanced around. Satisfied that no one was eavesdropping on their conversation, Lucky continued in a low voice. "It seems as though I found the murder weapon accidentally in the bramble along the fence near the water gap out at the dam construction site."

Angie leaned back and leveled her gaze at Lucky. "You found the murder weapon?"

"Yes, ma'am. It was a coil of clothesline rope about four or five-foot long."

"Wow. So now you're even more famous with the sheriff." Angie laughed softly.

"We theorize that was what was behind the attempted break-in of my truck."

"If the killer is still running around loose, you need to be more careful."

"What did you do this week?" Lucky asked. "Besides jogging and lifting weights and reading the Gospel of John."

"I met with my financial planner," Angie said. "We meet every six months to see how things are going. My main concern, of course, is having enough to let Auronia succeed."

"You don't worry about your future?"

"Well. Sure, I do. But, making sure Auronia has a good life is my first priority. How are your kids doing?"

"Oh, they're doing just fine. Each has their interests, and they go off and do their thing every morning. We all come back together at night and regroup—get ready for the next day."

"That's great," Angie said. "It sounds so family-like—so homey."

* * *

"Do you think we'll be able to study the Bible in this restaurant? It's noisy now, and even then, when it empties, it's likely to be uncomfortable with the echoing," Lucky suggested.

"Probably not," Angie admitted looking around the room. "But, there's a church just up the street. Why don't we go up there?"

"What kind of church is it? Lucky asked."

"I think it's Catholic."

"That's okay," Lucky said. "Since I'm a Lutheran now, there's not a huge difference between the Lutheran and Catholic services."

"What about between Methodist and Catholic?" Angie asked.

"I don't know about that," Lucky said and grinned. "I've never been to a Methodist service."

"I think that Methodist and Baptist services are really pretty similar," Angie offered.

"In that case, since I've been to a Baptist church, then there's a huge difference between a Methodist and a Catholic."

"You think?"

"I know," Lucky said smugly.

When the waitress arrived with their drinks, she asked, "Are you ready to order?"

"I'll have the Country Fried Steak," Angie said. "With Coleslaw and pinto beans."

"I'll have the same," Lucky said.

"How did your kids do in the parade yesterday?" Angie asked.

"Oh, they were great. All the kids took turns riding on the float for a few blocks each. Jason was dressed up as a shepherd. Olly and Sophia were dressed as biblical ladies."

"Did you get pictures?"

"Yes, ma'am. You want to see them?"

Lucky showed Angie the pictures on his cell phone, offering a brief commentary on each. "There's a whole Facebook page full of pictures. I'll write down the Church's Facebook page for you later," he said.

The waitress arrived with a tray loaded with dishes and bowls.

"That's enough food for four people," Lucky said, after surveying the plates arrayed in front of him. "It smells fabulous."

"That's why it's named *The Farmer's Platter*," Angie said. "I always leave here with a doggy box, which of course, since I don't have a dog, is for me to eat later."

Lucky was impressed with the dinner rolls. He ate most of his plate but waved off dessert.

Angie boxed up all the scraps. "You can take that for your kids."

"You take it," Lucky insisted. "In our house, Granny Watson and I are the only ones who eat leftovers. The kids rarely do."

Lucky followed as Angie drove north from downtown about six blocks to the church.

The sun was inching toward the tops of the trees along the western horizon, and a stiff southerly breeze brought warm air.

The sign indicated it was *St. Michael's Catholic Church*.

They parked and walked inside the church. A nun dressed in a white habit met them in the vestibule. A name tag on her habit read: *Sister Agnes*.

Lucky explained they were looking for a place to do Bible study.

The nun waved for them to follow her. "We have a study area open to all people that might be just what you need." She led them to a large room with an open door. There were tables and chairs arranged in no particular order. Along one wall was a built-in bookcase, holding about fifty books to a shelf. The number of Bibles on the shelves was impressive.

"Do you have Bibles?" the nun asked.

"Yes. Yes, we do," Angie said. "Out in our vehicles."

"You'll find Bible Dictionaries, Concordances, and other references in the bookcase if you need them." The nun turned to leave.

"Can we pay you something for using this?" Angie asked.

"We have an alms box out near the front door. You can give an anonymous donation in the envelopes provided."

"We'd like to come once a week, or so," Lucky said.

"That's wonderful," the nun purred. "We're always open—twenty-four-seven, and three-sixty-five. Feel free to use it once a day, if you like, or whenever you want."

After retrieving their Bibles, they rearranged a table and two chairs in the corner.

"How far did you get into John?" Lucky asked after they got comfortable.

"We need to talk about Chapter five."

"Are we making any real progress?" Lucky asked after he'd turned to the chapter.

"I think so," Angie said, "slowly."

"Still more pink tabs than green," Lucky observed.

"I told you I needed help." Angie opened her Bible, picking a particular tab that she had marked. She watched as Lucky leafed through his Bible to the same spot. "I'm at verse eighteen, which is titled *Jesus' Equality with God.*"

Lucky moved a few more pages.

Angie continued, "If I'm reading this right, apparently, the Jews are trying to find a reason to execute Jesus. They have asked him questions, and he answers them. It says, 'Therefore Jesus answered and was saying to them, "Truly, truly, I say to you, the Son can do nothing of Himself, unless it is something He sees the Father doing, for whatever the Father does, these things the Son also does in like manner.'

'For the Father loves the Son, and shows Him all things that He Himself is doing; and the Father will show Him greater works than these, so that you will marvel.'"

"Okay," Lucky said. "Do you have a question?"

Angie shrugged. "Is there something special about this section—talking about fathers and sons?"

"Several places in the gospels, the gospel writers have Jesus educating his listeners about the true relationship between God and Jesus as the Son," Lucky said. He paused to read the scripture. "In this Gospel, John treated Jesus as the Son of God—Jesus as a deity, and in it, Jesus is telling the world that he learned from God the Father, just as we all learn from our fathers. We learn from and take our cues from our fathers. And that is what Jesus is talking about here—"

Angie sighed audibly.

"Are you okay?" Lucky said, looking at her intently.

Angie waited a long time before speaking. "When you talk about learning from your father, I know that is true. It's just … it's just that my dad was killed when I was five years old, and …"

"I'm sorry," Lucky said. "I didn't know that. Do you want to talk about it?"

"I'm okay," Angie said quickly, then added, "Yes. Maybe I do need to talk about it."

"I'm listening," Lucky said.

Angie went silent for a long time. "I remember my mother taking us kids over to her folks' place about a mile outside of town. We always loved going there—to the farm. My mother left us and didn't come back for a long time—three or four days, I think. I had two older brothers, Bertrand, who I think was eight, and Lamar, who was probably seven. I was five years old. My little sister, Nicole, was still in diapers and I had to change her once in a while."

Angie paused and took a deep breath.

"Grandma Higgins told us that our dad was missing."

Tears began to leak from Angie's eyes and trickled down her cheeks.

Lucky laid his Bible down, and took Angie's hands into his across the table and squeezed them in support. He looked around the room and spotted a box of tissues on a nearby table. He got up and went to get the box of tissues and set it in front of Angie. She snapped a tissue from the box and daubed at her eyes.

"I'm such a baby," she whimpered.

"Not at all," Lucky soothed. "Goodness gracious, we all have sad memories that overwhelm us at times."

Angie looked at Lucky's face. He was calm. His face had a glow about it.

"Anyway," Angie said recovering. "My dad was a railroad engineer. The spring rains had weakened a trestle over the Mink River. The bridge gave way, and the engine fell into the flood. That big old engine was washed about a mile downstream by the water. That's how powerful the water was.

My dad's body was never found."

"I'm sorry," Lucky said again. "That is truly tragic, especially when there is no closure."

"My mother probably suffered the most from lack of closure. But, I'm sure it affected all of us kids, except maybe, Nicole."

"And, how are you feeling now?"

"Well, I do wonder where my dad is. Where did his body wind up? Did the animals eat him up?"

"Eventually, I think you'll be able to deal with this as you come to grips with the concept of body and spirit. The most important thing for you to know is that your father's spirit, his soul, left the body at some point and was taken up into heaven. So, what happened to your father's body after that is unimportant, especially now, what, thirty," Lucky looked at her with the question in his eyes, "years later?"

"I'd just like to know where he died," Angie said.

Lucky nodded understanding. "I assume they searched the river banks downstream."

"Oh, yeah. My mother kept calling the sheriff. She kept calling the railroad's office. She kept the pressure on them. I seem to remember they found one of his boots, his engineer's cap, and a lantern he carried in the engine. The lantern, I think, was found just upstream from Masonville's city limits. That would mean it floated about one-hundred miles from the accident scene."

"Have you ever gone to the place and walked the banks?"

"No. It was … it was northeast of Pleasant Valley. I've driven across the highway bridge near the railroad bridge they built to replace the washed away one. But, I've never got out and walked along the river bank."

"Maybe you should do that?"

"Would you go with me?"

"Sure."

They sat in silence for several minutes. Then Lucky said, "Are you ready for some more Bible study?"

"I think so," Angie said. "But, let's skip this part about the father—at least for a while."

"Okay with me," Lucky said. "What's next?"

"Still in Chapter Five, Verse forty-four, headed *Witness of the Scripture.*" Angie leafed to the next page. "It says, 'How can you believe, when you receive glory from one another and you do not seek the glory that is from the one and only God? Do not think that I will accuse you before the Father; the one who accuses you is Moses, in whom you have set your hope. For if you believed Moses, you would believe in Me, for he wrote about Me. But, if you do not believe his writings, how will you believe My words?'"

Angie paused to read her writing on the pink sticky note. "Jesus says, I'm not the one accusing you, but 'the one who accuses you is Moses. How did Moses get into the picture?"

"Great question," Lucky said. "Moses is the great lawgiver, so to speak. Moses went up on Mount Sinai and received the two tablets containing the Ten Commandments from God. You probably remember that story from Sunday school, right?"

Angie nodded.

"You can read that story in the Book of Exodus, Chapters nineteen and twenty. The Ten Commandments were the first rules and regulations sent down from God since his instruction to Adam and Eve about the Tree of Knowledge. When they ate the forbidden fruit, they committed the original sin. Original sin is discussed in Romans, Chapter Five." Lucky thumbed through the pages to Romans.

"Verse twelve through fourteen, says, 'Therefore, just as through one man, sin entered into the world, and death through sin, and so death spread to all men, because all sinned—for until the Law sin was in the world, but sin is not imputed when there is no law. Nevertheless, death reigned from Adam until Moses, even over those who had not sinned in the likeness of the offense of Adam, who is a type of Him who was to come.' What they're talking about here is that after Adam had introduced sin, by violating God's commandment, every person on earth was a sinner and the result of sin was eternal death. It may be a little hard to understand, but every man, woman, and child walking the face of the earth was a sinner, and their souls were condemned to eternal death—until Moses received the Ten Commandments." Lucky shuffled pages.

"To rectify this condition, God issued the Ten Commandments, through Moses, which gave humankind a point of reference with regard to sin. If you obeyed God's ten commandments, God would grant you eternal life. Thus, the promise of salvation."

Angie sat staring at Lucky. "How do you keep all of this straight?"

"It gets easier as you progress in your studies. Further along in Romans Five, it basically says, that codifying the rules would increase the amount of sin, but would increase salvation even more." Lucky leafed a few pages. "The last of that part says, 'as sin reigned in death, even so grace would reign through righteousness to eternal life through Jesus Christ our Lord.' That's our goal in life, eternal life through the salvation our Lord, Jesus Christ paid for on the cross."

"We are all sinners, huh?" Angie said.

"Yes, we are. Jesus makes that plain."

"Why was eating that fruit so awful?" Angie asked, frowning. "What is wrong with knowledge?"

Lucky looked at Angie. "Who do you think knows more about the world—the universe? God the creator, or His creation?"

"That would be God."

"Okay," Lucky continued, "Then with a little bit of knowledge, can you—a creature of God's creation—make all the right decisions? Can anyone?"

"Probably not. As a racecar driver, I need a lot of knowledge, I need to know a lot of things to make decisions. I also have to practice a lot."

"The race car analogy is a good one," Lucky said. "Adam and Eve did other things wrong. They lied to God. They passed the blame to the serpent. They tried to hide from God. Did He end their lives right then?"

"No."

"So, He is a merciful God."

Angie nodded. "Go on."

Lucky gave a quick nod. "In the Fifty-First Psalm, David says, 'For I was born a sinner—yes, from the moment my mother conceived me.'"

Angie sat staring at her Bible for a long time, then said, "If I were to sum up what you've told me tonight," she drew a breath. "Excluding the part about the father teaching us, it would be that from the time of Adam until Moses, there weren't any commandments for man to live by." She looked at Lucky, and he mouthed, "yes," so as not to interrupt her. She continued, "and so every human being was a sinner and condemned to eternal hell at death for sin. But, Moses was given the Ten Commandments, and the laws of God were codified so everyone could know what they were. If you violated them, then you were condemned to eternal death. Then Jesus Christ came to us and died on the cross to atone for mankind's sins and offered us eternal salvation if we believed in him and lived as he directed us to—promising us eternal life in heaven."

"Pretty close," Lucky said. "Keep reading your Bible, and next time we'll cover some more of John."

"Why do you like John so much?" Angie asked.

"The first reason is that the Gospel of John is an excellent synopsis of the entire New Testament. John captured and presented Jesus in his deity, from the perspective of Jesus as the Messiah, as the Son of God. The Gospel of Matthew looks at Jesus from the perspective of his earthly kingdom. The Gospel of Mark looks at Jesus from the perspective of his servanthood. Luke looks at Jesus from the perspective of his humanness— the son of man. So, most Bible scholars don't start to understand Jesus Christ until after they study the Gospel of John."

"That's interesting," Angie said. "I never realized the different gospel books were anything more than just a story of Jesus' life and times rehashed four times."

"Each gospel has its nuances the others miss. You'll see similarities, but that's not what matters in the reading. It's understanding what is important in each book. The biggest reason why John is so important is that John was the only Apostle who followed Jesus all the way to the cross. He understood something the others did not."

"Really? The only one?"

"When the large crowd of armed soldiers sent by the Chief Priest arrived to arrest Jesus, nine of the remaining eleven Apostles fled to safety. Only Peter and John remained with Jesus at that point. Then Peter denied Jesus three times before the cock crowed, and since Jesus had told him he would, he went out to weep, leaving only John."

"Is that in the Bible?" Angie asked. "I didn't see anything about it."

"You have to study the Bible closely, to follow that story through all the gospels. But, it's there."

"I want to learn to study the Bible that way," Angie said.

"You see," Lucky said, and grinned. "You're already looking forward to studying the Bible."

"How long is it going to take me? How long have you been studying the Bible?"

"Since I met Jesus in Iraq. Going on seven years now."

"You must know the Bible frontwards and backwards," Angie said.

"Not really," Lucky said quickly. "I have studied the Bible steadily, but it is still a gigantic mystery to me. As you read, again and again, there are things that you see revealed; where you didn't understand before, just because you've experienced it. There is so much I haven't studied, and I need to."

"And you expect me to understand it in a few weeks?" Angie gasped.

"Not at all. I expect you're as confused by it all as I was when I started," Lucky smiled. "Relax, you're doing wonderfully."

"You think?"

"I know. Just relax."

CHAPTER ELEVEN

Lucky gave up trying to dodge the random sprays from 2-liter of Coke and Pepsi bottles and moved several yards off the edge of the Winner's Circle. The solid blue number 4 Ford Fusion sitting at the center of the Winner's Circle was getting drenched in the sticky spray. In addition to its white number 4 markings, there were large red *TRUE VALUE* logos on both doors, the hood, and the trunk lid.

The Winner's Circle was in the shade of the grandstand, which also blocked any breeze. The air was heavy. The low cloud layer trapped the heat and humidity. There had been a fear of rain   until after the start of the third heat. After that everyone forgot about it.

A fan wearing a blue number 4 cap moved next to Lucky just out of range of the sprays. "Dave hasn't won a race in so long, I can't remember the last time," the fan said.

"His sponsors are sure happy about it," Lucky said, staying ready to dodge streams of cola.

"Yeah. Those three can get pretty wild at times."

Lucky caught the motion of Angie coming toward him, still clad in her gold and red racing uniform, walking with a second woman, whom he didn't know. Angie had finished today's race in second place, and Lucky was disappointed about that.

"Peggy, this is Lucky, uh, Kyle O'Rourke," Angie said. "Lucky, this is Patricia Kellogg, Dave Kellogg's wife."

"Call me Peggy," The woman said. She was the same age, height, weight, and coloration as Angie, except she wore long blond hair, where Angie's black hair was cut short and matted down from her helmet's headgear.

"Hello, Peggy," Lucky said. "Call me Lucky."

"Your luck on me ran out today," Angie said, showing a small pout. "Dave beat me in the last lap."

"You went too high in turn two and Davy shot under you," Peggy said.

"I couldn't see from the pit how—"

"Yeah, it was really my fault," Angie confessed. "So, it didn't have anything to do with your luck on me."

"I'm glad to hear that," Lucky said, and smiled.

Another woman, a few years older than Angie and Peggy walked toward them. She wore a name tag above her right breast that read *SUSAN BURPEE / LYLE'S TRUE VALUE*

Angie and Peggy hugged the newcomer.

Angie moved next to Lucky and said to him: "Susan is the wife of Leonard Burpee, Dave Kellogg's sponsor. The three guys whooping it up the most, besides Dave Kellogg, are the co-owners of Lyle's True Value hardware store in East Centralia."

"We're setting up a victory party at the Convention Center," Susan said. "I'm on my way over there now to finish setting it up. You all are coming, aren't you?"

Angie and Peggy both bobbed their heads. "Did you invite Kurt and Christina?" Angie asked.

"Yes. I was sitting with Christina in the stands watching the race. Lenny called me during the last lap and said, 'if we win, set up a party at the Convention Center.' I called the Center and told them we were coming over. Christina said they would stop by for a while."

"We're going to another victory party," Angie said to Lucky.

Lucky had allowed time for a party in his plans for the day, but with the hope they would be celebrating Angie's win. His plans included driving back to Masonville tonight, leaving Maplewood about 8:00 and getting home about 11:00. "Did you want to do some studying?" Lucky asked Angie in a low voice.

"Yeah. We'll have a little time after the party," Angie said. "Probably for an hour or so."

Susan waved "later," and walked toward the parking lot. Lucky saw Kurt and Christina Maxxon coming toward them.

"Congratulations, Peggy," Christina said as she neared the group. "If we have to lose, we like losing to one of the older teams in the association."

Kurt smiled and nodded agreement; then he looked at Angie. "You did great today, Angie. I'm proud of you."

"Second place isn't a win," Angie said. "I'm sorry."

"Listen, young lady," Kurt said, "You are not going to win them all. That's an impossibility. But, remember, you still get ninety points for placing second, and you got additional points for leading several laps. You win in this league by getting as many points as you can. And you're doing just fine."

"I guess you're right," Angie said. "But, after today, I'm going to win all the rest of them."

"Okay by me," Kurt said. He shook Lucky's hand. "You've been a good influence on her."

"I hope so," Lucky said.

"Are you two going to the party?" Christina asked Angie and then looked at Lucky.

"Yeah, we're going," Angie said. "Aren't we, Mr. Lucky?"

"I'm in," Lucky said.

"Let me go and grab a quick shower and get out of these racing clothes," Angie said. "I'll meet all of you at the party."

* * *

When she arrived at the Maplewood Furniture City Hotel and Convention Center, Angie sat in her car for several minutes thinking. *This party shouldn't last too long since I don't have to stay for the whole thing. Lucky and I should be able to go off and spend an hour or so in Bible study. I've got some questions I need Lucky to answer.*

She watched Lucky arrive and park his service truck at the back of the lot. He got out and walked briskly toward the ballroom entrance. Angie glanced at her Bible laying on the passenger seat. Her cell phone chimed, and she looked at the caller ID. Then she answered it on speaker phone. "Hello, mother. What's up?"

"Auronia and I were thinking about getting an ice cream cone. I was wondering what time you'd be home. We listened to the race. You didn't win. So, there isn't a victory party for you, is there?"

"No, mother; not for me. But, there is a—"

"Are you on your way home now? When will you be here?"

"There *is a party*," Angie said. "It's for Dave Kellogg, the winner. He invited Lucky and me to join them. I'm at the Convention Center now."

"You're still in Maplewood?"

"Yes. And I'm probably going to stay here tonight."

"With that Lucky fella?"

"No, mother, Not *with* Lucky. I'm completely worn out, and so I'll just get a room up here for the night. However, I'll be by myself. Alone. Solo."

"Do you have clean clothes? Clean underwear?"

"Yes mother, they were clean when I put them on after I showered. They'll be okay to put on tomorrow morning."

"What about pajamas?"

"I don't need pajamas, mother. I can sleep just fine without pajamas." She smiled because she had thrown her Baby Doll PJs into her duffle bag, just in case she won.

"Alright, dear. Auronia and I will walk up and get an ice cream cone at Magic's Ice Cream Parlor."

"That's good, mother. I'll be home tomorrow morning early. Tell Auronia I love her and miss her."

"Uh-huh. I'll do that."

Angie punched the button to close the call.

That made my decision a lot easier.

She got out of her car and walked toward the lobby door, instead of the ballroom entrance.

After securing a key card to a room, Angie walked toward the doors into the ballroom.

She pushed through the doors into the ballroom and stood to look around. A long table had been set up near the entrance doors, next to the bar. Susan Burpee sat at one end of the table.

Dave Kellogg was wandering around behind the table, talking on his cell phone. Peggy Kellogg was sitting at the center of the table chatting with Christina and Kurt Maxxon, and Lucky. Peggy stood and waved Angie toward the table. Lucky got up and slid a chair out for her.

"A glass of Chardonnay?" Kurt said as he stood.

"Yes, please."

"You want a Budweiser, Lucky?"

"No. I'm drinking coffee," Lucky said. "I have to drive back to Masonville yet tonight."

* * *

"You're not staying here tonight?" Kurt asked Lucky.

"No. I have to go home tonight," Lucky said. "I have to take the girls to Bible Camp tomorrow morning."

"The one over on Skunk Hollow Lake?" Peggy asked.

"Yes. Near Cotonana."

"I went there when I was a teenager," Peggy said, letting her eyes wander to the ceiling above Lucky's head. "That is such a neat place. Hiking, canoeing, campfires, roasting marshmallows, storytelling, God, I remember it like it was just yesterday."

"My girls are looking forward to it," Lucky said.

"How many do you have? How old are they?" Peggy asked.

"I have two girls; both of them are thirteen," Lucky said.

"You have twins?"

"No. They're not twins," Lucky said. "They aren't even sisters. But, it's a long story. One of the girls is my daughter. The other girl is her cousin who I took guardianship over when my sister died of cancer."

Peggy stopped and digested what Lucky had just told her. "That's wonderful," she said.

Angie reached into Lucky's shirt pocket and took out his little black Bible. "Is there anything in here about parents abusing their children mentally?"

"What's that all about?" Lucky asked.

"My mother—," Angie started to say, and then stopped and looked around. "Oh, I'm sorry. I shouldn't intrude into the party this way."

"Is that a Bible?" Peggy asked.

Lucky looked at her and bobbed his head in the affirmative. "It's the New Testament only."

"Are you a preacher?" Peggy asked.

"No. I'm just a born-again Christian."

"Oh." Peggy watched Dave Kellogg come over and sit down next to her.

"Oh, good, you've met Lucky," Dave said. "He's a born-again Christian like Kurt and Christina."

"I hope you're not as fanatical about it as Roland," Peggy blurted.

"Who is Roland?" Christina asked.

"Davy's older brother," Peggy said, stressing each word. "He just recently decided he's a born-again Christian. And none of the family has been spared his incessant preaching and his *holier-than-thou* attitude ever since."

Lucky paused, looking at Peggy. "Does it bother you that he is born-again?"

"Being born-again doesn't bother me—" Peggy started to say.

Dave interrupted her. "My brother is just that way. Everything he gets into, it's always pedal-to-the-metal, gung-ho, damn-the-torpedoes-full-speed-ahead. He's always been that way." He shrugged and smiled at Peggy.

Peggy scooted back in her chair and stared at Dave, then she looked back at Lucky. "It doesn't bother me that he's a born-again Christian," she said slowly. "What bothers me is that he says, 'I'm a born-again Christian, and that makes me better than all the rest of you.' That's what bothers me." She straightened up and glared at Dave. "I'm sorry if you disagree with me."

"I don't disagree with you, my love," Dave said. "In fact, I agree with you."

Lucky saw the fight go out of Peggy.

"Lucky is helping me learn about Jesus," Angie announced. She looked at Peggy. "I hope to understand what Jesus meant about being born-again one of these days soon."

"That's wonderful," Peggy said. "Just don't treat the rest of your friends and relatives like they are beneath you because you made it. I think we all are striving for that condition."

"You think everyone is striving to be born-again?" Lucky asked.

"Well. I think most rational people are," Peggy said. "Maybe not every single one."

"But you are?"

"Yes. I definitely am."

"Me, too," Dave said quickly.

"That's great. What keeps you from doing it?" Lucky asked.

Dave said, "Time. Circumstances. Work. Bills to pay."

"The kids," Peggy said, then looked up at the ceiling. "I mean, we have three kids, ages nine months, two years, and four years old."

"At any rate," Kurt said, his deep basal voice commanding attention, "We are of one mind that being born-again Christians is a desirable condition. Christina and I thank you all for thinking that way."

"Hear, hear," Christina said.

Angie handed Lucky his little black Bible. Lucky took it and opened it to the back pages. He took out his magnifying reading glasses and read.

Then he thumbed pages back into the middle of the book. "As to your question," Lucky said. "In Ephesians chapter six, it talks about children and parents. It starts with 'Children, obey your parents because you belong to the Lord, for this is the right thing to do.' Then in verse four, it says, 'Fathers, do not provoke your children to anger by the way you treat them. Rather, bring them up with the discipline and instruction that comes from the Lord.' That verse talks about fathers, but it obviously would apply equally to mothers."

"I just wish; I just wish my mother—" Angie realized she was stuttering

"Does your mother have a problem with you racing cars for a living?" Peggy asked.

"No. No, it's not the racing, I don't think," Angie said, fighting down her anger. "It's the constant harping about me being alone—a single mother with a child to raise. The 'When are you going to get a man?' Kind of thing." Suddenly Angie realized that every face within earshot was staring at her. She jumped up and fled through the doors to the restrooms.

"I suspected something like this was happening all along," Christina said. She stood, said, "Excuse me," and walked toward the restroom doors.

Kurt looked at Lucky with a blank expression. "It's probably best that we just stay out of this."

Lucky grinned. "That sounds like very sage advice, Colonel."

* * *

Angie sat in the chair in the women's restroom. When Christina pushed through the doors, she wasn't surprised. Christina washed her hands in one of the sinks.

"Do you want to talk to someone about it?" Christina asked.

"You're probably the perfect person for me to talk to about it," Angie said. "But, I'm not sure there's a lot to talk about. I doubt anyone can convince my mother that I'm not suffering terribly from being a single mother. Just because I'm not doing the nightlife and chasing men, doesn't mean I'm defective."

"Mothers are like that," Christina said. "They want the best for their daughters. They want their daughters' lives to turn out better than they had. And then, well, they rely on the old norms of our society to develop the concept of what that better life should look like."

"I don't fit those norms," Angie said.

"The important thing is what's right for you. But, your mother may be having difficulties dealing with what's acceptable for the modern day. In her heart of hearts, your mother probably recognizes you as a successful young woman. But she probably has no point of reference to guide her thinking on what that means. Women in our generation—mine *and* your mother's—made a home for her family. If they worked outside of the home, they were school teachers or nurses. But, for a woman to be a successful race car driver wasn't even considered. Nor was a woman supposed to be a successful lawyer or doctor. So, you and thousands of other young women have gone out and made careers in areas that used to be the domain of men. Your mother is probably just having difficulties dealing with the new order of things."

Angie nodded understanding.

"And that means," Christina continued. "Your mother still thinks in terms of, 'one man, one woman, and baby makes three.' If you don't have all three of those people, then you don't have a viable family."

"Lucky is probably in the same boat," Angie said slowly. "But, I don't think his mother is carping at him about being single—raising three teenagers by himself."

"And his mother would have no reason to. Not in our modern society."

"It's still supposed to be a man's world, huh?"

"Yes. It's supposed to be. But, we both know that's not the way it is anymore." Christina studied Angie's face for a few seconds. "Do you want me to talk to your mother? Maybe try to ease the tension a little?"

Angie sat silently. "No. That would probably just make matters worse."

"Your mother is not doing anything unusual. She's thinking of you. It's just that her way of thinking about you is nowhere near what you would like her to be thinking about you. If that makes any sense."

Angie stood up and hugged Christina. It makes perfect sense, in a nonsensical way,"

Angie walked to look at her face in the mirror. "It's a good thing I don't wear any makeup," she said.

"No mascara to run. That helps." Christina smiled. "You are a very pretty woman."

"Thank you," Angie said and followed Christina back to the table.

Angie picked up her untouched wine glass and took a sip.

"What time were you planning to leave to drive home?" she asked

Lucky.

"Anytime up till eight o'clock. It's about a three-and-a-half-hour drive. If I get home by midnight, I'll be okay."

"I'm going to wave off any Bible study tonight," Angie said. "I've got a room upstairs, and I'm going up and just collapse into bed."

"That race today was tiring," Lucky offered. "The heat and humidity wore us all out. I could tell you were wearing down towards the end."

"You're getting to know me pretty well, Mr. Lucky."

"And it seems like you're getting to know me, too."

"I like what I see," Angie said.

"Me, too."

Angie sipped on her wine and ordered a second one. The party seemed a little dull, and she talked with Lucky, Christina, and Kurt about various subjects. Eventually, she just began to tire.

I don't want to start yawning.

She pushed back from the table and said, "I'm going to turn in. That race wore me out today," She turned to Lucky and said, "I thank you for helping me today."

"You're more than welcome," Lucky said and grinned. "I'm going to go ahead and leave for home. I'll call you about next week's Bible study times."

"Good. I'll be waiting."

Angie took her time, mingling with others on her way to the lobby door. At one point she stopped to watch Lucky as he walked out to his truck. She thought about catching up to him and walking with him—saying a proper good night there.

Dave Kellogg came up beside her and said, "Lucky's a real nice fellow. I hope it all works out for you guys."

Angie started to reply, then thought better of it. "Thank you," she said. "I'm sure it's going to."

In her room, Angie poured another glass of wine and took several large sips. She undressed and donned her Baby Doll pajamas and climbed into bed. She fluffed the pillows behind her and laid back against the headboard. She reached to turn on the television. *I'm so tired.*

She tuned into a fashion competition just as the evening gown models were parading down the runway. "This week's winner will determine who gets the advantage in next week's wedding gown competition," she heard the host announce. Angie laid the control next to her and relaxed into the pillows.

* * *

Angie stood viewing herself in the full-length mirror on the closet door. She turned several times to get different views. The dress fit nearly perfectly.

My bust and my butt look good. The butt is a little bigger than when you bought the dress. But in only a few hours, I'll climb out of this dress and into my new life. I'll still be Angelica Beverly Prescotte. But, I'll also be Mrs. Kyle Tipton O'Rourke.

The light lavender dress was knee length—modest and appropriate—for a woman who, while never officially married, had a baby out of wedlock, and thus was viewed as tainted in the eyes of many of the conservative elders in the church. She sensed that some of the older women in the church, tacitly, did not approve of Lucky marrying her. *To each his own.*

She smiled to herself in the mirror. *Today is going to be the happiest day of my life.*

When she walked up that aisle toward the altar, all her past was going to be just that—*the past.*

At a soft tap on the door, Angie moved to open the door. Christina Maxxon pushed the door open and smiled as she viewed Angie standing in the middle of the tiny dressing room. "You look absolutely beautiful," Christina said.

"I feel even prettier," Angie said and smiled broadly.

"Are you decent?" she heard Kurt ask from outside the door.

"You've seen me worse," Angie yelled.

Kurt pushed around the door. "My, my, young lady, you are a stunning bride."

"Thank you."

Kurt would be a stand-in for her father, walking her to the altar and giving her away to Lucky. When she took the wedding dress out of the bag and stood dreaming about the coming event, she had gone through the sad memories of what she remembered about her father's disappearance; the weeks of searching. But her father was never found. He had just vanished off the face of the earth.

Today, Kurt was going to represent her father, and she was proud of that. If anyone came close to being the man her father would have been, it would be Kurt Maxxon.

Angie's thoughts darted through her brief life with Tugs Matthews—

the best memory from that part of her life was Auronia Michelle Matthews, born nineteen days after her daddy was buried. Angie's mother and Auronia arrived at the church with Angie earlier. They were sitting in the pews near the front of the church waiting for the spectacular to begin.

"There's a big crowd of people out there," Kurt said.

"That's because you're going to walk me up the aisle," Angie said and broadened her smile. "You are a celebrity around this town."

"I think it's really because the most popular current race driver and this congregation's own poster boy are getting hitched," Kurt said.

"And a very lovely race driver to boot," Christina said.

Angie heard the organ begin playing and knew that was a ten-minute notice to her and the bridesmaids. "Is everyone else ready?" Angie asked Christina.

"Yes. They've been ready for an hour now," Christina said, as she handed Angie her bouquet, after straightening some of the flowers and leaves.

Angie looked at the tailored suit she had made for the reception. In just a few hours, Angie thought, I can get out of this dress and into that suit. And then, a little while after that, I can get out of any clothes and into the arms of …

Kurt said, "It's time to go."

Angie walked with Kurt and Christina followed them. They went out into a mirrored hallway and floated up the stairs to the huge double doors that led to the cathedral. Kurt opened the door and looked. Angie saw movement on either side of the doors. When the doors were pushed open wide, Christina whispered, "It's standing room only in there."

Angie took Kurt's arm and let him guide and support her up the aisle toward the altar. Only in the last few feet did she realize that Lucky was standing watching her approach. *His smile is captivating.*

As they stood side by side, she looked down and saw a flowing white gown.

Angie repeated the vows and then Lucky was lifting her veil and kissing her. It wasn't the best kiss they had ever shared, but it served the purpose. They fled down the aisle and out into the welcome air.

And then a noise broke the silence. *What is that noise?* Her eyes flew open.

My cell phone. I was dreaming! The dream was so real. It's probably Mother, and I don't want to talk to her right now.

The ringing stopped. Angie laid back against the pillows and tried to reenter her dream.

Then curiosity overwhelmed her. Angie picked up her phone and viewed the last caller. She frantically punched buttons. Then she heard Lucky say, "Hey Angie." She relaxed a little.

"I—I was in the bathroom—"

"I thought maybe you'd already gone to bed."

"No," she lied. "As a matter of fact, I was thinking about you.'

"Good thoughts, I hope."

"Oh, the best."

CHAPTER TWELVE

Angie noticed the blue light blinking on her cell phone as she walked out of the kitchen toward her car in the garage. A voice mail—probably from Maurey Kennedy about this morning's car check. She laid the phone on the passenger's seat, started the engine and backed out onto the garage apron.

Did Maurey give me any special instructions for today? Am I forgetting something?

Sitting on the garage apron, Angie picked up her phone and looked at the voice mail caller ID. That told her that Lucky—not Maurey—had left the message about three hours before.

She punched the buttons to get the voice mail on speakerphone. "Good morning, Angie," she heard Lucky's voice say. "I'm on my way over to Marysville. Borsche just started a new job over there, and Jiggs wants me to check out the rental equipment delivered yesterday and will be delivering today. Jiggs told me to just get a motel room over there for tonight and tomorrow night."

Angie shut the engine off and listened.

"Since the three kids are all at Bible Camp this week and next, and Granny Watson drove down to Sinclaire to see the family; I'm home all by myself. Good timing for this trip. Have you ever been to Marysville?"

Lucky paused, and Angie shifted the phone from one hand to the other.

"I was wondering if you'd like to come over to Marysville this evening and meet me for supper. We could do some Bible study. Since you're going to Centralia today for the car check with Maurey; you could come over to Marysville on the way home. Getting to Marysville is kind of tricky with Skunk Hollow Lake between it and Masonville. Marysville is on the west side of the lake. It's about one-hundred-sixty-five mile trip to get about seventy miles as the crow flies. I haven't been there before, but Jiggs recommended a good place to eat—Uh, *The Outlaw Diner.* Just the name piques my interest. If you'd like to come over, you can get a room at the same motel as mine. We can probably find someplace to do our Bible study in the motel. Give me a call and tell me what you think. Leave a voicemail if I don't answer. Hoping to hear from you soon."

Angie sat for several minutes, thinking about the upcoming day. Then she climbed out of her car and went back into the house. She threw undies and toiletries into an overnight bag, then took two tank tops and two pairs of blue jeans hanging in the closet and put them into her clothes bag; along with her hot-pink jogging shoes. She decided to wait to return Lucky's call until after the car check with Maurey Kennedy.

Maurey can probably tell me the fastest way get to Marysville, if there is one.

Angie stopped in the door to Auronia's room. Auronia and Nana were reading a book. "After I finish the car check with Maurey, I'm going over to Marysville and will stay there tonight. I'll be home early tomorrow morning."

"That came up rather quickly," her mother said. "Are you going to be seeing Lucky?"

"As a matter of fact, mother, I will be seeing Lucky this evening."

"Okay, dear. Just be careful."

"I'm always careful, mother. In everything I do."

Auronia ran to Angie. "Can I go with you, Mommy?"

"No, Baby. I'm going to meet Lucky for supper and then do some Bible study."

"In Marysville?" her mother asked.

"Yes."

"Okay, dear."

Angie kissed Auronia and patted her on the shoulder. "You be good and do what Nana tells you to, all right?"

Auronia bobbed her head. Angie could see the sadness in her eyes and wished she didn't leave her so much. Then Angie spun on her heel and walked back out to the car, carrying her overnight bag and clothes bag.

As Angie drove toward Centralia, thoughts of Lucky fluttered through her mind. *He helps me in and out of the car during the race. He helps me understand the Bible.*

"My good luck charm is traipsing all over the valley," she said to herself. I might as well traipse along with him."

* * *

"This has been a week to remember," Lucky said as he sat down opposite Angie. "I was in the field, working on equipment, every single day this week. Outside in the hot sun all day long. I'll bet I drank at least ten gallons of water every day just to stay hydrated."

"I've had a rather trying week also." Angie moved her menu to read it. "The septic tank backed up, and they had to dig down to unclog it. Then the guy tells me that the tank is old and I should think about putting in a new one—and he also tells me that the sewer pipe is probably old and should be replaced."

"Sounds like he's just trying to make work for himself," Lucky said.

"I thought so too until the neighbor across the road came over, and she told me she had the same problem a few years back, just before I bought my place. She had the county inspector come out, and he verified that it was all bad. So, she had it all replaced."

"Were your houses built about the same time?"

"Yes, they were, and by the same contractor. The houses are thirty-seven years old. When I bought my place, it hadn't been properly cared for in several years. The owners were both in a nursing home, and their daughter didn't do anything around the place."

"Have they started replacing your tank?"

"Not yet. They delivered the new tank and pipe yesterday. I hired another contractor to do the installation. He was a little cheaper than the first guy, He'll start work next Wednesday."

The waitress arrived to take their orders. "Enough about septic tanks," Lucky said. "I'm hungry."

"I'm going to have the Smoked Chicken Platter," Angie said, pointing to it on the menu. "With baked potato and BBQ beans."

"I want the Pulled Pork plate," Lucky said. "Baked potato, roasted corn. And I'll have a dinner salad with Thousand Island salad dressing."

"This looks to be a fabulous smoke house," Angie said. "I like to try different fried chicken recipes. How about you?"

"I'm not a big chicken eater," Lucky said., "Three, four times a year is about all the chicken I want. If we have chicken, the kids prefer KFC."

"My mother does a pretty good version of fried chicken. Auronia loves it. I'd probably just as soon have Extra Crispy KFC, too."

"Granny Watson fixed fried chicken one time shortly after she moved in with us. All three of the kids voted it too greasy. So, they just told her, next time, we'll order KFC."

"Did that hurt Granny Watson's feelings?"

Lucky wobbled his head. "Nothing can hurt Granny Watson's feelings. She's a tough old bird."

"Do you talk to your folks?" Angie asked.

"They phone and talk to Granny Watson. I talk to them when they call. I don't call them much."

"Do you get along with your moth—I mean your folks?"

"Sure. We love each other. But we've all gone our separate ways and have our own lives."

"Does your mother ever ask you about raising three kids by yourself?"

Lucky stared at Angie for a long while. "Does my mother ever ask me about raising three kids by myself?" Lucky parroted Angie's question. He leaned toward her and said, "My mother raised ten kids of her own, I doubt there's much she would need to ask me about how to do it."

Angie chuckled and smiled. "I mean, without a wife—raising three kids without a wife."

Lucky continued to stare at Angie, and he started chuckling. "I doubt my mother ever thinks about me raising three kids without a wife." Then Lucky drew back. "Does your mother have a problem with you raising Auronia by yourself?"

"Incessantly."

Lucky's eyebrows shot up and then blended into a frown. "Your mother … your mother is old-fashioned."

"Heavy on the OLD."

The waitress arrived with their food and both focused on their meal.

"Next weekend is the Centralia Race," Angie said, as she finished emptying her plate. "Are you going to it?"

"Yes. I already have a reservation at Freeman's Hotel."

"That's a great hotel," Angie said. "That's where I always stay. It sounds like you were influenced by Kurt Maxxon."

"Guilty," Lucky said and grinned. "I asked Kurt where to stay in Centralia, and he told me Freeman's.

"After I win the race, that's where Kurt will throw my victory party."

"You're planning to win the race, then?"

"Certainly."

"Anyway, about tonight's Bible study," Lucky said. "They told me over at the motel that we can use the breakfast room. There are several tables in it. My service truck is parked in front of my room—number eighteen."

"Do you want to ride over in my car?" Angie asked.

"You drove over here after you checked in? It's just across the street."

"I saw your service truck parked toward the back and didn't know if you were in the diner or not. I figured if you weren't here yet, I'd go back out and sit in my car until you arrived. But, then I saw you coming across the street, so I came in and got a table."

"Okay. I'll meet you across the street in about two minutes."

* * *

Lucky stood beside Angie in the archway into the breakfast room and studied the arrangement of tables and chairs. Lucky led the way to a table in a well-lit corner and laid his Bible on the table. He moved a chair for Angie to sit next to him.

Angie opened her Bible at the ribbon marker. "I've haven't gone further than John Chapter Twelve," she said.

"That's good," Lucky said. "There's no time limit on this Bible study."

"It's discussing Jesus predicting his death."

Lucky opened his Bible and leafed through his book. He looked at Angie's book laying open on the table. "How many pink tabs do we have left to go through?"

"Fifteen or sixteen."

"Good thing there's only twenty-one chapters in John," Lucky said and grinned.

"Are you making fun of me, again?" Angie said with an exaggerated pout.

"You know I'm not making fun of you."

"I'm just trying to understand this stuff completely," Angie said. "It's not the most interesting reading, you know."

"Maybe not the most interesting, but definitely the most beneficial." Lucky smiled.

"I'm trying to see the big picture," Angie said. "You, know, the complete racetrack in front of me, so to speak."

"Got it," Lucky said. "Why is there a green tab and a pink tab at the same place there?"

"That means I've resolved most of the issues and only have minor questions for you."

"That's neat." Lucky leaned over to read Angie's Bible. "Where are you in John Twelve?"

"At verse twenty-seven, actually."

Lucky turned the pages.

Angie waited until Lucky laid the open Bible on the table and looked at her. Then she read, "It says: *Now my soul has become troubled; and what shall I say, 'Father, save Me from this hour'? But for this purpose I came to this hour. Father, glorify Your name.' Then a voice came out of heaven: 'I have glorified it, and will glorify it again.' So the crowd of people who stood by and heard it were saying that it had thundered; others were saying 'An angel has spoken to Him.' Jesus answered and said, 'This voice has not come for My sake, but for yours.' 'Now judgment is upon this world; now the ruler of this world will be cast out. And I, if I am lifted up from the earth, will draw all men to Myself. But He was saying this to indicated the kind of death by which He was to die."*

Lucky sat back. "Okay. What is the question?"

Angie flipped to pages further back. "So, it's pretty obvious, even though the people Jesus was speaking to are different, that He was speaking to the Father and was answered. Some people heard, and some didn't." She paused to collect her thoughts.

"In John, Jesus says, *I told you, and you do not believe.* But before that, in the reference to Luke, Jesus says, *If I tell you, you will not believe.* Angie laid her Bible on the table. "First Jesus says *If I tell you, you will not believe.* Then Jesus says, *I told you, and you don't believe it.*

"Exactly what is he telling us here?" Angie asked.

Lucky glanced at Angie sideways. *Maybe she's finally asked the question I can't answer.*

Lucky looked toward the door. "I'll have to look into your questions, and figure out exactly when Jesus told them He is the Christ. It sounds like a disconnect, but I never jump to conclusions. The verses you cited were Jesus telling us that he will be killed. The difference appears to be a challenge from the crowd versus the Sanhedrin, but the words are similar."

"It's just a question that popped into my mind," Angie said.

"That's good," Lucky said. "It's good you think for yourself. I like that. Now, about the sitting at the right-hand issue in Luke twenty-two. I think Jesus is just referring to his direct connection to the Father. There is always the confusion between *the Son of Man* and *Son of God.* We know today that

Jesus Christ was the son of a woman, in the sense that he was born to Mary, and for all intents and purposes, his father was considered to be Joseph. But, Christ was first and foremost, the Son of God, as part of the holy trinity, God, the Son, and the Holy Spirit. Jesus very carefully avoids using the *Son of God* designation because of the mood of the Jews at the time. However, at the end of John 8, John writes that He had referred to His deity when He said, *before Abraham was, I am.* At that point, we know that he is referring to something outside of the normal relationship that humans had to God. They were asking if He was the Messiah that prophecies foretold. To me, that's a pretty clear indication. "Christ," if you look up in a Strongs Concordance, you'd see means "anointed one" in Greek as it was translated to our English over the years. The Jews likely used the Hebrew word "Messiah." Earlier in John, at Three, fourteen to sixteen, we read, *As Moses lifted up the serpent in the wilderness, even so must the Son of Man be lifted up so that whoever believes will in Him have eternal life. For God so loved the world, that He gave His only begotten Son, that whoever believes in Him shall not perish, but have eternal life.* After Jesus' death and resurrection, the disciples confirmed that Jesus was the Christ. It says in First Corinthians, Chapter one, verse nine, *God is faithful, through whom you were called into fellowship with His Son, Jesus Christ our Lord.'* Lucky leafed through his book. "Again, in Romans One, we read, *concerning His Son, who was born of a descendant of David according to the flesh, who was declared the Son of God with power by the resurrection from the dead, according to the Spirit of holiness, Jesus Christ our Lord.*"

"The wording is really kind of awkward, even in this edition," Angie said. "What was that about power?"

"Through the power of the resurrection. Jesus Christ assumed all our sins and took them to the cross, where he died to cleanse us of sin. The resurrection demonstrates his power over death, he arose and lives eternally with the Father."

"In heaven—"

"Yes, ma'am, the promise of eternal life means life in paradise, which most people describe as heaven.0"

"I don't know if I'll ever understand it all," Angie said. "I mean the concept of God controlling the world."

"It is a huge subject, isn't it?" Lucky said. "You know?" Lucky let his gaze focus on a spot on the wall. "I'm reminded of one of my early experiences as a born-again Christian." He put his hands on the top of the open Bible.

"I remember it like it just happened yesterday." He paused to reflect for a moment. "After I got back stateside from Iraq, after my conversion, I went to meet with the preacher of a church one of my buddies attended near Clarksville, Tennessee. It was a large, very prosperous Southern Baptist congregation. He lived in a rambling brick house across the road from his church. He took me down into his basement, where he had a huge model railroad layout on five sheets of plywood forming an ell shape in the corner of it."

"His train layout was very realistic. He had six full trains running on the tracks that ran around the outside of the layout and that crisscrossed in various configurations. He had three little towns set up along the tracks, each with streets, stop lights that worked, water towers, train stations, churches, store buildings, gas stations, and grain elevators. There were miniature trucks and cars on the streets and roads, and little people on the sidewalks in the towns. There were farmers on tractors in the fields. As the trains approached a road, crossing guards started blinking red, and little arms came down to block the road. It was all so realistic."

Lucky paused momentarily in his memories. "The preacher could see the entire train layout from his seat on a stool in the ell of the layout. He sat and moved levers, toggled switches on and off, and turned dials. The preacher said, 'I control this little world just like God controls the big universe all around us out there.'" Lucky paused and looked at Angie.

"What a comparison," he said slowly. "It made a huge impression on me. It sent a chill down my spine then and still does today. It was a world smaller than the one I live in, but just as real to him, and me. Then, as you scale up; there's the real world all around us—all the continents floating around on the globe. And, then, beyond our planetary system is the huge—gigantic—universe outside of our world as well as the tiny universe that we can't comprehend unless we went down to the level of microorganisms and atoms that we see in electron microscopes. That whole universe is what God controls. I think of God looking just like that preacher, sitting on his stool in the corner of the operation, flipping switches, pushing buttons, turning knobs to make it all unfold. That preacher made things so understandable."

"Did you join his church?" Angie asked.

"I sure did. I loved that model train layout. The preacher held Bible Study classes in that basement every Saturday morning. I did not miss one of them. There were a couple of other fellows who liked the trains also. The preacher ran the trains for us after the class ended."

"You need to set up your own model railroad," Angie said. "That sounds like fun."

"I would if I had the room. But in my little house, there's barely room for the people, let alone a model railroad layout."

"I've got plenty of room," Angie said. "You're welcome to set up your railroad at my house and come play with it anytime you want to."

"That's a wonderful offer," Lucky said and grinned. "Someday, I'll have the room," "Granny Watson may decide to go back down to her place in Sinclaire. The kids will grow up and leave the nest."

"Your kids are closer to flying the nest than Auronia is," Angie said and grinned. "Just think, Mr. Lucky, someday we'll both be empty nesters." She laughed. "After that happens, we can meet for Bible study anytime we want to, huh?"

"I'm not in any hurry for that to happen," Lucky said. "Oh, I enjoy our Bible studies, but, being realistic, I'm not looking forward to being alone every night."

"That's the hard part." Angie nodded.

"Everything worth having is worth waiting for, right?" Lucky smiled.

Angie and Lucky stopped as a man came through the archway toward them." Are you two reading the Bible?" the man asked.

"Yes. Yes, sir, we are," Lucky said. "We occasionally meet for Bible study."

"That's wonderful," the man said, and he extended his hand toward Lucky. "I'm Chester Drescher—the pastor at the Trinity Lutheran Church here in Marysville. My sister and her husband own this motel. Everybody around here calls me Pastor Chet."

Pastor Chet was a portly man of just under six feet tall. He was bald except for a scraggly ring of hair just above his ears. Once black, it was now a dirty gray. His heavy eyebrows showed the same mixture. His dark brown eyes added a glint of happiness to his face, and his perpetual smile capped it off.

"My name is Lucky, uh, Kyle O'Rourke," Lucky said. "I belong to the United Lutheran Church in Masonville. And this is Angie Prescotte, she lives in Copperville and …" Lucky paused since he didn't know anything about Angie's church attendance.

Angie said, "We go to the United Methodist Church in Copperville."

"You both attend *United* churches," Pastor Chet said and grinned broadly. "That's interesting. What synod is your Lutheran church in?" he asked Lucky.

"It's in the Evangelical Lutheran Churches in America."

"The ELCA," Pastor Chet said. "My church is in the AALC—the American Association of Lutheran Churches."

"I'm kind of a new Lutheran," Lucky said. "I was confirmed into the church a year ago. I went through the Catechism with my nephew, Jason. He and his sister lost their mother, and I took guardianship of them. Jason and I were confirmed together."

"That's interesting. I've never met anyone who was confirmed at the same time as their child."

"This man is full of surprises," Angie said and smiled.

"What church did you attend before getting confirmed?"

"I was in the Army for fifteen years," Lucky said. "I always favored the Catholic Chaplains; since they were more lenient about things. I didn't attend church regularly until I met Jesus in Iraq."

Pastor Chet smiled "I'll bet that's a story I'd like to hear. Unfortunately, I must run. It's great that you're seeking his grace," he said to Angie. "And it's wonderful that you're living your life in Jesus Christ. If either or both of you are in town Sunday morning, we have services at nine and eleven. We're just south of town about a mile. You can't miss it."

Lucky and Angie watched Pastor Chet go out of the building to his car, then sat down and tried to pick up where they left off.

"I'm bushed," Lucky said. "I need to hit the hay."

"Yeah, I'm worn out, too."

Lucky walked with Angie out to her car and carried her overnight bag and clothes bag into the lobby and put them on a cart. "What room are you in?" Lucky asked.

Angie dug her keycard out of her hip pocket. "Two-twenty-one."

When the elevator door opened, Lucky pushed the cart into the car, said, "Goodnight, sleep tight," and then backed out into the hallway.

Angie pushed the DOOR OPEN button. "You're not going up?"

"I've got to run out to my truck and get my log book."

"Do you want to meet for breakfast?" Angie asked.

"Sure, what time?"

"Whatever works for you."

"We'll have to eat breakfast here in the motel. The Outlaw isn't open for breakfast. Six o'clock too early?"

"Six is fine with me. I'll see you then."

After retrieving his log book, Lucky looked up into the dark sky above him and his younger days came flashing back as he recognized the Summer Triangle—a Triangle much like a pyramid standing in the desert composed of stars from three different constellations. He squinted as he tried to remember the names.

It's such a beautiful night, Lord. Your sky is gorgeous. I wonder if I should ask Angie to come out and walk with me while we enjoy your universe. As he gazed up at the heavens, one by one, the names came to mind.

The top star is Vega, in the constellation Lyra. The left base star is Deneb in the constellation Cygnus. The right base star is Altair in the constellation of—What's the name of that constellation? It's called the Eagle.

I'll have to look it up when I get home.

* * *

Angie tried to recall what Lucky had told her during their Bible study.

Jesus convinced the Jews he was descended from David. He let them think he was the Son of God, and they hated him for it.

Does any of that make any sense?

And who, exactly, is this God? Is he really like a model train operator sitting at the control panel of the layout?

A model train layout from Fischer's Toy Store in Carpentier Falls from when she was a child came to mind.

But then her mind transformed the model train operator into a man wearing a striped engineer's hat and striped bib overalls—her father from the one picture her mother kept framed on her nightstand.

If God controls the universe in the same way—is he wearing a striped engineer's cap? Bib overalls? Does he have a red bandanna around his neck?

She remembered the blue bandanna she found in the garage several months after her father disappeared. She'd secreted it in one of the drawers of the old wood workbench where her father spent a lot of his spare time tinkering with gadgets she never recognized. She still had it in a special box in her garage.

If I walked along the river down from where the bridge collapsed, I wonder if I could find the red bandanna Daddy was wearing the day he died? It's been thirty years. Would it have lasted that long? Lucky said he would go with me if I wanted to walk the river. I'll ask him. If he goes with me, I'll do it.

CHAPTER THIRTEEN

Lucky drove through the hotel's parking lot and parked his service truck off to the side, toward the back of the lot.

I don't want to depreciate the value of the Jaguars, Porsches, BMWs, and Cadillacs scattered around the lot.

Angie's red Porsche isn't here yet.

He glanced at the clock in the dash: 2:35.

I'm so early I shouldn't expect her to be here.

The rain had stopped. But, the low, thick, roiling cloud layer made Lucky reach for his yellow and orange rain slicker behind the passenger's seat.

I'll just wear it to get to the door and take it off before anyone sees how ratty it is.

Since its opening in 1919, Freeman's Hotel had been *The Place* to stay in Centralia. Its popularity demanded expansion from time to time that resulted in a conglomeration of adjoining structures. Each expansion reflected the architecture and décor of the time. The original hotel building still housed the lobby and offices of the complex.

Lucky got out of the truck and swung into his rain gear as he walked around to the passenger's side to get his luggage. Even though the suitcase was only slightly larger than an overnight case, it had wheels, and Lucky extended the handle to drag it along behind. He looked at the Bible—wrapped in Saran Wrap—lying on the passenger seat.

"I'll get you when I need you," he whispered to the book.

He drug his suitcase behind as he walked toward the lobby entrance.

After getting his room key, Lucky walked around the lobby taking in all the large paintings hanging on the walls and artworks in display cases. The elevator expressed luxury in design and colors.

In his room, Lucky was amazed at how plush it was. The living room had a sofa and an easy chair with a coffee table. There was a full-size desk in the corner with an office chair. The small kitchen was mostly a dinette table, a microwave oven on a shelf over a small refrigerator. Lucky walked into the huge bedroom with adjoining bath. He noted that a hallway was formed by a mechanical room on one side and a closet on the other, isolating the bedroom. The polished walnut wood furniture along with the colorful wall hangings made the room seem private and comforting. The bathroom featured polished brass hardware and gleaming white porcelain fixtures.

Definitely not the flop-house class I'm used to.

How much is this costing me? Buddy, you've got to stop trying to run in the world's Kurt Maxxon social class.

Lucky put his suitcase on the bed. He glanced at the clock radio on the nightstand. 2:50. He went out to investigate the small refrigerator in the corner of the kitchen. An assortment of single shot bottles of wine and whiskey filled a large wicker basket on top. A small sign on the back of the basket listed the prices for each that would be added to the bill—*IF OPENED.* Another note indicated that bottled beer was in the refrigerator for $7.00 per bottle.

Lucky opened the refrigerator door and studied the six bottles of beer. All the name brands of both regular and light beer were there. He picked up a long-neck bottle of Budweiser and looked at it.

Seven bucks! Lucky put the bottle back into the refrigerator.

Maybe later.

He thought about his Bible, out in the truck.

I should have brought it in.

So far, I've been able to answer Angie's questions about the Gospel of John. I hope my luck holds up.

His cell phone jangled, and he looked at the caller ID. He answered on speaker phone. "Hey Angie, how are you doing?"

"I'm fine. Where are you?" Angie asked.

"I'm in my room."

"You're there already. Good gosh, I'm only about half-way to Centralia. You're early."

"Yes, ma'am," Lucky said. "I was down in Marysville. This morning I looked at a couple of dozers they delivered last night. Then I just moseyed on up here. I got here early, but they had a room for me."

"I usually get there about three-thirty," Angie said. "I check into the hotel and then suit up to drive the Qualification Runs. I usually get to the track about four-fifteen or four-thirty. There are only a half-dozen drivers there to run qualifications, so I usually can get right in line."

"I'll be at the track to watch you run."

"Oh. Okay. Plan on being there for four and I should be there shortly after that."

"Take your time. I'll be there."

"Are you still planning on doing a Bible study after dinner?" Angie asked.

"Yes, ma'am. I asked the front desk if I could use one of the guest offices in the lobby. They said I could. So, that's where we'll do the study."

"Works for me," Angie said.

"Man, this is plush," Lucky said and whistled lowly.

"Yeah. Freeman's is the place to stay in Centralia," Angie said. "All the big shots and royalty stay there."

"I walked past the restaurant," Lucky said. "That looks awfully fancy. You want to do early supper?"

"Yes. I love Romanov's. It has great food."

* * *

Angie drove around Freeman's parking lot looking for Lucky's service truck. When she spotted it, she parked next to it. As she stood out of her car, Angie surveyed the cloudy sky. She glanced at the umbrella on the tiny back seat but decided against carrying it with her.

Angie walked into the hotel's lobby. She had stayed at Freeman's each year she raced in the races in Centralia. The July race was a regular SRVSCRA race, while the Centralia "Shootout" was the last race of the season, a By-Invitation-Only race, in which only the top ten points scorers for the year were invited to race for the grand prize—a big purse and a trophy.

Just inside the door, Angie stopped to let her eyes adjust. She looked up at a gigantic full-length painting of a woman in evening gown from what she thought might be the 1920s. The colors and talent of the artist intrigued her. She read the name of the woman on the brass plate below; *Alexandria Freeman, wife of the founder, Adolf Freeman.*

Each time Angie visited Freeman's she was impressed anew by the amenities.

Angie went to the front desk to register. Then she led the porter with a cart out to her car. He put Angie's luggage on the cart and led her back to the elevators, and up to her suite.

Once she was settled in her room, Angie dialed the front desk and asked for "Lucky O'Rourke."

After a long silence, the operator said, "I'm sorry, but we don't have a *Lucky O'Rourke* registered. Another pause. "We do, however, have a Kyle T. O'Rourke."

"That's who I want," Angie said. "That's my Lucky."

The phone buzzed with no answer. Angie glanced at her wristwatch. *3:50. Maybe he has already gone to the track.*

Angie dressed in her racing togs and went down the back stairs to her car. At the track, she parked next to Lucky's service truck in the driver's lot and walked to the pits.

As she neared the grandstand, she saw Nikki, her blue flame engulfed number 27 Ford Fusion sitting several pit stalls back. One car was in the first stall, waiting for the go-ahead to begin his Qualification Run. Once Angie made her way beyond that pit, she heard the car accelerate onto the track as another car exited the track and pulled in behind Nikki.

Kurt saw Angie coming and waved. She stopped and watched as Kurt, Maurey, and Lucky pushed Nikki toward the first pit stall. A track official materialized and said, "You ready to start number twenty-seven?"

Angie nodded.

The official stood with Angie as Nikki came to the stall. Angie walked around and reached in for her helmet and handed it to Lucky. She inserted the earplugs into her ears, and then Lucky helped her put it on, adjust it, and buckle the chin strap. Lucky helped her climb into the cockpit through the window. Angie strapped the safety harness in place and gave Maurey the thumbs up. Maurey nodded, and Angie started the engine. The three men grabbed earplugs and shoved them into their ears.

Angie watched the track official in front of her, who held a green flag in his hand, and pointed it directly at her. As he raised the green flag and stepped back, Angie released the parking brake and floored the accelerator. Nikki leaped forward onto the track. Angie's heart beat faster. She felt the thrill of speed once again.

She drove into turn one a little too fast, and Nikki's rear end slipped a little. Angie let up on the gas pedal, then floored it again as she exited the turn.

* * *

Lucky stood with Kurt and Maurey just behind the concrete barrier wall in the pit stall. Kurt used his wrist chronometer to time Angie's lap time each lap. Lucky watched Kurt's face each time Angie whizzed by on the track, and he knew Kurt was not happy with what was happening.

As Angie flew past into her final lap, Lucky looked up at the Leader Board Pole at the back of the Winner's Circle. It showed that the number 114 car was in the pole position; car number 29 was in second; car number 90 was in third, and car number 34 was in fourth. He hoped to see the numbers change and show the number 27 car in first. Angie finished the Qualification runs and pulled off the track into the pit area several stalls back. There were no other cars on the track. Kurt and Lucky moved to the driver's side window and looked down at Angie. Maurey undid the hood latches and listened to the idling engine. He moved from driver's side to passenger's side.

Finally, Maurey lowered the hood but did not latch it. "Drive it to the garage," Maurey said.

Angie drove through the gap in the bleachers that led to the garages. She parked Nikki on the apron and shut off the engine. She sat waiting for Lucky, Kurt, and Maurey to walk up. Then she let Lucky help her out of the car.

"What room are you in?" she asked Lucky.

"Uh, four-fourteen."

"I'm going over to my room to clean up. I'll call you when I'm ready."

* * *

Angie brushed her hair to finish drying it. It was short enough that it dried fast. She checked her appearance in the full-length mirror on the closet door. Light blue tank top, blue jeans, and white sneakers. She glanced at the bright pink sneakers sitting next to her bed, ready for tomorrow morning's trip to the hotel's fitness center and a three-mile jog on the treadmill.

In the living room, she looked at her Bible lying on the coffee table in front of the sofa.

I'll come back up for you after dinner.

She picked up the phone and dialed Lucky's room.

When Lucky answered, Angie said, "I'm hungry. How about you?"

"I'm famished," Lucky said. "I'll meet you in the lobby."

Angie walked off the elevator and didn't see Lucky. She stood in front of one of the giant portraits on the wall. She heard the elevator ding and turned to see Lucky exiting the car.

He walked toward her. She stepped up and kissed Lucky on the cheek.

"Are you enjoying the artwork?" Lucky asked.

"I'm an absolute novice at identifying the art and architecture," Angie said. "All this is quite attractive. Soothing and calming."

"I was totally awed by all the art when I arrived," Lucky said. "You said you were hungry."

"Yeah. But I suspect you are even hungrier."

Lucky smiled broadly. "How quickly a woman learns what a man likes."

They walked around the corner and down the long hall that led to Romanov's Restaurant. The Maître'd led them to a table next to a window looking out over a grassy lawn. Only a few of the tables were occupied. The dark mahogany paneling made the room whisper-quiet.

As they studied their menus, Lucky said, "The only thing I think I recognize is the Beef Wellington. You're probably used to this kind of food."

"The Beef Wellington here is excellent. I think I'll have the Ducketta Plate."

"Is that with duck, as in waterfowl?"

"Yes. It's stuffed duck breasts. This looks to be a Russian recipe. I've had it with Asian stuffing."

"What's it stuffed with?"

"Oh, cheeses, spices, pasta. I'm not sure since I've never had it here before, and it's a Russian dish."

"I think we ate duck once in a while when I was a kid growing up," Lucky said. "It didn't impress me then. So, I think I'll skip it now and stick with the beef."

A waiter arrived. Angie ordered a glass of Chardonnay. Lucky ordered a long-neck Budweiser. He noted that the waiter looked at him over his bifocals for a long time, but left to get the drinks.

"A bottle of Bud is seven-fifty in this restaurant. If I had drunk one in the room, it would have only cost me seven bucks. That's highway robbery, even if it is cheaper in the room."

The waiter delivered their drinks.

"Has anyone ever challenged your drinking beer?" Angie asked.

"I've never had any qualms about drinking beer," Lucky said. "I've been drinking beer for years. When the Baptist Preacher challenged me about drinking beer, I simply told him, *I believe Jesus Christ is my Savior, and so long that he doesn't tell me it's forbidden, then I'll continue to drink beer.*

"Is that the only thing you drink?"

"Pretty much. Granny Watson is pretty strict on me. Once in a while, she buys a bottle of red wine to cook with. She and I will sample a shot glass full. But other than that, the house is pretty much alcohol-free."

While they waited for the food, Angie and Lucky talked about the latest activities of their children.

"My tribe all got back from Bible Camp this morning," Lucky said. "All three of them called me just after noon to tell me they were home."

"Too bad you couldn't have been there to welcome them back."

"Oh, I imagine all three of them went to their friends' houses and then went back home to crash. They are usually worn out from two weeks at camp."

"Auronia just became interested in reading the Bible," Angie announced, "Since I told her that was what I was doing."

"That's great. You can't start children reading the Bible too early," Lucky said, then frowned. "But, can she read yet?"

"She's learning the alphabet right now. We work with her on reading some. It'll be a while before she is studying the Gospel of John, however." Angie laughed softly.

"Well, yes, but once she starts, you probably won't be able to slow her down."

The waiter delivered their entrees.

Lucky looked at Angie's platter and was amazed at the amount of food.

Lucky ate all of his meal including one of Angie's dinner rolls.

Angie declined dessert. But Lucky ordered a specially concocted cheesecake.

"You'll be too full to study the Bible," Angie chided.

"That will never happen," Lucky said, with a glint of humor in his eyes.

* * *

Lucky led Angie into the guest office off the hotel lobby. They both set their Bibles on the conference table, and Angie sat down, gesturing to the chair next to her.

Angie looked up at Lucky, "I'm so lucky to have you helping me," she said. "Only the Pope is more patient than you."

Lucky grinned. "I've got a long way to go for that to be true." He paused. "Where were we?"

"Chapter Fourteen," Angie's voice trailed off as she turned to the page. She sat looking at the page for a long time and then said, "I had some trouble dealing with this part. It brought back some bitter memories that I am going to have to deal with."

Lucky leaned close as he sat down to see what verse Angie was looking at. "John fourteen. This is a key chapter for Christians."

"I know," Angie whispered. "The preacher used part of it in Tugs' funeral service." Angie paused and looked past Lucky. Her face clouded slightly. "That's the part I'm trying to deal with."

Lucky glanced at Angie. "John fourteen is a frequently used passage at funerals. *In My Father's house are many dwelling places; if it were not so, I would have told you; I go to prepare a place for you. If I go and prepare a place for you, I will come again and receive you to Myself, that where I am, there you may be also.* There's a lot said in that verse. 'Then I will come again and receive you to Myself, that where I am, there you may be also' is a direct promise of the second coming of Jesus. That's what all Christians take from it." Lucky paused studying Angie's face.

"Personally," Lucky continued, I like the King James Version of this verse better, just because it says In My Father's house are *many mansions*. I like the word *mansions* better than *dwelling places*."

Angie studied Lucky's face for several seconds. "That was a sad time in my life." Angie returned her gaze to the Bible lying open in front of her. "It's just that—"

Lucky waited, then leaned back to look at Angie. "You still miss Tugs."

Angie bobbed her head. "But, I know I have to move on. Get my life in order."

"Getting to know Jesus Christ, and accepting him as your savior, will do wonders for your loss," Lucky said.

Angie picked up her Bible. "Do not let your heart be troubled;" she read aloud from the book. "believe in God, believe also in Me—"

Angie looked at Lucky with a blank expression. Her breathing was sharp. Her eyes were moist.

"The next few verses are the key to this whole discussion," Lucky said as he took over the reading. Jesus says, *If you had known Me, you would have known My Father also; from now on you know Him, and have seen Him."*

Lucky paused and looked at Angie.

Angie was gazing into space. Lucky waited until he thought she had returned to the present. "Are you okay?"

"I think so," Angie said slowly. She took a shuddering breath in. "Yes, I'm fine."

Lucky continued reading. *"Whatever you ask in My name, that will I do, so that the Father may be glorified in the Son. If you ask Me anything in My name, I will do it. If you love Me, you will keep My commandments."*

Lucky leaned down and looked at Angie's Bible. "You didn't have any sticky notes on that page."

"When I read those verses, I remembered Tugs' funeral," Angie said. "Tugs was a good man." She paused and twined her fingers together and laid her hands on the Bible. "He was honest to a fault, hard-working, and absolutely dedicated to the people he loved. Just like—just the same as you are, Lucky." She pulled back and looked directly into Lucky's eyes. "Just like you."

Lucky smiled. "It's easy to love those people who love you in return." He flipped the page in his Bible. "And that's exactly what Jesus is talking about here." He patted the open page.

Angie continued. "After a couple of days, I read the rest of this chapter. About the Holy Spirit."

"Jesus promises," Lucky said, and picked up his Bible to read it. *"I will ask the Father, and He will give you another Helper, that He may be with you forever; that is the Spirit of truth, whom the world cannot receive, because it does not see Him or know Him, but you know Him because He abides with you and will be in you. I will not leave you as orphans; I will come to you."'*

Lucky glanced at Angie. "That's Jesus' promise to us about giving us the Holy Spirit," he said.

"I still have trouble imagining the Trinity," Angie said. "I understand who the Father is. I understand who the Son is. But the Holy Spirit, or Holy Ghost, as my mother calls it, what is that?"

"The Holy Spirit is probably the most difficult part of Christianity to understand," Lucky said and looked at Angie. "It's just my own interpretation, but I believe that every human being recognizes that he or she is composed of a body and a mind. The thoughts of the mind make up the spirit of the person. Once you understand how Jesus relates to God, and accept Jesus Christ as your savior, then your human spirit accepts the Holy Spirit who guides your life from then on."

Angie frowned slightly. "So, as we sit here right now, and I say to you, I'm not sure I understand this religious stuff, which means I haven't been born again, then I do not have the Holy Spirit yet?"

"Unfortunately, that's the way I see it," Lucky said and shrugged. "Non-believers and people who can't relate to being born again don't have the Holy Spirit within them. Once you accept Jesus, your spirit welcomes the Holy Spirit in. You realize your life has changed dramatically. That it has a whole new guidance system."

"So, God just leaves people alone, and won't help them until they accept Jesus?"

"No. I think God lets hints of his goodness show. He guides people in their understanding of him." Lucky paused and studied Angie for a beat. "You see, you need to hear Him, which you did as a child, and you're now doing by reading His words. Then believe Him, what He says about Himself, and His promises to live with you, and guide you. Then accept Him. Then He comes into your heart and lives in you."

"So, what you are saying is that if I become a believer, and accept Jesus, then my current mind will be filled with the Holy Spirit?" Angie leveled her gaze on Lucky.

Lucky bobbed his head. "You cannot have the Holy Spirit except you also have the Father and the Son—the Holy Trinity." Lucky ran his finger over the page. "Down here in verse twenty-six, Jesus says, *'But the Helper, the Holy Spirit, whom the Father will send in My name, He will teach you all things, and bring to your remembrance all that I said to you.'*

Paraphrasing the rest of this section, Jesus says, *Peace I leave with you. I go away, and I will come to you.' If you loved Me, you would have rejoiced because I go to the Father, for the Father is greater than I.*"

Angie sat for several moments looking at Lucky. Once again, she thought she saw a glow about his face. "That makes some sense to me," she said. "Just as soon as I accept Jesus as my savior, I, uh—"

Lucky swung to look at her face. "You're not into this yet. But in Chapter sixteen, verse seven, Jesus says, *It's for your own good that I go away. Unless I go away, the Comforter cannot come.*

"I can accept Jesus in private, or I can go to church and do it publicly, huh?"

"Whenever you're ready, accepting Jesus is personal, and it's between you and God, no matter where you are," Lucky said. "It doesn't matter how."

"I don't know," Angie said slowly. "It's such a big decision."

"It surely is. It will change your life forever. But, when you're ready, you'll know it.""

"I think I do need to change my life," Angie said. "I know I'm in a rut."

Lucky chuckled slightly. "Ruts aren't too bad. It's not a problem until they become ravines."

"Ravines?" Angie giggled.

"I sometimes feel like my ruts have become ravines," Lucky said.

Angie giggled, "Me, too." She leaned against Lucky's arm and squeezed it. "I need to get some shut-eye. I have to drive the race tomorrow."

Lucky nodded understanding.

They carried their Bibles and walked to the elevator.

"How are you feeling about this Bible stuff?" Lucky asked as they waited for the car.

Angie turned to face him. "I feel a little confused about the Trinity. But, at the same time, I feel like you will be able to help me understand it."

"Good," Lucky said. "That's good. If you keep studying, I'm sure it'll come to you."

CHAPTER FOURTEEN

Lucky was studying one of the huge tapestries hanging on the hotel wall, noting its Christian overtones, when Angie walked up to him and stepped up to kiss him on the cheek. They walked toward the restaurant. The main entrance into Romanov's was closed, but a door across the across the hall was open and exhibiting a Breakfast Menu.

"I'm going to try the Eggs Benedict," Lucky announced. "I've never had them before, but now is the time for new things in my life."

"I'm going with a double order of bacon and eggs," Angie said. "No potatoes. One slice of toast."

"Are bacon and eggs your get-ready-for-the-race breakfast?"

"Yeah. Every race day morning."

"Are you superstitious about anything?"

"I used to be. But, I've given them all up. Well—except for you," Angie said and winked at him.

"That's good," Lucky said. "All you need to do is put your trust in Jesus, and he will take care of you."

A hostess led them to a table near a window and left them with open menus.

"Will Jesus *guarantee* that I'll win today's race?" Angie asked.

"No. That's not what you rely on Jesus for."

"Will Jesus *help me* win the race?" she persisted.

"No. Jesus will do everything he can—short of building a shield around you—to prevent evil from happening to you." Lucky sat back and watched the waitress approach with their coffee and Coke. The waitress took their breakfast order, double checking with Angie on her double order of bacon and eggs.

"Yeah, and just one slice of wheat toast," she reiterated.

"Is there a special reason—?"

"I'll be driving the number 27 car in this afternoon's race," Angie said. "So, I need a high protein, low carb breakfast."

"Yes, ma'am. Thank you, ma'am." The waitress walked away, but glanced back, over her shoulder, at Angie.

Lucky chuckled. "As I was saying, Jesus will be watching over you. Jesus is there to help guide your life through the storms, through the vicissitudes, of life."

"The vicissitudes of life?" Angie mimicked Lucky.

"The ups and downs. The good times and the bad times. Jesus walks next to you every step of the way, ready to help you decide what to do next, where to go next."

"I thought that was what the Holy Spirit does."

"Jesus is such an essential part of the Trinity," Lucky said. "You never have one without the others."

Lucky looked out the window. "I remember a little sign I saw in that first church I went to in Clarksville. It showed this man looking up into the heavens, and he asked: 'Lord, why did you lead me through those deep waters?' The next line said 'Because your enemies can't swim.' I have always loved that little sign. I made one of my own. It's on my wall at home. That little sign captures the essence of my relationship with Jesus so well."

Angie sat looking at Lucky for a long time. "You can teach me so much. I'm really glad we've started the Bible study."

The waitress delivered their meals.

While they ate breakfast, they talked about the weather, being thankful the rain had stopped, and the sun was shining. "Good racing weather," Angie said.

"What do you normally do on race day between breakfast and time to go to the track?" Lucky asked.

"What I plan to do this morning," Angie said slowly. "Go to my room and relax. Watch TV and rest. About ten-thirty I'll get dressed and get ready to drive over to the track."

"I assume that doesn't mean an evening gown and high heels," Lucky said and grinned at her.

"Nope. It means an ill-fitting Nomex suit and super traction racing flats," Angie said. "Along with a skid lid that musses up my hair. Then, there are the racing gloves that invariably screw up my manicure."

Lucky swung his wristwatch into view. "That's only about an hour and a half from now."

"Right. Today, I plan on reading some more of the Bible. That seems to help me relax."

"That's good; the Bible is always relaxing reading for me, too," Lucky said. "Why do you put up with all the negatives?"

"It's the money, honey. The money and the thrill of it all."

"Plus, you have more wins and points than any other driver so far this year."

"That, too."

Lucky walked with Angie through the lobby to the elevators. He leaned over to kiss her, and said, "Until the pits."

She looked up, nodded, and then laughed. "Okay!"

Lucky stepped into the elevator and punched her floor; then he turned to leave the car as he looked at Angie.

Beautiful. Just absolutely, totally beautiful.

"You're not going up?" Angie asked.

"No, I'm going out to walk around the outside of the building for a little while," Lucky said. "Get some fresh air. Stretch a bit."

He strolled out through the lobby door and walked around the parking lot. He often stopped to study the different structures and their unique architectures. The sun was bright, and the sky was cloudless. Eventually, he walked back to the lobby.

As the elevator rose to the fourth floor, Lucky rummaged through his mind:

Do I have anything I'm supposed to do tomorrow morning with the kids? For the kids? Other than heading to work early?

Did I promise any of the kids—Olivia Maye, Sophia, or Jason—that I'd do something tomorrow morning?

The elevator stopped, and Lucky walked toward room four-fourteen.

The kids—all three of them have been leaving the house each morning even before I leave for work.

In his room, Lucky walked to the window and pulled the curtains open. Sunlight filled the room.

The kids are growing up fast. They'll be out on their own sooner than I like to think about.

Satisfied that he had no obligations for Monday morning, Lucky set about brewing another pot of coffee. He sat down to finish working the crossword puzzle.

Thank you, Lord.

* * *

Angie surfed the TV stations and accidentally found one broadcasting a local church service. The congregation was singing a hymn as the station came into tune.

I need to buy some gospel music to listen to; at home, and in the car. Does Lucky like gospel music? I have no idea, but I would think so. I'll have to ask him.

She sat down on the sofa and picked up her Bible from the coffee table. She opened it to the ribbon maker and began reading.

I wonder what Lucky is doing right now.

I should have spent the morning visiting with him.

What's wrong with you lady? Lucky is the best thing that's happened to you in a long while.

* * *

When Lucky walked over to take a good look out his window, he realized he was looking at the Greene County Fairgrounds directly across the street from the hotel. He could see the grandstand only a couple of blocks away.

This hotel is certainly convenient to the racetrack.

Lucky sat down at the desk with his Bible in front of him. He studied the gold *Kyle O'Rourke* emblazoned on the cover.

What a wonderful gift. From a thoughtful lady.

He opened his Bible as it lay on the desk, and flipped pages toward one of his favorite epistles, Ephesians.

I wonder what Angie's doing right now?

He looked at his wristwatch. *Nine-thirty.*

Why sit here? The action is over at the racetrack.

* * *

Lucky drove through the gate and parked his service truck in the driver's parking lot. He looked around to orient himself. The grandstand was visible from the hotel room, and now he was right next to it, just on the other side. He heard the roar of engines as drivers practiced on the racetrack. Lucky knew the practice laps would stop at ten o'clock, to allow race officials time to inspect the entire track for potential problems before the race started.

He walked into the grandstand area and stopped at the steps down to the track. A striped crosswalk led to the pit area, which the track had delineated with wide white lines. A heavy welded-pipe gate blocked passage onto the track. At ten o'clock the access would be unlocked. He glanced at his wristwatch.

Seven minutes.

Then he remembered Angie's disappointment with having qualified in the third position. Lucky looked at the third stall in the pit area and saw the blue, flame engulfed, number 27 Ford Fusion sitting motionless. As Lucky focused on the car, his imagination visualized the car's front wheels pawing at the ground—like a raging bull—chomping at the bit to get going.

But, Nikki, you need Angie to drive you. You can't do it by yourself.

A loud bell clanged all around the track, and it seemed like the track noise started decaying immediately. Two cars streamed by on the track, both decelerating and growing quieter.

Lucky stood motionless at the top of the stairs. Then a loud click as the electronic lock opened the access gate. He started to walk down the steps when he saw Kurt Maxxon and Maurey Kennedy walking toward him from the driver's lounge area. He waited for them.

"Great weather for racing," Lucky said as the two men neared.

"A little hot," Maurey said. "But, no rain."

Kurt bobbed his head.

"How soon will Angie get here?" Lucky asked.

"Oh, she'll probably be here around eleven o'clock, eleven-fifteen," Kurt said as he led the way down the steps and out onto the track. "Angie doesn't like sitting in the pit area when it's hot like this."

"Probably that racing suit she wears gets kind of hot," Lucky offered.

"It's made of Nomex, a flame-retardant material," Kurt offered. "So, it doesn't breathe like cotton. I can tell you from experience, it doesn't breathe at all."

All three men laughed.

Maurey lifted the hood of Nikki and propped it open. Kurt leaned in and started the engine. Maurey walked around listening and frowning. He moved from driver's side to passenger's side; then reversed the process, stopping every few minutes to lean in to hear what only he could hear— eight pistons bouncing up and down in their cylinders, a camshaft flipping valve lifters, and a crankshaft driving it all. Maurey reminded Lucky of a hunting dog his boyhood friend had while growing up. An English Pointer, it had a regular routine while zoning in on pheasants. *Stop. Freeze. Listen.*

Stop. Freeze. Listen.

Eventually, Maurey swiped his two fingers across his throat, and Kurt leaned in and turned the engine off.

At the same time, Lucky saw Angie get out of an ATV and walk toward him. Kurt and Maurey stopped and watched her.

"You're early," Maurey said.

"I'm anxious to get this race going."

"Do you feel good about it?" Kurt asked.

"I feel great about it," Angie said. "How about you, Mr. Lucky?"

"You're going to win it," Lucky said. "I feel it in my bones."

"That's my good luck charm speaking," Angie said and grinned.

Lucky watched Maurey close Nikki's hood and lock the latch pins in place. "She's the best she's ever been," Maurey declared.

"Are you talking about the car or me?" Angie asked.

"Both!" Maurey said diplomatically. "Both you gals are the best you've ever been."

At fifteen minutes before twelve, the officials clanged the bells again, and the race teams went into action, getting drivers into the cars, and ready to roll for the parade lap—the uncounted lap where the drivers line up in their starting order and drive around the track.

Angie moved to the edge of Nikki and waited for Lucky to help her climb through the driver's side window.

* * *

Angie started the race in the third position and went as far back as the fifth position before finishing the heat in fourth place. During the second heat, Angie moved up to second, but finished the heat in fourth place, running behind Eugenios Christofides in first, Dave Kellogg in second, and Jiggs Borsche in third. Immediately behind her were Hermann Nordstradt and Nelson Greene.

During the third, and final heat, the race seemed to slip into a steady-state condition. Lap after lap the positions didn't change much. Each lap, as the pack raced past, Lucky stood just behind the concrete barrier wall, yelling and waving Angie on.

At the beginning of lap forty-nine, Angie was running third behind Dave Kellogg and Eugenios Christofides. Lucky waved his fist hoping to empower Angie to move past Kellogg and Christofides. As they flew past headed into lap fifty, Angie was in second place, running behind only Dave

Kellogg.

Heading into turn four, Kellogg maintained a high line at the top of the banking. Angie steered Nikki into a low line hoping she had enough tires left to pull off the pass. Nikki glided low past Kellogg. Angie saw in her side mirror that Clyde Bird, Nelson Greene, Jiggs Borsche, and Christofides following her low route and passing Kellogg.

As she steered Nikki out of turn four onto the flat straightaway to the Finish Line, she was contented. She was two full car lengths ahead of the number 90 car with the number 34 car immediately behind him.

A quarter lap to go!

"We've got this race in the bag, Ms. Nikki," she shouted. She was sure she heard, "Let's do it!"

Suddenly Nikki coughed, shuddered and started slowing down.

"No. No…." Angie pounded on the gas pedal. Nothing.

With the engine off, the power steering wasn't working. Steering Nikki took all of Angie's strength. She fought the wheel and steered toward the outside of the track to get out of everyone else's way. But, then she realized she could coast across the finish line. She didn't brake. Nikki came to a creaking stop with her rear bumper just one foot beyond the finish line.

* * *

Lucky, Kurt and Maurey stood near the concrete barrier watching as the cars came off turn four and headed for the finish line.

As Lucky watched Angie come out of turn four toward the finish line, he focused on the flames seemingly engulfing the blue car and started shouting, "She's winning! Go, Nikki! Go, Angie!"

Then, suddenly he heard a cough and Nikki's engine went silent.

"Good, Lord, what's happening?" Lucky yelled.

The flag man grabbed the yellow flag and started waving it.

Other cars came around turn four and began to slow. The number 34 car couldn't slow fast enough appeared to clip the right corner of the number 90 car and send that car fishtailing wildly. Lucky watched wide-eyed. He realized the number 90 car was careening straight toward Angie's car on the driver's side.

"Oh, Dear God," Lucky cried. Kurt looked to see what Lucky was gasping at. Then they both dashed toward the track. The remaining cars were crashing into each other and nearly choked off the track with wreckage.

* * *

After Nikki had stopped rolling, Angie looked in her left-side mirror and saw that she was past the finish line.

Thank you, Lord. We did it.

Then the unmistakable sound of metal crunching and squeal of tires drew her attention. She looked in the rearview mirror and saw a mess of cars banging together coming out of turn four. But, she also saw the 90 car spinning after colliding with the 34 car, careening directly toward her. She grabbed and jerked on the emergency seat-belt harness release.

But where do I go?

If I go out the driver's side window, the oncoming car hits me.

If I go out the passenger's side, the careening wreckage pins me against the wall—sure death!

Her heart in her throat, she prayed. "Dear God. Keep Auronia safe, please. And oh, I forgive you!"

She heard tires screeching. She scooted toward the center of Nikki. Her eyes widened as the black and white number 90 car slid toward her door in slow motion.

She felt frozen. She saw a flash of white, and then nothing. Total silence.

Stunned, Angie looked around.

Am I dead?

As her head cleared, she saw the car that was about to hit her had stopped—but not with the loud noise of a crash. She stared at the black and white hood just a cat hair's distance from her door.

Lucky flew up onto the black and white hood next to Angie's door and tore away the protective webbing in the window. He leaned into the car and came face to face with Angie. "Are you okay?" Lucky shouted.

Startled, she replied, "Yes, I'm… I'm fine."

Then she kissed him full on the lips—holding his head against her for a long time.

Lucky and Kurt helped Angie out of Nikki, and the crowd cheered loudly. Angie shrugged out of her helmet and tossed it into Nikki.

The emergency crews raced to the pileup just up the track. Other pit crew members and track officials helped move the cars apart. Clyde Bird climbed out of his car, looking just as rattled as Angie. He looked toward his car, angled across the finish line—but with only the left front fender past it. He looked at Angie's door and shook his head as if to clear it. One of his fans ran up to offer a supportive arm, while others began to push his car away from Angie's car.

It was quickly determined that none of the drivers were seriously injured and no one in the stands or pits had been hurt.

The race officials announced that the race was over because the number 27 car had coasted past the Finish Line and had won the race.

The number 90 car driven by Clyde Bird and the number 34 car driven by Nelson Greene both stopped short of crossing the Finish line. They both drew a *DNF—did not finish designation.*

Eugenios Christofides and Jiggs Borsche had slammed together and then, careened side-by-side across the finish line, but not before Angie had coasted across.

Dave Kellogg's engine stalled when he braked to avoid the pileup. He was banged into by a couple of cars, but he was able to get his engine restarted, and he drove across the finish line to take fourth place.

To help clear the track, Maurey and Kurt pushed Nikki across to the pit area. Lucky held Angie close and walked with her to the pit area and helped her sit down on the concrete barrier.

But Angie preferred standing, cradled in Lucky's arms. They watched Maurey Kennedy lift the hood and lean under it to fiddle with various parts. She shivered occasionally, and Lucky tightened the embrace.

Maurey stood up and said, "The damn throttle wire came loose on the carburetor. It's fixed now."

* * *

As the crowd of drivers and officials stood, reliving the crash, many drivers said they saw a flash of white light. A few of them declared they'd seen an angel in action. Angie just listened, absorbing their recollections.

An angel of the Lord saved me.

Kurt and Maurey shook hands with each other, shrugged and started pushing Nikki toward the Winner's Circle several stalls down in the middle of the pit row. As they neared the Winner's Circle, Lucky saw Christina Maxxon waiting to be allowed to walk across the track. A uniformed track official was guarding the gate.

A couple of race cars drove by and then there was quiet. The guard opened the gate, and Christina led a pack of people over into the Winner's Circle. The number 27 Ford Fusion crept toward the circle, by human power. When the officials waved, Lucky and Kurt pushed Nikki to the center of the Winner's Circle.

Angie took a two-liter bottle of Diet Coke from a wash tub filled with cans and ice. She took a long drink. A band of Angie's fans arrived with armloads of diet Coke and Pepsi two-liter bottles, but few of them were in the mood for celebration—with a dozen wreckers pulling cars apart and hauling them off only a few feet up the track.

Angie stepped back from Lucky's embrace and looked at Lucky. "I told you I was going to win, didn't I?" Angie said.

Lucky smiled. "I'll never doubt your prescience in the future."

"Was Christofides second?" Angie asked.

"He and Jiggs crossed the line so close they are looking at the photos now. One of them will finish second, and one will finish third," Kurt said. "Or they may just say they tied for second place."

"That's okay." Angie pulled Lucky's head down and kissed him again.

Lucky stood stunned, then looked around to see if anyone had paid attention to Angie's move. Kurt and Maurey were mingling with and chatting with the fans and well-wishers.

Christina walked up and hugged Angie.

"Is there going to be a party?" Someone yelled.

"Freeman's Ballroom," Kurt yelled back. "Right across the street."

The same TV13 television crew arrived and asked Angie for an interview.

"I don't think so," Angie said. "Not after the mess out there." She pointed to the cars and wreckers on the track.

Angie walked over to Lucky. "I'm going to the hotel to shower and clean up. I'll meet you at the party."

"Okay," Lucky said. He watched Angie walk toward the driver's parking lot. He noted that she turned north on the first cross street in fairground complex. *There must be a faster way out that way.*

* * *

Lucky walked to the main table in the corner of the ballroom. Christina pointed him to the chair in the same position as at the Evandale party. Lucky sat down and scanned the room. He recognized several drivers and super fans—some in the corners behind the tables, some in the bar area, and some were just sitting and watching the activity around them. He watched Dave Kellogg lead his wife, Peggy, to the table. Dave held the chair for Peggy.

Do you want a Budweiser?" Kurt asked Lucky. "I'm going over to the bar to get a glass of Chardonnay for Angie. She should be down any minute now."

Lucky sat up straight and leaned back. "Yes, sir. Please."

He stared off into space. His trance was broken when he heard Christina say, "Lucky, I think you've already met one of Kurt's long-time friends."

Lucky swung his focus to look at Pastor Chet and a woman standing next to him. "Pastor Chester Drescher and his wife, Lillian."

Lillian was a sturdy woman about five-foot-five, with a round face surrounded by blue-gray hair neatly coifed. Her blue eyes accented her hair. The red lipstick she wore was the only contrast to the blue and gray theme. Pastor Chet shook Lucky's hand. Lillian extended her hand and Lucky gently shook it.

"Chester told me about you and the girl doing Bible study at the motel," Lillian said.

"Yes, ma'am. Angie and I have met several places around the valley to do Bible study."

"Angie is searching for Jesus," Christina said.

When the lobby door swung open again, they all turned to watch Angie enter the ballroom. Her smile was radiant. She surveyed the room as she walked to the table. Before Lucky could react, Angie pulled out a chair and sat down next to him. When she saw Lucky staring at her, her smile brightened and widened considerably.

Kurt walked up at that moment and set the glass of Chardonnay in front of Angie's place at the table. Then he handed Lucky the long-neck Budweiser. He put his hand on Pastor Chet's shoulder. "I've known this guy almost forever, it seems like."

"We met him down in Marysville," Lucky said.

"I think we first met at a Marine Corps birthday party in Jacksonville, Florida," Kurt said. "In about seventy-three."

"Yes. It was the same year that our daughter, Sherri, was born." Pastor Chet petted Lillian's arm.

"When I retired out of the Marine Corps," Kurt said, "My wife, Vicki, and I came to my hometown of Albertstown. My best friend and buddy during my Marine Corps days, Brad Langley, told me that Chet Drescher had gone to seminary and was a preacher somewhere around Marysville. The nicest motel in the area was the Pinetree Motel in Marysville; so we decided to stay there. When we checked in, I asked the lady if she knew Chester Drescher. She looked at me kind of funny and said. "Well, naturally I know Chester Drescher. He's my brother." Kurt chuckled. "Talk about luck."

"My sister graduated from college in 1986. I had just been assigned to the Trinity Lutheran Church in Marysville, and Teresa came to visit Lillian and me in our new home. The next thing I know, Teresa is engaged to the mayor's son. Then she had me marry her to Daniel. He worked as a representative for a local industrial laundry service. Then he and Teresa bought the old motel on the edge of town and fixed it up into what it is now."

Jiggs Borsche and Katy came in and sat next to Angie and Lucky. Even with the couples chatting, the table was relatively quiet until Eugenios Christofides and Don Epperley arrived. The two men came into the ballroom from different directions and went straight to the bar. Christofides for a snifter full of ouzo; Don Epperley for a highball glass of Scotch and water. When they met at the table, they immediately started taunting each other.

Lucky declined a second Budweiser, but Angie accepted a second glass of Chardonnay.

Jiggs was the first driver to leave the party. "I'm going out to the motorhome." He stood and led Katy out the door.

Pastor Chet stood and walked around to sit down in the chair vacated by Jiggs, next to Lucky. "Christina told me about your conversion in Iraq," Pastor Chet said. "I had a similar experience in Vietnam."

Lucky moved in his chair so he could hear Pastor Chet better.

Pastor Chet continued. "I was a medivac helicopter pilot in the Marine Corps. "I ferried the wounded out to hospital ships in the Gulf. One time as I went in to evacuate the wounded, I got hit with small arms fire, and I went down hard. I was strapped in the seat, and I couldn't move my arms. My body felt numb. *Spinal cord nerve damage* flashed through my mind. The reality of the location also flashed through my mind. If the shooters were close enough to knock me out of the air; they were close enough to come in and finish the job. I couldn't move my head, but I could move my eyes. Sure enough, I saw the brush moving and the VC, in their black pajamas, scurrying toward me. About the time the first of them broke into the clearing around me, I heard friendly fire from behind me. The VC got off a few shots, but they turned tail and ran. Then a corpsman was there talking to me. Pretty soon I was surrounded by friendly units. They muscled my chopper off to the side and brought in the second chopper. While they loaded the wounded, they dug me out and got me on a canvas. They took me out to the hospital ship. When I woke up, the nurse said, "You want to get up?"

I said "Yes." That nurse helped me get out of bed. I couldn't walk. I just stood there. But I could stand. And, by God, if I could stand, I'd walk again. As I stood there—wobbling on my feet—I know I saw Jesus walk out of my room and go down the hall. The next day they got me up and helped me take a step. The next day, I took two steps. I asked a nurse. 'Where did Jesus go the other day after he visited me?' She looked at me kind of funny, then said, 'Probably to the chapel. It's at the end of that hall.'"

Lucky sat silent for a long time. Several people had related their "moments with Jesus" to him, and each was unique and fascinating to hear. But Lucky savored those testimonies that involved difficult and trying times like he had experienced. "That's a fabulous story," Lucky said. "I'm always so thankful to hear of interventions He's involved with. Thank you for sharing it with me."

"You're more than welcome, Mr. Lucky. And may God bless you and Miss Angie there in her quest."

Christofides was next to leave saying he had to drive back to Kings Rapids yet tonight. Then Dave Kellogg begged off. The party was slowing down.

Don Epperley picked up his third drink and walked to another table.

Pastor Chet stood and said, "We need to get going. It's already two hours past our bedtime."

Angie looked at Lucky. "It's kind of early. Do you want to study the Bible?"

"You look bushed," Lucky said. "Maybe we should wave it off tonight and do it another time."

"You're probably right. I wouldn't last too long."

"There's no need to hurry," Lucky said. "You're doing fabulously. Your moment will come when it wants to."

Angie said. "It's a good bet that it arrived this afternoon. I should have been severely injured at the very least. How did I come out without a scratch?"

Lucky studied her face for a long time. Then he raised his hands above his head and shrugged.

"Yeah," Angie said, and kissed him on the cheek. "Goodnight."

CHAPTER FIFTEEN

Lucky walked into the office area to get coffee. He noted that Jiggs' office door was closed and the room dark. Jiggs' secretary, Juanita Suarez, was around somewhere because her computer screen was alive.

Jiggs is probably only a few minutes away. He'll be here shortly.

During the four-hour drive from Centralia to Masonville, Lucky had occasionally chastised himself for not staying to have breakfast with Angie. Last night, he had decided to leave for Masonville at least by five o'clock in the morning so he wouldn't be terribly late getting to work.

Thoughts of yesterday's race-ending crash flashed through Lucky's mind again.

Angie won the race after a frighteningly close call. Jiggs and Eugenios Christofides careened across the finish line, their cars welded together from the impact, and tied for second place. That pile of wreckage just a few feet up the track was such a mess. It took a long time and effort to get the cars pried apart and taken off to the storage lot.

As Lucky drew a mug of hot coffee, he saw Juanita rush to her office and answer her ringing phone. She stood and looked around holding the receiver to her ear. When she spotted Lucky at the coffee pot, she waved for him to come to her.

"Angie's on the phone," Juanita said, as Lucky stepped into her office. "You can take the call in the conference room if you wish."

Lucky walked into the conference room and sat down in a chair. He pushed the speaker phone button. "Hello."

"You made it to work, huh?" He heard Angie say.

"Yes. I just got here. Where are you?"

"I'm about half-way to Masonville," Angie answered. "Are you going to be there for awhile?"

"Yes. I have to look around and see what's going on. I'll be here in the shop all morning at least."

"Good. I'm coming straight to the shop. I need to talk to you."

"About what?"

"Everything," Angie said quickly. "Jesus, God, the Holy Spirit."

"Okay," Lucky said, stretching the word out.

"Stay right there," Angie directed. "I'll be there as fast as I can get there."

"Stay safe," Lucky cautioned.

Lucky walked with his mug of coffee out to his workstation and sat down on his stool. A clipboard of papers hung from a screw in the toolbox wall. He looked at the newspaper he'd bought at the Quik-Trip convenience store in north Masonville. He took the clipboard off the hook and thumbed through the pages. Nothing earth shattering on it. He folded the crossword puzzle and slipped it into the clipboard.

He saw Samantha Corning walk toward him. She was the company's maintenance scheduling maven. "We've got a scraper transmission being brought in this morning. Priority One."

She handed him a printed Maintenance Order.

"Any idea of what's wrong with it?"

"Just that it won't shift from high-range back down to low-range."

Lucky scanned the Order and realized it was one of the gigantic twin-engine earth scrapers—the biggest pieces of equipment in Borsche's fleet. There were four of those behemoths in the fleet, and every one of them was expected to be operating full time all the time.

"I've already fixed one of these before," Lucky said. "I think I know what the problem is."

"If you need new gears, we'll have to order them," Samantha said. "That always takes a couple of days to get them."

"As I remember, it wasn't the gears," Lucky said. "It was that the shift-lever arm was bent, where it moves the gears along the spline. Hopefully, that's what the problem is. We'll see."

"Can you fix that faster?"

"Yes, ma'am. In one day."

"Okay, Wonderboy," Samantha said. "The truck's supposed to be here mid-morning with the transmission."

Lucky and Samantha watched Jiggs' motor home drive into the lot and park near the office complex.

"How did Jiggs take the end of the race yesterday?"

"Oh, he was about as normal as possible."

"Okay. Let me get back to my office at the other end of the building in case he comes in to talk to you about it." She smiled and left.

Lucky worked the crossword puzzle as he sipped his coffee. He heard Jiggs talking as he approached, and looked up to see Jiggs, on his cell phone, coming toward him talking.

Jiggs put his phone in his shirt pocket. "That was the truck driver with the transmission coming in this morning," Jiggs said. "He's about ten minutes away. Have you heard about that transmission?"

"Yes, sir," Lucky said. "I fixed that one from the Route 20 project and it was just a bent shifter lever bar. Hopefully, this is the same problem."

"I hope so," Jiggs said. "It's one of the big Cat six-five-sevens. At this stage of the project, when the big one goes down, the whole project slows to a snail's pace, and the schedule goes to hell."

"When I fixed the one on Route Twenty, I ordered an extra shifter-lever bar," Lucky said.

"That was smart," Jiggs said. "You'll have to replace one of the hydraulic hoses. When they were taking the transmission out of the machine, they screwed up the hoses."

"We always have plenty of hoses," Lucky said. "Do you want me to go up and put the transmission back into the rig?"

"No. Let them do it. I need you here," Jiggs said.

"What's going on?"

"The insurance agent will be here tomorrow to talk about our coverage. I want you in on those discussions."

"Okay. If that's everything, Angie called," Lucky said, and paused. "She's on her way here to talk to me."

"Oh, yeah. About what?"

Lucky took a deep breath. "I don't know. But I hope she hasn't given up on her quest to be born again."

"Me, too," Jiggs said. "She was pretty shaken up after the crash yesterday, wasn't she?"

"Yes, sir. But, last night, I thought she had pretty much dealt with it, even though she looked like she was ready to drop."

"Let me know." Jiggs turned and walked toward the office. "If Angie needs help, do what you can," Jiggs called over his shoulder.

* * *

Angie parked next to Lucky's service truck in the Borsche employee lot. She wrestled her Bible into her arm and walked to the big roll-up door close to Lucky's workstation.

Lucky spotted her come through the door and stood to let her sit down on his stool after putting her Bible down on the workbench. He frowned as he studied her face. Her eyes were red from crying, but her face was full of radiant beauty.

What is going on?

Lucky quickly decided to go to the conference room. He picked up Angie's Bible and said, "Let's go into the conference room and get comfortable."

Angie hadn't sat down on his stool, so she merely nodded and moved to follow him.

They walked into the office area and toward the conference room. Lucky noted that Juanita was not at her desk and that Jiggs was on the phone talking.

He held a chair out for Angie who took her Bible from him and sat down. She laid the Bible on the table in front of her.

Lucky nodded at her.

"Last night," Angie started slowly. "I tossed and turned for quite awhile and then finally fell asleep. But, I had a nightmare about the crash, and it startled me wide awake. I got up and poured a glass of wine. Then I decided I would read the Bible for a little while. The flash of white light kept running through my head. How strange it was. When I sat down and opened my Bible, I remembered you telling me to start a search with the Concordance at the back. So I went there and looked up *Light*."

Lucky nodded.

Angie opened her Bible and turned pages over until she was at the back of the book. She flipped pages slowly until she found the one she wanted. "Under *Light*, the annotation drew my attention and intrigued me. It says *In the Scriptures light is used frequently as a metaphor for Christ and the Christian's proper lifestyle.* That made me take note. *Frequently used as a metaphor for Christ.* Wow. I kept reading and as you told me to do, reading the citations."

Angie moved pages back to the center of the book. "In Isaiah 60:1, it says *Arise, shine; for your light has come, And the glory of the Lord has risen upon you.*" She thumbed pages. "Then in John 8:12," Angie continued, "Jesus says, *I am the Light of the world; he who follows Me will not walk in the darkness, but will have the Light of Life.* Then in John 12:35, Jesus continues, *For a little while longer the Light is among you. Walk while you have the Light,* and in verse 36, *While you have the Light, believe in the Light, so that you may become sons of Light."*

She paused to flip more pages. "Then in Second Corinthians 4:4, *the god of this world has blinded the minds of the unbelieving so that they might not see the light of the gospel of the glory of Christ, who is the image of God."*

Angie stopped and took a deep breath. She looked at Lucky. Her eyes were full of joy.

Lucky reached over the table and took her hand in his. He studied her shining face. "Keep going, sweet one. Your recitations of those verses are making my heart leap."

Angie nodded and turned more pages. "Then in Ephesians 5:8, we read, *you were formerly darkness, but now you are Light in the Lord; walk as children of Light."*

Angie glanced at Lucky and then said, "Finally, in First John: 7, it says, *but if we walk in the Light, we have fellowship with one another, and the blood of Jesus His Son cleanses us from all sin."*

Angie closed the Bible and set it on the table. "After I finished reading those Scriptures, I sat for a long time staring at the wall. Jesus is Light. If we walk in the Light, we walk with Jesus, with him who gives us the Light of Life. Suddenly, I felt totally relaxed. My body simply went limp." Angie pushed back into the chair.

"Then I saw Jesus standing in the motel room wall. He said to me, *'The bright light you saw during the crash was not an Angel. It was me. Come. Take my hand and walk with me."*

Angie paused as if reliving the scene in her mind. "I started crying. But I got up and walked to take his hand. I felt his hand in mine. Then He said, 'You are a child of the Light. Welcome to the Light of Life.'"

Angie stopped and looked directly at Lucky, who was merely looking at her with understanding eyes.

"Then he was gone. My hand was flat against the wall. But it was still warm. My whole body felt satisfied like I'd just climbed out of a hot bath. I sat down, and I wanted to pray. So, I recited the Lord's Prayer, just like you taught me."

"That's wonderful," Lucky said. "You made it. I'd say you've been born of the spirit. One sign of that is that you have a really healthy glow about you."

Lucky leaned back in his chair. "Now you must guard your ways. You might even have trouble with what you hear from others. But, I'll share with you something I heard, shortly after I gave my life into His hands. You can find three verses that will affirm the truth of what you hear. Anyone can take one verse and make it sound like they're telling you the truth."

Lucky took a sip of his coffee. "Are you ready for a Coke yet?"

Angie bobbed her head. "Yeah. That would be good."

Lucky retrieved a can of Coke from the small refrigerator, popped the top and handed it to Angie.

She took a long draught, set the can on the table and smiled radiantly at Lucky.

"You'll be wanting to learn everything you can about Christ," Lucky continued, and noted that Angie was nodding *yes, yes.* "You'll see things that He taught about Himself in the Old Testament as you read and study. You'll come to know Him as the lover of our souls."

"The Lover of our souls?" Angie asked "That's deep. How is he the lover of our souls?"

"You already know that Jesus willingly gave his life to welcome all who would ask his blessing. When you studied John 3, we talked about the second birth and how much God loved the world."

Angie nodded.

"You can use your concordance to learn about the bridegroom, and you'll see many references to God referring to His people as the bride or wife. Later, in John 10, Jesus tells us that his sheep hear His voice and recognize it. So, we are both a bride and a sheep."

Angie giggled slightly, then looked away.

Lucky sipped on his coffee. "At the same time, Jesus is the Lamb of Sacrifice. So, Jesus is both sheep and," Lucky paused to put air quotes around: "and Master of the sheep, or shepherd."

Angie felt more relaxed as she listened to Lucky talking. "So, is 'Lover of our souls,' a verse somewhere?"

"It's a song written by Charles Wesley, entitled *Jesus, Lover of my Soul.*"

Angie bobbed her head. "I want to hear that song."

"Last night," Lucky said slowly. "When Jesus held your hand, Did you feel loved?"

"Oh, yeah!" Angie blurted. "Oh, man; I felt loved and at peace with the world." Angie's eyes teared up. "I've waited so long."

Lucky stood and picked Angie up out of her seat and held her in his arms.

After a few moments, Angie calmed down and her sobs were mere hiccups. Lucky lowered her down into the chair. She took a long drink of her Coke. "I feel so good about life, except—except I wonder if—if I could have prevented the crash in the first place? When Nikki stalled, I did what I was supposed to do, get it to the side of the track; out of everyone else's way. Did the cars behind me crash trying to avoid me?"

"I don't think so," Lucky said. "I didn't hear anyone talking about anything you did or didn't do."

"I feel so sorry for all the drivers who self-finance their racing hobby," Angie said slowly. "Good, Lord, they use the rent money and the grocery, money to keep their cars running so they can race. Now all they have is a crumpled pile of metal. What are their wives going to do? Their kids? The money is gone."

"That includes about ninety percent of the drivers," Lucky said. "But it wasn't anything you did. It wasn't your fault."

"Would God think bad of me—"

"God allows things to happen, so we learn to reflect on our lives," Lucky said. "Otherwise, Jesus would not have died on the cross. We wouldn't celebrate Easter. And we all would be subject to eternal death for our sins. But, God loves us. He wants us to love him in return. Why do bad things happen to good people? Because God set it up that way. In the end, however, when we realize His loving care and know that He has provided us with a way to love Him in return; our eternal walk with Him is assured."

"I still feel terrible for those drivers who wrecked their cars."

Lucky grinned. "You will achieve sainthood someday, but, you can't do it while you're still alive—it's not allowed. The crash wasn't your fault!"

Jiggs popped into the room. He studied Angie and Lucky for a minute. "Is there a problem?"

"Angie feels responsible for the crash yesterday," Lucky said. "Since Nikki stalled and she thinks that caused the pileup."

"Nikki stalling didn't cause the crash," Jiggs said and frowned. "Coming out of turn four, Clyde Bird's car got loose and went sideways. Someone said his right rear tire blew. Then Nelson Greene ran into him. I swerved to miss those two guys spinning around and got into the side of

Christofides' car. Fortunately, Christofides and I careened against the inside wall, but we kept moving and eventually coasted across the Finish Line. Everybody else behind us just naturally reacted and that resulted in one gigantic pileup."

Jiggs started toward the door, then stopped and turned back. "You did not cause the crash, Ms. Angie Prescotte. It was caused by Bird's number 90 Chevy Impala getting sideways."

"I saw Bird's car coming at me," Angie said and shuddered. "I figured he was going to destroy me. I remember thinking about my options; go out the driver's window and get hit by the car coming at me, or go out the passenger side window and get crushed between my car and the concrete wall. That's when I saw the flash of white light that I now know was Jesus."

"How do you know that?" Jiggs asked.

"He told me so, last night."

Jiggs studied Angie for a long moment and then looked at Lucky.

Lucky gave an abrupt nod.

Angie looked at Jiggs for a long time. "I feel bad for those drivers who wrecked their cars. The families. The kids."

"You know about the racing association hardship assistance fund, don't you?" Jiggs asked.

Angie wobbled her head. Lucky looked at Jiggs and said, "What's that all about?"

Jiggs sat down at the end of the conference table. "Part of our membership dues and part of our entrance fees go into what we call a *Distress Fund.* Whenever we have a major pileup like this one, drivers can apply for help. Kurt Maxxon has already indicated the fund is open. Any driver who needs it can get up to four thousand dollars from the fund to help get back up and running."

"That's interesting," Lucky said. "Kurt has never mentioned it to me."

"Me either," Angie agreed.

"Well, neither of you would qualify for it," Jiggs said matter-of-factly. "Of the nine or ten drivers who had their cars totaled in the crash, only three or four will qualify for it. Like Christofides and me, neither of us qualify since we have the wherewithal to deal with the wreck. I have another car out back of the building here that we can get ready for the next race. Eugenios Christofides also has a backup car."

Lucky bobbed his head, "Yes, sir, I've seen that car out back here and wondered what it was for. So if you're wealthy, you keep a backup car ready?" He grinned.

"You don't need to be wealthy, so much as prudent." Jiggs looked at both Lucky and Angie.

"Nelson Greene, who tangled with Clyde Bird, comes from a well-to-do family," Jiggs continued. "So he doesn't qualify. Clyde Bird, on the other hand, is not so well off. Clyde will get four thousand dollars to help him recover. Clyde was driving an old Chevy Impala. He'll go find another one in a junk yard, someplace, and create a new car."

"What does that involve?" Lucky asked.

"He'll lift the body off it and reinforce the chassis. He'll salvage his old steering system, repair the driver's roll cage from his wrecked car, including the seat and safety harness, and install it on the new chassis. Then he'll remove all the upholstery and unnecessary weight from the body, and weld the doors and trunk lid shut. He'll salvage his engine, transmission and drive train from his wrecked car and set them into the new one. Since he'll do most of the work himself, his total cost will probably be about the four thousand he gets from the association. He may have to come up with some extra money, but it won't be much. And other drivers, like myself and Nelson Greene, will help him with that. Clyde will be okay. He might miss the next race, but he'll be back shortly after that."

"That's wonderful," Angie said. "I didn't know about any of this."

"Well now you know," Jiggs said and stood up to walk out the door.

Angie looked at Lucky. "Why didn't you tell me how the wreck happened?"

"Because I didn't know how it happened. I was in the pits, remember?"

"I guess Jiggs was an eyewitness, huh?"

"I'd sure think so," Lucky said. "He was right there in the middle of the action—in a position to see it all."

Angie smiled. "I feel a little better about it all. But, I'm still concerned for those drivers who lost it all."

"They'll be just fine." Lucky took a sip of his coffee. "If it were the first for anyone, they'd have learned from it. Trust God. He knows what He's doing. Even if it seems bad to us."

"But—"

"You'll understand more as you mature in your faith, Angie. Look at how He rescued you. You can even think back at times in your life and see

His care to save you for this day."

"You think—"

"Yes. Look at John Nine, and read about the man born blind." Lucky paused to let Angie flip pages in her Bible.

"All of Nine?"

Lucky swung Angie's Bible so he could read it. "In this chapter, Jesus encounters a man born blind. His disciples ask Him: *who sinned, this man or his parents, that he would be born blind.* And Jesus answers *It was neither that this man sinned, nor his parents; but it was so that the works of God might be displayed in him.*"

Angie kept reading. "Look at verse five: *While I am in the world, I am the Light of the world.*"

Lucky smiled. "There, you see. Jesus is the light of the world."

Angie shook her head. "Amazing."

CHAPTER SIXTEEN

Lucky listened intently as he drove through Pleasant Valley and out onto the open highway.

No annoying rattle in the truck's door. So far, so good.

"One of the screws holding the window bracket to the door panel worked itself loose," the Pleasant Valley Ford service manager explained to him. "We just had to put in a new screw and tightened it good with a little Lok-tight. I'm sorry about that."

"Will it hold?" Lucky asked.

"If it doesn't, bring it back and we'll weld it in place."

"I'm a perfectionist," Lucky said and smiled. "Especially with mechanical things that should not make noises."

"That's fine," the service manager replied. "We want you entirely satisfied with our work."

Whoever shot that window out should be made to fix it. But Lucky stopped before he got off onto that line of thought again. The sniping had upset him, but there was no need to let it continue to impinge upon his life.

As he drove across the railroad tracks west of town, Lucky looked directly at the door.

Good, they fixed it. Thank you, Lord, for the small things.

The late July sun was midway toward setting in the west. A light breeze moved the hot and muggy air enough to rustle the leaves, but not enough to cool anything.

Lucky let his mind wander to thoughts of Angie. He was looking forward to seeing her and being with her again this afternoon. Lucky surveyed the road ahead, trying to guess where he was.

About half-way to Copperville.

He glanced at the clock on the radio.

I'm only about twenty minutes late.

As he drove into the downtown area of Copperville, Lucky was amazed at how many parking spaces were available. He saw Angie's red Porsche parked a dozen spaces down from the door into the Farmer's Platter. He parked next to her.

Angie was sitting in her car and looked up at Lucky's service truck as it pulled in next to her. When she realized who it was, she scrambled out of her car and hurried around the truck and walked into Lucky's embrace. She kissed him on the cheek.

"Have you been waiting long?" Lucky asked.

"No. Only arrived a few minutes ago. Whew, is it hot or what?"

"Where are all the people?" Lucky asked, sweeping his hand in an arc to indicate the dozens of empty parking spaces. "It's five-forty-five."

"It's Wednesday afternoon. This old town still closes down on Wednesday afternoons so people can go home and get ready for evening prayer meeting."

"Oh, yes. I remember when I was a kid," Lucky said. "Sinclaire was deserted every Wednesday afternoon." He looked toward the restaurant door. "Is the Farmer's Platter open?"

"It sure smells like it, doesn't it," Angie said and giggled. "I guess there are enough people who don't go to church to keep them busy on Wednesday nights."

Lucky led her to the door, opened it for her, and followed her into the restaurant. They followed the waitress to a table at the back of the room, off by themselves, even though there were several booths and tables available close to the door.

Lucky helped Angie with her chair and sat down next to her. They studied their menus briefly then set them aside. The waitress arrived. Angie ordered diet Coke, and Lucky wanted a cup of coffee.

When the waitress brought their drinks, they both ordered the Country Fried Steak with Coleslaw and pinto beans.

The waitress gathered their menus and walked away writing on her order pad.

"Did they fix the rattle in your truck?" Angie asked.

"Yes, ma'am. They got it fixed. Thankfully, it didn't take them too long. I was afraid they might take a long time to figure out what was causing it, and I would have to call and cancel tonight."

"I'm really glad you didn't have to cancel," Angie said. "God, I've been like a teenager thinking about seeing you again today."

"What did you do today?"

"I bought Auronia a Jungle Gym. Mother and I spent most of the day assembling it in the backyard."

"Those things can get complicated. How'd that go?"

"Don't ask," Angie said. "*Some assembly required* means a box with a gazillion bolts, nuts, washers, screws, latches, hinges, pegs, spacers, and chains. A hundred pieces of plastic of various shapes, sizes, lengths, and colors—all clearly marked, except for the pieces where the tags have fallen off."

"You're braver than I am to undertake a project like that," Lucky said. "I'm mechanically inclined when dealing with complicated gearboxes. But, when it comes to putting kid's toys together, well, it's always been one of my challenges." He chuckled audibly.

"We finished it, fortunately, just before I was ready to throw the toolbox across the yard."

"I bet Auronia appreciates your efforts," Lucky said, then paused. "But she's only a two-year-old. Is she big enough to play on it?"

"We blocked off the slide, and other high stuff that the instructions said were not recommended for children under four years old. She can still use the swing and the seesaw. There are a lot of hidey-holes and spaces for her to climb into and around and several boxes are full of plastic balls."

"I'm sure she's going to love it."

"Oh, yeah. She was still playing on it when I left to come over here," Angie said. "I doubt she even missed me leaving. And, I wouldn't be surprised if I found her sleeping in it when I get home tonight."

"Are there any other children in your neighborhood her age?"

"No. There are only a half dozen kids in the whole development, and they're all teenagers in high school or college. That's been a problem with that location I didn't think about when I bought it. No kid her age to help socialize her. My mother takes her to a daycare center two, three, mornings a week just so she can get used to playing with other kids. It took a while to teach her social mores, like just because she wanted a toy to play with didn't mean she could just take it away from another child."

"That can be a problem," Lucky agreed. "So, she won't have any friends coming over to play with her on her new jungle gym."

"Nope. My cousin lives up near Centralia. She has a two-year-old and a four-year-old. She brings them down often. Now Auronia and the boys will have something to play on when they come."

The waitress arrived with their food.

Lucky reached for Angie's hand, and they bowed their heads to say Grace.

As they ate, Angie asked Lucky for an update regarding the killer of the girl he found under the trailer.

"Nothing new that I've heard about," Lucky said.

"I worry about you wandering around with some nutcase killer loose out there. He knows who you are. He shot at you once already."

"I'm extra cautious," Lucky said. "I'm constantly aware of the people around me. My training in the military did that."

After the waitress had cleared their plates, Lucky scooted his chair back. "Did you bring your Bible?"

"Sure. I always have it with me. Do you want to go up to the church and study some?"

"I'm ready," Lucky said. "We can do a short study."

* * *

They drove to St. Michaels Church and went in. Lucky took one of the envelopes from the rack under the alms box and followed Angie to the study room. Sister Agnes made a brief appearance to see who had entered the church and then went down the hall.

Lucky rearranged a table with two chairs and sat down. Angie scooted her chair close to Lucky's side and opened her Bible to the ribbon marker. "The last time I was having a hard time dealing with John Fourteen. I think I've come to grips with it all."

"It's okay if you still miss Tugs," Lucky said.

Angie nodded her head. "And it's okay if I fall in love with someone else, right?"

"We can love more that one person at a time," Lucky said. "I love Jesus, I love Olivia Maye. I love Sophia. I love Jason. I love Granny Watson. And I love you."

"You do?"

"Do what?"

"You love me?"

"Yes! I do," Lucky said. "So, you see—"

"You're in love with me?" Angie said.

"Yes. Yes. I'm in love with you."

Angie stared at Lucky. "I'm—I'm in love with you, too."

Lucky looked at Angie for a long time, cleared his throat and said. "So, you see that I have a lot of love to share. And you do, too. Love is not a finite quantity given to each of us to use sparingly. Our love for others expands as the need grows. And, very often, we continue to love someone who has been taken from us."

Angie moved closer to Lucky. Then she buried her face in his chest. Her sobs were controlled but clearly visible.

Lucky stroked her hair.

"I love you," Angie said in a squeaky voice. "And, I love Auronia just as much." She rubbed away the tears trickling down her cheeks. "I love Jesus, and," Angie paused for breath. "And I'm sure I'll love all your family, too."

"And now you're walking with Jesus," Lucky said, "who is the epitome of love."

"You know," Angie said, then paused. "I can feel his love in my heart. It's such a wonderful feeling."

"And, it just keeps getting better," Lucky said.

Angie nodded. "I just want to go up on the highest mountain and yell, 'I love you, Jesus!' I want the whole wide world to know."

Lucky smiled. He took Angie's hands in his and squeezed them.

"I want to get up in church and tell everyone there that I love Jesus."

"You can do that if you want," Lucky said softly. "But, you don't have to."

"Yeah. But, I want to. Next Sunday morning."

"We can talk to Pastor Judith and see if we do that."

"Can we do that now?" Angie asked.

"Probably not," Lucky said after swinging his arm up to look at his watch. "This is Wednesday night, remember. Pastor Judith is getting ready to start the Prayer Meeting."

"Oh, yeah. You're right. Have you seen someone do it in church before?" Angie asked.

"Not here in this church," Lucky said. "It was a fairly regular occurrence in the Baptist Church I attended down in Tennessee."

"Would it be different here?"

"I've seen it in the Lutheran Manual. There appears to be a structured ritual. I didn't read it, I just saw it."

"How long do you think it'll take?" Angie asked, frowning slightly.

"Not too long. It's done as part of the regular Sunday Service; so probably ten minutes, tops."

"I'm ready! I want to do it next Sunday."

"I'll call Pastor Judith tomorrow morning, and see what she says."

"I know Jesus saved my life last Sunday, during the race," Angie said slowly. "He saved me. Now I have to tell the world."

"That's fine with me," Lucky said, stroking Angie's back. "You know I'll be there alongside you, cheering you on, supporting you all the way."

Lucky leaned down and kissed her.

Angie leaned into the kiss. Then she pulled back. "Hold me," Angie whispered. "Wrap those long arms around me and hold me—hold me tight. Don't let go."

CHAPTER SEVENTEEN

Angie sat at the breakfast bar finishing a Diet Coke and reading her Bible.

She heard Auronia running up the hall toward her.

"I'm done with my letters and numbers," Auronia shouted. "Can I go play on my new gym, Mommy?" She ran toward the sliding patio door.

"For just a few minutes, Baby," Angie said. "We'll be leaving soon,"

"Mommy, I'm all grown up. I'm not a baby any more," Auronia stomped her foot. "Where are we going?"

Angie giggled at Auronia's quick change of pace. "We're going down Lucky's place in Masonville."

"Oh, yeah. I remember now."

Angie's mother came out of her room off the corner of the kitchen. "Are you still going to do it?"

"Yes, Mother, Of course, I'm still going to do it."

Auronia stood motionless listening to her mother and Nana talk.

"Go out and play on your gym," Angie said. "I'll call you when we need to leave."

"I don't want to," Auronia whined. "Nana is mad at you."

Angie glared at her mother. "Go on out and play, Baby," she said in a soft voice. "Nana and I will talk about this."

Auronia hesitantly turned, slid the door open, and walked slowly out. "How soon are we leaving?" she asked again.

"In about an hour."

"What time will that be?"

'The big hand will be on twelve, and the little hand will be on the four."

After Auronia had slid the door shut and they watched her amble slowly toward the Jungle Gym, Angie said, "Mother, I've asked you not to involve Auronia in our disputes. She's too young to understand that people can disagree on things and still love one another."

"I didn't say anything to her," Angie's mother pleaded.

"Then what is she talking about?"

"I have no idea. She's only two years old."

"She's nearly three now, Mother, and perceptive enough to pick up on comments you make and interpret them by the tone of your voice. What have you been grousing about? What's bothering you?"

"I'm just concerned that you're going to make a spectacle of yourself in front of that church on Sunday."

"Are you serious?" Angie gasped. "Mother, I'm born again. One of my duties now is to let people know that God is in my life. A spiritual baptism is one way people can do that."

"Angie, you were born a Christian. You were already baptized. Adults don't get baptized. Your Daddy and I never had any other religion."

Angie sighed. "Mother, I know you'll understand some day. You'll meet Lucky, and you'll realize how much Christ can make a difference in people's lives. Now, have you been talking to Auronia about your concerns about being a spectacle in Church? You could come and be proud of what's going on, instead of worried."

"I haven't been talking to Auronia about it, and no, I won't come watch." Angie's mother stood resolutely.

"Alright, Mother. I can't force you. But, you've been making comments about it?" Angie asked, cocking her head.

"I don't know," Angie's mother said, turned on her heel, and walked into her room. She closed the door with a bang.

Angie scrubbed her forehead. Sighing, she turned to look at Auronia. The little girl was sitting on a crossbar, chewing her lower lip, and staring at the house. Angie slid the door open and said, "Come on, Aurie. Let's get ready and leave for Masonville."

Auronia jumped up and ran up the steps into the kitchen. "Is everything okay, Mommy?"

"It will be. Grandma's just not ready to go visiting right now. Did you pack your favorite doll to take on the trip?"

"I have two of them."

"Two of them?"

"Yes, Nana said there should always be a boy and a girl together."

"Uh-huh," Angie grunted. "Is there anything else you want to take besides what we put in your suitcase earlier?"

"I don't think so."

"Good. Go out to the garage," Angie said. "I'll get our suitcases and come out to buckle you into your car seat."

Angie put the suitcases on the front passenger seat of her car.

That's the major drawback to owning a sports car. No trunk space and almost no back seat.

Auronia stood beside the car. "Can I ride so I can see where we're going?"

Angie smiled at her. "Yes. I think so. I can turn your car seat around, so it's front facing. You're a big girl now, aren't you?"

"Yes!" Auronia yelled. "I am a big girl now."

Angie moved the car seat to center of the backseat and laughed as she helped her daughter jump into the car and then watched her scramble up into her seat. She looked at Auronia playing with the toy wheel on the age-adjustable seat Kurt and Christina had purchased for her and smiled. *Like mother, like daughter!* After she finished buckling Auronia in, Angie went back into the house. She closed the door. "Mother," she yelled. "We're leaving now."

She waited for a response. When none came, she turned and went out to the car.

After Auronia settled in and stopped jabbering nonstop, Angie let her mind wander to the upcoming events.

Lucky has been a wonderful coach. I'm as ready for this as I'll ever be. But, what am I willing to do? Will this become a spectacle as mother fears? No. Lucky will get me through it. Jesus will. Please, Lord, Jesus. Help me. Help Lucky get me through this.

* * *

Lucky walked from the office area to his workbench in the garage area. He set the fresh cup of coffee on his workbench and sat down on the stool. With the large garage door open, the morning sun gleamed on his tool boxes and the metal workbench. He moved the folded crossword puzzle laying open next to his calendar into the shadow cast by his tool box. He decided to go ahead and finish working it rather than wait until later. He sipped on his coffee and filled in blank boxes. He glanced at the clock on the wall.

Lucky added letters to the crossword puzzle.

Jiggs Borsche came out of the office area and walked to Lucky's area.

"It's another scorcher," Jiggs said. He looked behind the workbench and drug out a second stool. "Lars called from the Highway Sixty-Five Project. He's got a dozer down. I called Craig and told him to plan on going down there tomorrow morning and fix it."

"I can take care of it," Lucky said.

"No, you can't," Jiggs retorted. "Not with Angie coming to town today. Not with Sunday being her big day at church. When Angie hits the city limits, you get in your truck and go meet her. Craig can handle the dozer."

"Yes, sir."

"What time do you expect her?"

"Probably about five."

"Good." Jiggs watched Lucky studying the crossword puzzle. "I keep meaning to ask if you've had a chance to look over the new shop tools budget; and if you've decided what we need to buy?"

"I just gave it to Juanita."

"That's good," Jiggs said. He pointed to the crossword puzzle. "Ninety-eight down is *REAPER.*"

Lucky swung his gaze from Jiggs to his crossword puzzle. "Oh, yes, sir. You're right." He filled in the boxes.

Jiggs climbed down off the stool and started to leave.

Lucky's cell phone jangled. He answered it on speaker phone. He heard Angie say, "Hello, My Lucky Charm. How are you?"

Jiggs stopped where he was and listened. Lucky wished he hadn't answered on speaker.

"I'm great," Lucky said. "How are you?"

"We're fine. We just left the house."

"You're already on the road?"

"Yeah, we left a little earlier than I planned. I'll tell you about it later. We should be to the motel about three-thirty. I hope they have a room ready. Auronia will be cranky after the trip—even though it's a short one."

"That's great."

"Auronia and I are just singing our way to Masonville."

"Singing your way to Masonville?"

"I tuned into a radio station with gospel music. Some of the songs Auronia knows from Sunday School, and she started singing along. So cute. A couple of them I even remembered."

"If you call me when you hit the city limits, I can be at the motel about the time you arrive. Then I can go over to Lucy's and get your sandwiches."

"You can get off work?"

"He's free to go when you need him," Jiggs yelled.

"Is that you, Jiggs?"

"Yes, ma'am. I just told Lucky that when you hit the city limits, he should take off the rest of the day and get up with you."

"You are a wonderful man, Jiggs Borsche, "Angie said. "I don't care what everybody else says about you."

"Thank you, ma'am."

Lucky could see Jiggs shaking with mirth as he walked back to talk to Juanita.

* * *

Lucky punched the phone off to end Angie's call and looked around his work area. Everything was in order. He'd cleaned his tools and packed them away a few minutes before and locked the boxes. He walked out and climbed into his service truck.

When he turned into the motel entrance, he saw Angie's red Porsche parked under the covered entryway. He parked and walked toward the lobby. As he pushed through the doors, he saw Auronia sitting quietly on a sofa, observing Angie as she stood at the counter.

When Angie saw him coming, she walked to him and leaned into his embrace and kissed him on the cheek.

Lucky noted that Auronia did not miss a moment of their encounter. She stared totally engrossed on her mother and Lucky.

Angie returned her attention to the clerk checking her in.

"Will you need one or two keys?" the clerk asked.

"Just one," Angie answered.

Angie accepted the envelope of key card and then led Lucky over to Auronia. "Auronia, baby, this is Kyle O'Rourke. He is Mommy's new friend that I love."

Auronia's eyes lit up. "Hello, Mr. Kyle. Mommy, is he the man Nana says you need?"

Angie looked at Lucky as they shared the humor of the awkward situation. "Yes. This is the man I need in my life."

"Me. Too, huh?" Auronia said.

"Yes. You need him in your life, too."

"He's tall," Auronia said.

"Yes, he is," Angie said.

Lucky bent down and squatted next to Auronia. "I've been waiting a long time to meet you in person. Your mother showed me the pictures she has in her purse. Every one of them was of you! You're even cuter in person. I love your dimples."

"Everyone tells me that," Auronia said and blushed.

" Oh. Well, I also love your golden curly hair."

"It's real."

Lucky laughed. "Yes, I know it's real, I can tell you're not wearing a wig."

"Noooo." Auronia giggled.

"I'll park my car, and then we can go up to the room," Angie said.

"I'll get a cart," Lucky offered.

After Lucky had helped Angie load her suitcases, he turned to push the luggage cart toward the doors.

"Auronia, you go with Mr. Lucky while I park my car."

Lucky stopped and looked at Auronia.

Auronia laughed. "Okay, Mommy." She walked alongside Lucky as he carefully pushed through the motel's automatic doors.

"Do you like my Mommy?" Auronia asked Lucky when they stopped in the motel lobby to wait for her mother.

Lucky looked at the little girl's folded arms and serious face. He smiled at her. "Oh, yes. I surely do."

"She's nice, isn't she?" Auronia persisted.

"Yes, she is," Lucky said. "And she's pretty, too, huh? Just like you."

"Yes!" Auronia said and giggled.

Auronia looked out the door her mother had gone out of. "Where are you going to stay tonight?" she asked Lucky. "Did you get a room here, too?"

"Oh, I'll just stay at my house tonight," Lucky said and grinned. "At supper, you're going to meet my kids."

"You have kids, too?" Auronia said in a loud voice.

"Yes, I have three kids."

"How old are they?"

"They're older than you. But, I'll bet you'll like them anyway."

"I like everybody."

Angie came through the door.

Auronia pointed to the cart. "Can I ride on that?"

"Sure," Lucky said and leaned down to help her climb up. Lucky led the way to the elevators. "Hang on tight."

Angie dug the keycard out of the envelope and handed it to Lucky. "We're in room three-twenty-six."

After the cart was empty, Lucky said, "I'll take this back down to the lobby. What kind of sandwiches do you guys want for lunch?"

"Tuna salad," Auronia said quickly.

Angie grinned and bobbed her head. "Me, too."

"That's my favorite sandwich, too," Lucky said. "I'll go over to Lucy's and see if they can rustle up some tuna salad sandwiches."

Lucy greeted him at the door and assured him they always had tuna salad sandwiches. In a few minutes, Lucky walked back to the motel with three square white boxes each containing a tuna salad sandwich, a dill pickle, and a small bag of potato chips.

After the sandwiches had been devoured, Angie found the Cartoon Channel on the TV and Auronia settled into the big easy chair to watch it. Angie led Lucky to the sofa, and they sat down.

"Where are we going for tonight's family dinner?"

"My gang likes the little pizza parlor near where we live. It's a family affair with clowns and a birthday party mood all the time. They also have hamburgers and hot dogs and malts and sodas. Anything you might want."

"All of which I can get along without. My girlish figure is getting a little dense."

"Looks great to me," Lucky said.

"Keep telling me that," Angie said, smiling. "However, I know when my jeans don't fit anymore."

"They don't fit anymore?"

"They're getting tight around the waist."

* * *

Angie watched happily as Auronia bonded with all three of Lucky's children during the supper at Mr. Jays Pizzeria.

Then Lucky led the way to his house, and they all settled in to get to know each other even better. Olivia Maye and Sophia took to Auronia as if she'd always been there. Very quickly, Auronia insisted she was going to move in to live with the girls.

Granny Watson had baked peach pies during the afternoon, and everyone topped off the pizza with peach pie ala mode.

"Can we have stuff like this at home, Mommy?" Auronia asked.

"Maybe we will," Angie said. "It is good, isn't it?"

When Angie decided it was time to put Auronia to bed for the night, she wasn't too surprised that Auronia didn't want to go back to the motel.

"I want to stay with here with Ollie and Sophie," Auronia whined.

Angie looked at Lucky.

Lucky shrugged. "It's okay with me. We have an extra bed in the garage."

After the kids were all down for the night, Angie led Lucky out into the kitchen. Granny Watson was watching TV in the den. "The kids are getting along great," Lucky said.

"They sure are," Angie said, bobbing her head and grinning. "They're like one big happy family."

"Did you bring your Bible?"

"It's in the car," Angie said. "Do you want to study?"

"We could dig out some of the more appropriate Scriptures about living with Jesus Christ." Lucky smiled. "you're heading into a whole new life."

"We can go over to the motel and use that meeting room in the lobby," Angie offered.

"I'm ready," Lucky said. "Let me get my Bible and tell Granny Watson where I'm going."

"Meet me at my car," Angie said.

* * *

When they arrived at the motel, they saw several people sitting in the meeting room off the lobby. They appeared to be in deep discussions. The breakfast room was locked.

"We can go up to my room," Angie said.

She moved suitcases and toys off the sofa, and she and Lucky laid their Bibles on the coffee table.

"You want coffee?" Angie asked.

"Yes, ma'am, but I can brew it." Lucky dug out the coffee fixings and set the pot to brewing.

Angie took a can of Diet Coke out of the small refrigerator in the corner.

Lucky flipped to the Concordance in the back of his Bible. "Ah, just as

I suspected, the best book for this is Ephesians." He thumbed pages back. "Look at Chapter four, verse twenty-one: 'if indeed you have heard Him and have been taught in Him, just as truth is in Jesus, that, in reference to your former life, you lay aside the old self, which is being corrupted in accordance with the lusts of deceit, and that you be renewed in the spirit of your mind, and put on the new self, which in *the likeness of* God has been created in righteousness and holiness of the truth. This is part of what is called *The Christian's Walk*." He scanned several pages. The rest of Chapter four and all of Chapters five and six are good reading for born-again Christians."

Angie opened her Bible and followed Lucky's instruction. She read several lines. "Look at this," she said. "Verse thirty, 'Do not grieve the Holy Spirit of God, by whom you were sealed for the day of redemption. Let all bitterness and wrath and anger and slander be put away from you, along with all malice. Be kind to one another, tender-hearted, forgiving each other, just of God in Christ also has forgiven you.'"

"I love the Book of Ephesians," Lucky said.

"This is great stuff," Angie said. "I'm going to start reading Ephesians." She pushed into Lucky's arm.

Lucky turned and looked at Angie for a long moment.

She leaned back and raised her head to look at him.

Lucky bent down, and he kissed her full on the mouth. Angie started to pull back but then leaned into the kiss. She turned and pressed her body against Lucky's arm. When Lucky moved to end the kiss, Angie reached up and pulled him back into it.

Lucky wiggled his arm from between him and Angie, and he wrapped it around her to pull her closer. She seemed to be enjoying their kiss.

Lucky was the first to pull back.

"What's wrong?" Angie asked.

Lucky shook his head. "Absolutely nothing is wrong," he murmured. "Everything is absolutely right."

Angie leaned close to Lucky for another kiss. After a few seconds, she pulled back. "Are we ready to take this to the next level?"

"We just had our first real kiss," Lucky said. "Don't we need to talk about important things before we get physical?"

Angie pulled back. "We're both adults. I don't understand. Why?"

"What's on your mind, right now?"

Angie blushed.

Lucky nodded and smiled gently. "Angie, we have to have God first, in everything we do. Our first priority is to obey Him. Our second priority is our children, which the Bible says are blessings from God."

Angie looked down. "You're right." She paused.

Lucky watched as Angie turned back to her Bible. She turned to the Concordance at the back. She read for a short time, then looked around for the notepad and pen on the desk. She jotted down some references.

One by one, she looked at each reference. Occasionally she'd flip to another page, holding her finger in the last one. She swung to face Lucky.

"Lucky," she said, her voice breaking. "I love my sweet little girl so much."

Angie began to cry softly.

"And, I love you. Auronia … Auronia needs a Daddy." She paused, then continued. "The Bible tells me that God blessed us with children and that we need to train them in the way they should go."

Lucky reached over and tilted her chin up. He kissed her. "I'd love to be her Daddy for the rest of her life, and mine."

Angie closed both Bibles, stood and reached for Lucky's hand. "Come on Daddy. Let's do what Mommies and Daddies do."

"Are you sure you want to do this?" Lucky asked.

"I couldn't be more certain."

"It means commitment. Don't hurt the children," Lucky persisted.

Angie paused, thinking. She nodded and continued toward the bed.

Lucky smiled and followed her.

* * *

When Lucky returned to the room from getting a morning paper, the coffee pot was finished. He poured a cup and then sat down at the small desk to work the crossword puzzle. Angie was sleeping. Lucky made sure the light didn't shine on her.

He finished the crossword puzzle and his second cup of coffee. He decided to go ahead and take a shower, hoping he didn't wake Angie up. As he exited the shower, Lucky noted that Angie was out of bed. Lucky put on his T-shirt and briefs and walked out into the living room. Angie was sitting on the sofa watching the muted news banner streaming across the bottom of the TV screen—completely nude.

She is so natural about everything.

Lucky dug a can of Diet Coke out of the refrigerator and handed it to Angie.

She looked at it and then set it on the coffee table. "What do you think of morning sex?" Angie asked, tilting her head seductively.

Lucky looked at her. "I've never tried it."

Angie stood and grabbed his hand and pulled him toward the bed. "Well, then. Let me demonstrate the benefits to you."

CHAPTER EIGHTEEN

Angie took a quick shower after they decided they should get back to Lucky's house before the kids got up and missed them. She was dressing in the bathroom.

Lucky picked up his cell phone, stopped and studied it for a moment. "I've got a voice mail," he said, as he dialed the numbers to retrieve it. He listened to the creepy voice as it whispered: "Hey dude. You got something I want back. I want my coil of clothesline rope back. The one you found up by the water gap. Take it to the party spot there on the creek near the water gap and leave it at the post with NO SWIMMING sign on it. If you don't give the rope back to me, and forget you ever saw it, I'll have to hurt your girlfriend and her cute little girl. I know who they are. I know where they live. If you don't want them hurt, give me back my rope. Do not, I repeat, *do not,* call the cops."

Lucky glanced at Angie who was sitting on the sofa apparently totally absorbed in the news. He was thankful he had not listened to it with the phone's speaker turned on.

This must be the killer talking to me. Good Lord, give me the strength to deal with this.

Lucky studied Angie for several seconds.

The killer knows who Angie and Auronia are. He knows my cell number. But does he know where they are right now?

Lucky waved for Angie to follow him and walked toward the door. "We've got a problem," he said in a stern voice. "We've *got* to get to my place."

Angie swung to look at Lucky but followed him out the door as he went down the hall to the stairway.

As they walked toward Angie's car, Lucky said, "Give me the keys. I'll drive."

As they exited the motel parking lot, Lucky handed Angie his cell phone. "Listen to the last voicemail message."

Angie punched buttons and sat listening to the message.

Suddenly Angie swung her head to look directly at Lucky. Her eyes were huge. "What is this all about?"

"The coil of clothesline rope was the murder weapon," Lucky said through clenched teeth. "That's the killer on the phone."

Angie dropped the phone into her lap. "Oh, my God."

"Relax. Don't panic," Lucky said in a quiet, soothing voice.

"That's easy for you to say," Angie said curtly. "My God, what if he's already at your house? What if he already has Auronia? Oh, my God. What's going on?"

"I doubt he's here yet," Lucky said. "He gave me the chance to return the rope. So, maybe, just maybe, we have some breathing room."

"Yeah, but what if he followed me to Masonville yesterday, and then followed us to your house last night? What if he knows where Auronia is now?"

"Calm down." Lucky looked in the rearview mirror and both side mirrors. "We'll check it all out. I'm going to come into my development from the back way. I should be able to tell if anything is amiss that way."

"Are you sure you can tell?"

"As sure as I can be about anything. Look through my contact list and see if there's a phone number for Sheriff Weinberger. It's an eight-one-nine area code number, as I remember."

Lucky drove as Angie poked buttons on his phone. "Here's an 819 starting with 335—"

"That's it. Call that number. Put it on speaker."

The dial tone sounded six times, and then there was a pause and click. Then a voice said. "Weinberger."

Angie handed the phone to Lucky. "Sheriff, this is Lucky O'Rourke."

"Yeah, I know. Do you think you can sneak up on me?"

"I think the killer called me during the night and left a message," Lucky said in a loud voice, worried about the road noise outside. "He wants his rope back, or he says he'll hurt Angie and Auronia if I don't give it to him."

"Oh, yeah?" Weinberger said, then paused. "Damn! This may be the lead we've been looking for."

"I'm serious," Lucky said.

Angie yelled. "I'm scared."

"Is that you, Angie?"

"Yes. You've got to find this guy and take him down," Angie pleaded.

"I agree," Weinberger said. "Where are you guys?"

"In Masonville," Lucky said. "We're headed toward my house."

"Alright. You two get to your house. I'll alert the Masonville Police and have them provide cover. Give me your address. Is the message still on your cell phone?"

"Yes."

"Good. The MPD has a pretty damn good lab, and they'll be able to analyze the message," Weinberger said. I'll contact them and have them set something up to get your cell phone without raising any suspicion in the neighborhood. It will probably involve something like a floral delivery, or something like that. A delivery girl from a local florist will show up at your house to make a delivery. You'll take the flowers and give the girl your cell phone. You've got a phone, don't you, Angie?"

"Yes."

"Give me the number."

Lucky wound around on side streets of his development.

"You two hole up at your place," Weinberger said. "And don't worry. We've got your backs."

"What will they be able to find on my cell phone?"

"Oh, you'd be amazed what they can determine from the message. Approximate age of the speaker. How nervous he is. How likely is he to do what he says he will. And they'll enhance it to hear things in the background—unique sounds that could pinpoint where he was when he called. Like is there a lot of truck traffic. Sirens. Sirens all are identifiable—the agency, division, etc."

"I just hope they can figure out who he is," Lucky said.

"Does this guy know who your kids are, Lucky?" Weinberger asked.

Lucky said, "I don't think so. But, I don't know what he knows."

"Are your kids at home?"

"They should be," Lucky said. "The two girls will wake up doting on Auronia. Jason usually is slower to get going." Lucky glanced at his watch. "Jason will be ready to leave the house in about an hour."

"We've probably got some time," Weinberger said. "The killer is getting antsy. He doesn't know what we're doing. As time goes by, the killer is thinking more and more about it, and then he polishes off a six-pack of beer and gets bold. He calls and threatens dire results. I doubt he's ready to act yet. Did he tell you to deliver the rope someplace?"

"Yes, sir. He told me to leave it at the party area there on the creek."

"How close are you to being home?"

"One more turn and I'll be able to see my house, two blocks away."

"Do you see anything unusual?"

"Not yet. There's my house. Nothing out of place so far."

"Stay on the phone with me until you're inside the house."

* * *

Angie jerked a double take and watched Granny Watson come back from her room with a shotgun in her hands. Angie looked uneasily from the shotgun to Auronia, who was sitting with Sophia watching TV in the den.

"What—what is that?" Angie asked.

"It's a sawed-off double-barrel twelve-gauge shotgun," Granny Watson said. She walked to the end cabinet drawer and dug out two red shotgun shells. She levered the weapon open and slid the shells into place. "We're ready for 'em, now," she said, and laid the shotgun on the counter next to the sink.

"Does that thing kick?" Angie asked, remembering her one and only foray into hunting as a teenage girl.

"Sure does," Granny Watson said. "The first time I shot that thing it rolled me back three loops. And that was just one barrel."

"How long ago was that?" Lucky asked.

"When I was five years old." Granny chuckled.

"Can you shoot both barrels at the same time?" Angie asked.

"Yeah. There's two triggers," Granny Watson said. "But you can pull them together. You'd have to be crazy to do that. But, if you wanted to make sure you hit what you're shooting at, it might be worth the pain."

Angie stood and walked into the den. Lucky went to fill his coffee cup and followed her. Angie sat in the middle next to the girls, and Lucky sat down on the end.

Auronia scrambled down from where she sat and climbed up into Lucky's lap. She snuggled in. Angie watched her little girl and dug at a tear in the corner of her eye with her knuckle.

Olivia Maye asked if anyone else wanted a cookie.

Angie noticed that even the temptation of a cookie could not distract Auronia from her spot on Lucky's lap.

Olivia Maye came into the room, munching on a cookie. "A flower delivery truck just pulled into the driveway," she announced.

"Oh, yes. I'll get it," Lucky said and walked to the front door just as the doorbell chimed. He opened the door wide enough for the girl to step inside. She had a small colorful arrangement in a glass vase with a huge balloon stretched above it that announced HAPPY BIRTHDAY. Lucky accepted the floral arrangement and handed the girl his cell phone.

The girl slipped the cell phone into her pants pocket and ran back to the delivery van. The van was moving before the girl was fully on board. Lucky set the flowers on the coffee table and walked in an arc so he could see the neighborhood out the bay window.

Nothing unusual. Maybe this will all work out okay after all.

Lucky poured a cup of coffee and sat down at the dinette table in the kitchen. Angie's phone chimed. Lucky looked at the caller ID. He answered it, "Hello, Sheriff."

He glanced toward the den and saw Angie and Granny Watson staring at him.

Fortunately, the kids have lost interest.

Lucky listened, not saying much.

Angie came into the kitchen, dug a coffee mug out of the cupboard and poured a cup of coffee. She opened the refrigerator and found the carton of milk. She poured a good portion of it into the mug and sat down next to Lucky.

"What did the sheriff say?"

"He just wanted to let me know that the MPD has my cell phone and they're working on it. The first thing they did was make a copy of the message and sent that up to the major crimes lab in Centralia. That lab is working on it, too."

"I guess that's good, huh?" Angie sat back. "If we need to know what the Centralia crime lab is doing, we can have Kurt call his buddy who runs the thing."

Lucky nodded. "Yes, ma'am. Brad Langley. I haven't met him, but I've heard a lot about him."

"Same here." Angie snuggled closer to Lucky.

Angie stared off into space. Her focus landed on the sawed-off shotgun, lying nearby on the counter. She looked at Lucky. "Do you think Granny Watson can react fast enough to get to that shotgun if the killer started breaking down the door right now?"

"I wouldn't want to be the one to test her." Lucky smiled and gripped Angie's hand and squeezed. "There's never a dull moment around this house. Are you sure you want to become a part of it?"

"It can't happen soon enough." Angie stood up and kissed Lucky. When she looked up, she saw three faces staring at her from the den door—Olivia Maye, Sophia, and Auronia. All three of them giggled.

Angie started chuckling and let it grow into a full roaring laugh.

Granny Watson prepared grilled cheese sandwiches for lunch which she served with homemade potato salad. The four kids sat at the breakfast bar while the adults sat at the kitchenette.

Auronia came to the table and tugged on Angie's shirt. "Mommy?"

"Yes, Aurie?" Angie asked as Lucky and Granny Watson looked on.

"My new favorite sandwich is a gilled cheese," Auronia announced.

"They are good, aren't they? Can you say 'Thank You' to Granny Watson?"

Auronia dashed around the table and gripped Granny Watson's apron. "Thank You, Granny."

Granny laughed. "You are welcome, Auronia."

Lucky chuckled and said, "You want Granny Watson to fix you another sandwich?"

"No! I'm full." Auronia kept hold of Granny Watson's apron.

"Too full for some of my pound cake?" Granny Watson asked.

Auronia stood looking at Granny Watson and then at Angie. Her brow furrowed. She looked up at Granny Watson. "Browned cake?" she asked aloud. "You cook so good, I always have room for some of your browned cake."

Angie's phone chimed. She looked at the caller ID and handed it to Lucky. Lucky whispered to Angie, "It's Weinberger again." He walked out the back door into the yard to answer it. Angie followed him, after sending Auronia back to the breakfast bar.

"Put it on speaker phone, so I can hear."

Weinberger said, "I wanted you to know what we are planning for the weekend. "We'll be staking out the party area on Hangman's Creek tonight with night vision equipment to see if someone shows up looking for the rope. Also, we've got the Thomas County Sheriff's office lined up to stake out Angie's house in Copperville. They'll be watching to see if someone shows up looking like they might want to hurt her. If that happens, they'll take him down."

"Angie's house is actually in Meeker County, Sheriff, even though Her address is Copperville, which is in Thomas County."

"Good thing you told me that," Weinberger said. "See how easy it is to get things screwed up?"

"Hopefully, the guy doesn't know where Angie and Auronia are," Lucky said.

"We're counting on that," Weinberger said. "But, we're planning for any and all contingencies."

"They're safe at my house, especially since Granny Watson got out her sawed-off twelve-gauge shotgun."

"Sawed-off shotguns are illegal everywhere," Weinberger said. "I don't want to know who Granny Watson is. The only question I have: *does she know how to use it?*"

Lucky chuckled, then said. "The short answer is *You can bet your bottom dollar she knows how to use it.*"

"So, you're secure in Masonville. Is your house in Copperville empty, Angie?"

"Oh, my God," Angie gasped. "My mother—my mother lives with me, and she's still at the house."

"Can you get her out of it without raising any suspicions?"

"I'll call my brother and have him go get her. He lives in Centralia, about an hour away."

"Do that," Weinberger said. "Let me know if there are any hitches." He hung up.

Angie called her brother, Bertrand, and explained the situation to him. "I can't give you very many details right now. But, Mother may be in real danger if she stays there tonight."

"She's been hinting to Irene that she would like to spend a few days up here with us. I'll go get her. Bring her up here. Are you okay?"

"Auronia and I are safe."

"Stay that way, sis. Please!"

"We will, Bert. I'll call you when we're past it," Angie punched the phone off and looked at Lucky. "I left home with us not talking. I don't want her to be gone, Lucky," She started crying.

Lucky held her close and let her sob.

Dear Jesus, I know you're here with us, and things will be okay. I know we have to learn, but it's easier to be more reckless ourselves than putting others in danger. Keep us all safe. Amen.

"God will take care of us," Lucky said. "We'll be okay."

CHAPTER NINETEEN

Lucky opened the drapes in the motel room. Outside, the sun was shining brightly on a rain-cleansed world. The world seemed to hold deeper and purer colors than he had seen before. Lucky smiled and bowed his head. "Thank you, Lord," he whispered. He sat back down at the desk where he was working on the morning's crossword puzzle and drinking his second cup of coffee.

From the bathroom, he heard Angie close the shower door and the shower come alive. He looked toward the bed and saw that Angie had laid out her undies and a new slip ready to dress for her big day.

Lucky returned to the crossword puzzle. He filled in a few boxes, but his mind kept wandering back to his family.

If anything had happened to the family, I would already know about it, right? The Masonville Police assured me they were watching and that all would be well. That's why Angie and I came back to the Hilltop Motel to spend the night. Was that the right thing to do?

Lucky sipped his coffee and read the clue for 24 Down.

What is the killer doing right now? Has the killer already decided he isn't going to get the rope back? What will he do next? Who is this guy anyhow?

Lucky looked up and watched Angie shrug into her bra, then pull the silk slip over her head.

Without blue jeans and tank tops, Angie seems so different. Absolutely, utterly beautiful, and different.

Angie's cell phone chimed, and Lucky picked it up. He didn't recognize the caller ID number. He punched the speaker button. "Lucky, here."

"Good morning, Mr. O'Rourke. This is Don Epperley. We met at one of Angie's victory parties."

"Yes, I remember you," Lucky said. "What can I do for you?"

"I'm going to meet you and Angie in the basement of the church. I'll be in the dining room. That's where you were planning to go when you arrive at the church, right?"

"Yes. Are you part of the police screen?"

"I am, in a peripheral way. I'll be wearing a vest and will be between you and Angie and any doors or windows. I just wanted to alert you, so you're not surprised when you get to church."

"I appreciate that," Lucky said. "Will there be other cops around?"

"Oh, yeah. There will be a bunch of them. But, you won't know who they are."

"I feel better about it. My real concern is for Angie and her little girl, Auronia. My three kids, too, and Granny Watson."

"I'd like you not to worry about them, but I know you will. Just let me say, you and your family have one very tight shield around you."

"Thank you," Lucky said.

Angie came out of the bathroom wearing a sun dress she bought. "Who was that?"

"Don Epperley. He'll be meeting us at church to help protect us."

"Oh, Lord," Angie said. "Don's already been through so much. Why is he involved?"

"Probably because you and I are familiar with him. I wouldn't be surprised if Kurt Maxxon didn't enlist Don's help."

"I need some breakfast," Angie said. "Do you want to go over to Lucy's?"

"I'm not all that hungry," Lucky said. "Let's just go on over to my house and have toast and jam, or maybe cereal, with the kids."

Breathing a sigh of relief, Angie nodded. "That sounds okay to me."

* * *

"I haven't heard from my mother," Angie said, as Lucky eased out of the motel parking lot into the traffic on the highway. "Bertrand was going to go get her and take her up to his place."

"But, you don't know if he did or not, or if she would go with him."

"That's true. But, if Auronia wasn't there to distract her, I'm pretty sure mother would agree to spend a few days with Bertrand and Irene."

"Does Bertrand have children?"

"They have a daughter they adopted from Korea over twenty years ago. She was six years old when she came to live with them. They were living in

Carpentier Falls at that time. Mother spent a lot of time with Kyung Soon. Kyung is doing her residency in pediatrics in Saint Louis right now. It doesn't seem possible that she's already a doctor."

"So, not a lot of attraction for your mother at your brother's house."

"Right. Plus, Irene and our Mother are not the best of buddies."

* * *

Lucky and Angie were too late to share breakfast with the kids. Jason was working on his computer in his room. The girls were playing in the den, entertaining Auronia, and watching TV.

The bright sunshine filled the kitchen.

"You want sausage and eggs?" Granny Watson asked.

"I don't," Lucky said. He looked at Angie.

"Toast is about all I want," Angie said.

"That'll do me, too," Lucky agreed.

"I made strawberry jam. You want some of that?"

"What's toast without Granny Watson's homemade strawberry jam?" Lucky asked, rolling his eyes toward the ceiling.

Angie laughed. "Were you expecting an answer from God?"

"Wait till you taste Granny Watson's strawberry jam," Lucky promised. "You'll never eat anyone else's jam again."

Granny Watson dipped her head and went about preparing the toast. She dug into the refrigerator and produced a pint mason jar with brilliantly red contents. She grabbed the butter tray and put both on the table.

After Granny Watson had set the plate of toast on the table, she said, "It's time to start getting the kids ready for church."

Lucky glanced at his wristwatch. "How long is it going to take you to get ready, Angie?"

"I just have to get into my new dress. That won't take very long."

"Do you want Granny Watson to help you?"

"You can help me, can't you?"

"I suppose. I was just trying to be chivalrous."

"I'm sure Granny Watson knows. I doubt she will be shocked if you help me with my dress."

"I was thinking more about Auronia."

"Oh, yeah. I forgot about her. Well, if she is traumatized by it, I suppose we'll have to get her therapy. But, she'll have to learn sooner or later that you and I are a pair and are going to spend our lives together."

"Another problem I just thought of is how are we going to get everyone to church. Can you drive in that getup?"

"Yes. I can drive wearing a dress," Angie said confidently. "I've done it before."

"When was that?"

"When I was in high school I wore dresses once in a while."

"I'll take Granny Watson and Jason in my truck. You can take the girls in your car."

"That gets us all to the church on time."

The zipper on Angie's dress caught once and was a fight to get undone. But, Angie and Lucky eventually emerged from his room ready to go.

"Pastor Judith wanted you guys there forty-five minutes early," Jason protested. "We're already late."

Angie followed Lucky's truck to the church and parked next to him in the lot after they drove around looking for two spaces together at the back of the lot. The bright sunlight highlighted the children's clothes, mostly new for the occasion.

The group climbed the steps toward the church. Lucky led Angie and the family to the front of the church and got the family settled into the first pew. Then he led Angie to a side door and down the steps into the basement of the church.

Pastor Judith met them in the hall and led them into a small meeting room off the side of the dining room, where she told them to be seated while she went to get the manual.

"When I bought this dress, it fit like a glove," Angie said, squirming in her seat. "Now, I'm not so sure it even fits."

You're just feeling self-conscious about being out of your element—and wearing a dress. You're usually wearing tomboy clothes.

Lucky pecked her on the cheek and chuckled. "By the way," he whispered, "You look adorable. I'm sure no one will notice. I don't plan on you fitting in that dress for very long anyway."

Angie shushed him and giggled.

When Pastor Judith returned, she was accompanied by Don Epperley. Don shook hands without saying a word and sat down off to the side. Pastor Judith sat down facing Lucky and Angie and opened the Lutheran Worship book and leafed through it. "The ritual is short and fairly straightforward," she said.

"Angelica," Pastor Judith said, "Christina Maxxon will escort you from the Narthex to the end of the aisle."

The use of her given name *Angelica* made Angie wonder, for a moment, who the pastor was talking to. She quickly regained her bearings and smiled, nodding her head.

"Kyle will be waiting for you there and will take your hand and bring you to the Altar Rail where I will be standing. Kyle will introduce you to me, and then you will both turn to face the congregation, and I will introduce you to the congregation. Then you will both turn back to face me." She paused to turn the page in the book. "We'll do this thing in short parts."

"The actual ritual consists of me reading the Introduction. *Blessed be the Holy Trinity, one God, who forgives all our sin, whose mercy endures forever. You have come to make confession before God. You are free to confess before me, a pastor in the Church of Christ, Sins of which you are aware and which trouble you.*"

She paused to read ahead.

"Then the three of us and the congregation will say *Amen.*"

She turned the page in the book. "Then I will ask you to repeat after me: *Merciful God, I confess that I have sinned, in thought, word and deed, by what I have done and by what I have left undone, I repent all my sins, known and unknown, I am truly sorry, and I pray for forgiveness. I firmly intend to amend my life, and seek help in mending what is broken. I ask for strength to turn away from sin and to serve you in newness of life.*"

"Then I will give you instructions: *Cling to this promise; the word of forgiveness I give to you comes from God.*

"Then I will give you your charge: *By water and the Holy Spirit God gives you a new birth,*

And through the death and resurrection of Jesus Christ, God forgives you all your sins. May the Almighty God strengthen you in all goodness and keep you in eternal life."

Pastor Judith looked directly at Angie.

"Then I will ask the congregation to rise, and I will say: *The peace of God, which passes all understanding, keep your heart and your mind in Christ Jesus.*

"All of us will say: *Amen.*"

"And then, you will leave the Altar having been reborn in Jesus Christ and living a new life."

"I don't have to memorize anything?" Angie asked.

"If you're going to be a good Christian," Lucky said, "You better be able to recite the Lord's Prayer without notes."

He smiled broadly.

Pastor Judith smiled also and nodded agreement. "I'll lead you all during the ritual. If you forget what I asked you to repeat, just pause and look me in the eye. I'll repeat it."

Angie shrugged her head slightly. "We can do this."

"You have an option to speak to the congregation regarding your new birth. Would you like to do that?"

Angie stared off into space for a long while. "Probably not," she said. "If I talk about how I came to this I'd probably never get through the experience. Just saying I know Jesus lives, yesterday, today, and forever, would be all I could get out."

Pastor Judith laughed. "Just let me know if you change your mind."

Lucky put his arm around her shoulders and squeezed. "Easy as falling off a log."

"If you fall off a log," Pastor Judith said, "you might break an arm or a leg. I guarantee no broken bones by being reborn in Christ on my watch."

* * *

Lucky led Angie up the stairs. Don Epperley shadowed them. At the top of the stairs, Kurt and Christina Maxxon were waiting for them in the Narthex. They greeted each other all around. Don Epperley moved off to the side, acting like he didn't know any of them. Lucky noticed that Angie was uncomfortable sitting down with her knee-length dress riding higher.

"Is everything a go?" Kurt asked.

Angie bobbed her head and beamed. "I'm ready," Angie said. "And Pastor Judith said I would not have to memorize the entire Sermon on the Mount."

Christina frowned and looked at Angie. "Who told you you'd have to memorize the Sermon on the—" Christina stepped back and glared at Kurt. "Did you tell her that?"

Kurt's face took on a guilty look. "Did I say the entire Sermon on the Mount?"

Angie bobbed her head violently.

"I was just talking about the Lord's Prayer part of the Sermon on the Mount," Kurt grinned and shrugged.

"You've been busted," Christina said. "You are in serious trouble, Mister."

Lucky was enjoying the banter, and he noted that Don Epperley was also enjoying it. Lucky studied Kurt's face and concluded he'd been in similar spots before and had survived them. "At any rate," Lucky said. "we are on stage here in about ten minutes."

"You're going to escort me to Lucky at the front of the church," Angie said to Christina.

"Yes. I'm ready," Christina said. "Kurt will take care of the kids. He's good at that."

"It'll be interesting to see who Auronia snuggles up to when she has to choose between Kurt and the two girls," Angie said.

The music started inside the church, and everyone moved to their places. Kurt and Lucky walked to the front of the church where Granny Watson sat with the four children. Kurt sat down at the end of the row.

Don Epperley waited and then followed Christina and Angie up the aisle.

Lucky watched as Auronia climbed over the other laps to get to Kurt, where she sat down, settled in, and confidently looked around the church.

Lucky was happy to see the people sitting close to the front row. He saw Jiggs and Katy Borsche; Sheriff Weinberger and his wife, Natascha, all of whom he had invited. The woman with carrot-colored hair sitting behind Jiggs caught his attention.

I know her from somewhere. But where?

Oh, yes. That's Alisa Sharpe. I haven't seen her since she helped me get custody of Olivia Maye.

* * *

"I feel like a human again," Angie said, as she wrestled her formal dress onto its matching padded hanger and hung it up in Lucky's closet. Lucky glanced at her. *She seems more natural and comfortable in blue jeans and a tank top.*

"You did wonderfully," Lucky said again. He'd said it a dozen times while they circulated among the congregation during the lunch after the church service was over.

"I don't feel a whole lot different," Angie said. They heard Auronia shrieking as she ran down the hallway past their door.

"Auronia is happy," Lucky said.

"I think she's happy all the strange activities are over, and she's back to her little world."

Angie opened the door and led the way to the den. Auronia and

Lucky's two girls were in the bedroom at the end of the hallway. They were calling to each other and laughing and screaming.

They sat down on the sofa, and Lucky turned on some instrumental gospel music.

"What smells so good?" Angie asked.

"Granny Watson bakes bread and dessert after church each Sunday," Lucky said and smiled. "If you think the toast was good this morning, with her strawberry jam on it, man, oh, man, wait until you put that jam on her fresh baked potato bread."

"Oh, well," Angie sighed, looking down at her jeans. "I can buy a new pair of jeans to fit."

"The kids have sure bonded," Lucky said. "That's great."

"Auronia is happy as a lark with Olivia Maye and Sophia doting on her," Angie said. "We need to start talking about how to merge the two families together. The first thing we have to decide is where this merged family going to live."

"Your place or mine?" Lucky asked, and grinned.

Angie giggled and gave him a playful slap on the thigh.

"You can live in Copperville and work at Borsche Excavating." Angie said and leaned back to look at Lucky. "My place is bigger, and we might need the space."

Lucky thought a moment, "I'll have to get up earlier, but I can live with that. I've not seen your place yet, so we'll have to do some planning before we let the family know."

"Let's do that after all this stuff with the murderer is past us. Okay? I don't want to try that and risk Granny Watson and your kids, too."

Lucky nodded. "You're a smart lady. I am one blessed fellow," he said and wrapped his arm around her. She laid her head on his shoulder and snuggled into the crook of his arm.

Lucky reached for the TV remote and found the news network with the banner streaming across the bottom of the screen. He noted that Angie seemed to have dozed off. Lucky thought he saw an aura framing her face. He quickly muted the channel.

She seems so at peace. I think you've brought a good thing to my life, Lord.

The afternoon sunlight brightened and warmed the room. Lucky let his gaze blur.

I wonder what the killer is up to? Where is he right now? Who the hell is he? What is he planning? How much does he really know about us? Have the cops found out anything from their surveillance activities?

Lucky stood up gently. Satisfied that he hadn't disturbed Angie, he walked into the living room and stood where he could see the neighborhood. He opened the front door and stood just inside the storm door which allowed him a much wider view of the surroundings. He noticed a Masonville PD car as it passed the intersection a block away.

Lucky sat down at the dinette table waiting for the coffee pot to finish brewing. Angie came out of the den and sat down beside him.

"I suddenly have a case of the nerves," Angie said. "Is there any wine in the house?"

"No. Granny Watson is pretty strict on me. I can have a beer once in a while, but I can't bring home a six-pack."

"I need a glass of wine," Angie said.

"After being called *Angelica* all afternoon?"

"Even then. Is there a liquor store close?"

"Four blocks over. I'll walk over and get you a bottle of wine. Do you want Chardonnay?"

"That's all I ever drink."

"The house is so quiet. I peeked in the girls' bedroom, and even the older girls were napping. I guess the morning was more exciting for them than we thought," Lucky said. "I'll be back in a little while."

"I'll walk over with you," Angie said.

"What about the kids? One of us should probably stay here with them just to make them feel safe."

"Do they know they are in danger of anything?" Angie asked. "Did you tell them there's a Boogie Man out there wanting to hurt us?"

"I didn't tell them."

Granny Watson came into the kitchen from her room. She checked the shotgun on the counter.

"Angie needs some wine to calm her nerves," Lucky said. "We're going to walk over to the liquor store and get a bottle."

"Bring me a fifth of brandy," Granny Watson ordered. "That's what you need for nerves young lady," she said, tapping her finger on the counter at every word.

"I've never had brandy," Angie said.

"If you're going to become part of this family, you best get used to it."

Granny Watson sat down across from Angie. "It works in lots of things. Hot Toddies when you're cold or have a cold. Spikes up Hot Cocoa, just fine."

"I didn't know you drank brandy," Lucky said.

"There's probably a lot of things you don't know about me," Granny Watson said as her eyes twinkled.

Lucky bobbed his head. "Most of which I don't need to know, right?"

"Right! Now you two get to getting for your wine and brandy. I got this place covered."

"Have we got soda pop for the kids?" Angie asked.

"They don't drink sodas." Granny Watson shot back. "When was the last time you saw a can of soda pop in the refrigerator, Kyle?"

Lucky stared at Granny Watson. "I guess—"

"Auronia doesn't drink soda pop, either," Angie added. "Fruit juices and sugar-free fruit drinks are the best for kids nowadays. I guess I'll get a bit of Diet Coke for me, keep it out of sight, and just add ice."

Granny Watson smiled, "Yup, young lady, you got that idea perfect. Those kids might get into soda pop out with their friends, but home is where they spend most of their time. If they know growing up healthy is important, they'll put up with it!"

"I guess I need to get modern, huh?" Lucky said and bobbed his head.

"That would be nice," Angie said.

"Amen." Granny Watson said. "Now get a move on."

CHAPTER TWENTY

Lucky was digging in a drawer of his toolbox when a Fed Ex delivery van pulled up to the roll-up door next to his work area. Lucky stopped and watched. The driver stayed sitting behind the wheel while a delivery person went into the back of the van and emerged carrying a small padded envelope. She walked directly toward Lucky.

"You should take that over to the Department Receiving," Lucky said as the woman neared, starting to point toward the other end of the building.

The delivery woman looked around and in a low voice said, "We're returning your cell phone, Mr. O'Rourke. It's in the envelope. Please don't open the envelope where others can see you."

Lucky quickly looked toward the other mechanics working in at various stations around the garage. He stared at the woman. "Oh! Uh. Okay."

Lucky signed on the clipboard proffered and noted that it was nothing more than a blank delivery form. "Thank you," he said as the woman turned to ran back to the Fed Ex van. He stood motionless and watched the van exit the Borsche lot onto the service road.

He walked inside behind his tool box and started to unzip the package. The phone inside started jangling. He quickly removed it from the packaging and looked at the caller ID.

He poked the button, put the phone to his ear, and listened. The eerie, whispering voice of the killer said: 'Hey, dude. No rope yet. Where's the rope? I told you what would happen if I didn't get the rope back. Do you remember me telling you what would happen if I don't get it back?'

"I don't have the rope," Lucky pleaded. "I lost that rope. I don't know where it is."

"I don't believe you, dude. Do you understand how serious I want that rope back?"

"It's the truth. I don't have the rope."

"Dude, if you already gave it to the cops then your girlfriend and her little blonde baby are in real trouble. I'm watching her and her little girl. I want that rope back. I'll give you another chance. You've got until sunrise tomorrow morning to leave it at the party area like I told you the first time. I'll be watching for it. And once again, don't go to the cops about this, understand?"

The line went to dial tone.

Lucky looked at the phone. *Geez. I've had my phone back two minutes, and it's already causing problems.*

Lucky looked through his contact list and dialed the number for Sheriff Weinberger. He told Weinberger about the latest call.

"Are Angie and Auronia still safe?" Weinberger asked.

"Yes, I think so. They're at my place here in Masonville. I haven't heard anything from them. But, the killer said he is watching them."

"We're still working on the intel we collected over the weekend surveillances. He may just be talking, hoping to scare you into something. He told you to take the rope to the party area, right?"

"Yes, sir, before sunrise tomorrow morning."

"Yes, sir. That's what he told me to do."

"He sounds more like Hollywood than a smart criminal," Weinberger said. "But he's probably a very determined criminal, and we have to worry about what he does next."

"Yes, sir. That's what I worry about. Can he hurt Angie or Auronia?"

"It sounds like he's probably over here in the Pleasant Valley area. So, he may not actually know where Angie and Auronia are. He may just be grasping at straws."

"That may be true," Lucky said. "But how do I know what he knows, or where he is? Who he is?"

"Calm down," Weinberger said. "We're working on getting that information as fast as we can."

"I know," Lucky said and paused. "By the way, I meant to ask, did they find any of the slugs that hit my truck?"

"Yes, they did," Weinberger said. "Hang on, my Chief Deputy, Bramley Rollo, is sitting here. He handled that part of it. Let me put you on speaker phone."

Lucky listened as the phone connection changed.

Weinberger said, "Lucky, meet Bramley Rollo."

"Did they find any of the slugs shot at Lucky's truck?"

"PV Ford dug one out of the passenger's side door padding," Bramley said. "It was a .44 caliber Winchester Cowboy Action load. That's not a real common load. It's used by shooters with a historical bent. I contacted the Herman County Sheriff and asked him to create a list of all the purchasers of .44 caliber Winchester Cowboy Action Loads. He hasn't gotten back to me on that yet. Let me call him."

You know what," Lucky said. "Thinking back on the shooting, the shooter must have been shooting a bolt action or lever action rifle because of the time between shots. Not a long time, but not like from a semi-automatic weapon."

"Lucky was in the Army for fifteen years," Weinberger said, confirming Lucky's background and knowledge of weapons to Bramley.

"I'll follow up with Herman County," Bramley said. "Let me go to my office and do that right now. I've got all the information there. Good talking to you, Lucky."

"Do you know Tony Brazinsky?" Weinberger asked.

"Yeah, I know Tony," Bramley said.

"He's a Herman County deputy, but better still, he belongs to a Black Powder group up in Herman County. He might know who shoots .44 caliber ammo."

"The sniper was not shooting black powder," Lucky said.

"Well, Tony is more into antique weapons," Weinberger said, "Not just black powder stuff. The .44 caliber Winchester load makes me think of early rifles—Winchesters and Henrys."

"You may be right, Clete. Let me follow up on this," Bramley said.

Lucky listened to the squeak of leather as Bramley stood and left.

* * *

Lucky stopped and thought about what he was doing. He realized he couldn't remember if he had tightened the bolts to the transmission cover in the right order.

If you didn't, there's a good chance that the cover will leak fluid. Maybe not today. Not tomorrow. But, about a week or two from now when it's at work on a job site. So, do it right.

He removed the nuts from all twelve of the cover bolts and went to get a new gasket from the shop's warehouse.

"What happened to the other gasket you got this morning?" the parts clerk asked Lucky.

"I didn't crush it right, so I have to replace it."

Lucky took the new gasket back to his work area. He saw his cell phone lying next to Angie's cell phone near his tool box. He picked up his cell phone and punched in a speed dial number.

Someone answered on the third ring. But, then the phone went dead.

"What?" Lucky felt a little panicky. He quickly dialed the number again. This time he heard Granny Watson say: "Hello."

"Granny, it's me. Lucky."

"Oh, Lordy, Kyle, when you called the first time I just automatically answered it, but even as I did, I saw your phone number on the caller ID, and I thought, Kyle doesn't have his cell phone. It scared me. I froze, and hung up."

"They brought my cell phone back to me just before lunch time. What's going on over there?"

"Not much. Jason went to a friend's house. The girls and Auronia are playing in their bedroom."

"Where's Angie?"

"Taking a nap," Granny said, then paused. "Oh, no. Angie's standing in the doorway staring at me. You want to talk to Kyle?"

"I always wonder who she's talking about when she talks about Kyle," Angie said. "I'll have to get used to that, huh?"

"That would be my recommendation," Lucky said and laughed. "Anything happening over there I should know about?"

"No. Calm down. We walked around the neighborhood a bit. Your girls are just loving having Auronia to take care of. I saw a Masonville squad car go by. But nothing else."

"The killer called me again, wanting his rope back. I—"

"How did he call you? Good Lord, he doesn't have my cell phone number, does he?"

"No. They brought my phone back just before lunch. I called Weinberger, and they are working on the case as fast as they can."

"Yeah, but will it be fast enough?"

"You and Auronia are safe there with Granny Watson and her shotgun. Is the shotgun still laying on the counter?"

"Same place she put it yesterday."

"I wish I had that level of protection. I pity the poor devil who tries to get at you or Auronia while you're under the protection of Granny Watson."

"She does make me feel safe," Angie said assuringly. "What time will you be home?"

"Probably the usual. Six-thirty, quarter to seven."

"I miss you."

"I'll get there as quick as I can. I love you."

Before he put the cover on again, Lucky decided to check the clearances on the gears one more time. He found that he had transposed the numbers on two different gears and decided to recheck all the clearances. Lucky forced himself to concentrate on the task at hand. Then he very carefully bolted the cover on, concentrating on the tightening pattern for the twelve bolts on the transmission cover. That made him satisfied the cover gasket would seal properly.

I'll know for sure later when I fill it with transmission fluid.

Lucky walked to get the equipment needed to fill the transmission. As he pushed the heavy wheeled tank into his work area, Angie's cell phone jangled. He looked at the number.

He answered it, "Hello Sheriff."

"We might have, I repeat *might have,* busted this case wide open. Do you remember a guy by the name of Marvin Lacombe?"

"Name doesn't ring a bell."

"He worked for Borsche Excavating on the dam project as a day laborer."

"I didn't pay much attention to any of the people on site, other than the operators I met. That's how he probably got my cell number."

"Okay. His description is pretty generic, five-foot-eleven, one-hundred-ninety-five pounds, brown eyes, blond hair."

"I've seen a lot of people who fit that description," Lucky said as he tried to put a face with the name.

"Yeah. Me, too," Weinberger said. "Anyway. Bramley talked to Tony Brazinsky up in Herman County. Tony told him about one guy who uses the .44 caliber Cowboy loads. His name is Jedidiah Lacombe. Jedidiah shoots .44 Cowboy loads because they are a nice fit for his antique Colt Peacemakers and Winchester Model 73 rifle, both of which were originally chambered for .44-40 loads. Now Jed is in his fifties, but he has a son, Marvin, who is mid-twenties. We did a quick make on the young Lacombe. Turns out, he's our man."

"He is?"

"It's his fingerprints on the girl's purse you found. The latents on the clothesline rope are close enough. We're pretty sure he's the one we saw on our surveillance tapes searching the party area. The guy who pulled into Angie's drive and went up to the house seems to match the surveillance tape on the party area. That guy was driving a Jeep Wrangler we know was stolen from the local dealer in Pleasant Valley. Surveillance tapes from that theft give us a pretty good image of the suspect, and we're absolutely certain that it was Marvin Lacombe."

"So, you're pretty sure, pretty sure, and absolutely sure it's him?" Lucky said.

"That's a good summation," Weinberger said. "Whittington, up in Herman County, is getting a warrant as we speak."

"Angie and I won't be able to relax until you have this guy behind bars."

"That should be within the next couple of hours, depending on where he is. We'll start looking for him down at the dam construction site. But, I doubt he's been working. He's driving a Ford Explorer, blue with a white top. It has oversize tires, but not riser shocks."

"I'll be on the lookout for a blue Ford Explorer," Lucky said. "I'll be going home in about an hour. I'll hunker down with the Angie and the kids with Granny Watson guarding the door, and wait for you guys to take this guy down."

"Do that," Weinberger said. "It shouldn't take us long to get him—now that we know who he is."

Lucky called his home phone again. Angie answered it. "Hello, Kyle."

Lucky laughed. "You've got our routine down pretty pat."

"I'm learning."

"The cops know who the killer is."

"They do, that's great. Have they arrested him yet?"

"They just figured out who he is. He worked at the dam site there. So, he probably lives in that area. He was probably a friend of the victim."

"We'll have to keep an eye out until he's in jail."

"Yes, ma'am. If he knows they're after him, he might do just about anything. I feel good about you and Auronia being there with Granny Watson. Just stay inside until this thing is over. Weinberger feels like they can get the guy pretty quickly. Is Jason home?"

"No, he's at a friend's house. He said he'd be home about five, which is not too long from now."

"My girls are there?"

"Oh, yeah. Wherever Auronia is, Olivia Maye and Sophia are close by."

"Okay. Keep all of them in the house for now. Please."

"Yeah. They're playing with dolls right now. I just heard them talking about having to fix supper. That'll keep them busy for a while."

"Good. I'll finish up here and get on my way home."

"I love you," Angie said. "Be careful you don't run into the killer."

"I'll do my best."

Lucky puttered around his work area waiting for the transmission to fill. He dug around looking for a crossword puzzle to work. But there wasn't one.

I need to buy a book of puzzles to keep here for times like this.

* * *

Angie's cell phone jangled and Lucky glanced at the screen. He answered it on the speaker. "Hello, Ollie, what's up?"

"I want to go to the library with Rosemary and her mom. But, they'll be staying late. Can you pick me up at the library on your way home from work?"

Lucky glanced at the gauges on the tank next to the transmission he was working on. "Yes, I can pick you up. I should be there about six-fifteen."

"That'll work great, Daddy. I'll see you then."

"Uh, Ollie—" Lucky hesitated.

We haven't told the kids about Marvin Lacombe. Should I let her go to the library?

But, the Masonville Police has all the information about Marvin. Can they intercept him if he comes to Masonville to harm the Angie or the kids?

So far Marvin has only shown knowledge of Angie and Auronia. Does Marvin know my kids?

"Yes, Daddy?" Olivia Maye said.

"Oh, uh, nothing," Lucky stammered. "We can talk about it later. Go to the library and do your thing."

"Okay, Daddy. I love you. See you later."

Lucky thought about going home to Angie, four kids, and Granny Watson.

How nice is that? A loving family.

The transmission was filling with fluid; no problems.

Angie was so beautiful yesterday when she declared Jesus Christ as her Savior before the congregation. I'm so proud of her for doing that.

Lucky turned off one of the fill valves and studied the gauges, again.

The transmission was full of fluid, and he turned off the last fill valve.

I don't have time to test this thing tonight. But, first thing tomorrow morning, I'll test this baby and then have it loaded into the truck to go back to the site.

CHAPTER TWENTY-ONE

Lucky decided to go home a bit early. He cleaned his tools and stowed them in the boxes, and then locked the boxes. He walked toward the employee parking lot out back.

I have to swing through downtown to pick up Ollie. If she's not there, I can wait for her.

Another night as a family unit—Angie, Aurie, Ollie, Sophie, Jase and Granny Watson. I can't believe how blessed we are. Angie loves it too.

Lucky climbed into his service truck. As he did, he caught motion on the floor on the passenger's side. He swung toward it. He saw a man holding a small-bore pistol, pointed directly at his chest.

"If you try anything funny, dude, you're dead," the man said. "Drive out of here like nothing is happening. And, don't try to attract attention or do anything strange."

"You're Marvin Lacombe, right?" Lucky said, eyeing the pistol in the man's hand.

"Yup, that's me."

"Where are we going?"

"For right now, just head towards Kings Rapids. The back way. I'll decide later."

"Why don't you think about giving this whole mess up. Quit now."

"You're right, dude, it is a mess. But, it's that damn Brit's fault. If she hadn't come on to me, none of this would have happened."

"She came on to you?"

"Yup. I was just sitting on the square, minding my own business and here she comes walking down the street and climbs into my car."

"So, you knew who she was?"

"Oh sure," Marvin said and laid the gun in his lap. "Everybody knows who she was. "

"I read she was active socially in school and town events."

Lucky avoided looking directly at the gun lying in Marvin's lap.

I might be able to grab it away from him. Stay sharp.

"Yup. She was into everything. So, I start my engine, and we drive over to the park, you know, where all the guys get their girls in the back seat. But after we get there, she turns *Miss Goody Two Shoes*. She's not cooperating. She don't want to get in the back seat. So, I ask her flat out, 'Do you want to have sex?' She says 'No!'"

"Wait a minute," Lucky said. "You asked if she wanted to have sex? Had you had sex with her before?"

"Oh, sure." Marvin relaxed a little. He hefted the gun in his lap, then laid it down and folded his arms across his chest. She was the Homecoming Queen during our senior year in high school. I was the Homecoming King. I was the captain of the football team. I could have any of the girls I wanted. But I chose Brit. She and I were dating steady and doing it in the backseat, too."

"Okay," Lucky said. You had known her. But you two weren't going together that night, right?"

"Right. Oh, hell, we broke up two, three years ago."

"So, why did she come up and get into your truck?"

"I really don't know, but she had done that one time before after she broke up with the second guy after me."

"Were you her first sexual partner?"

"Yeah, I was. I was the one who broke her cherry."

"So, did she keep coming back to you after each breakup?"

Not really, just that second one."

"Okay. So, she climbs into your truck, and you take her to the park."

"Yeah, dude. She scooted over and was sitting next to me. I could feel the heat. But, then she says she don't want sex. Then I said, 'well, I do, and you're the only girl close enough to help me out, so honey, you're it.' But, as I make my move, she starts fighting me off. And then, she gets this little knife out of her purse and cuts my arm. That pissed me off, and I lost my cool. I grabbed that piece of clothesline rope laying on the floor, hoping to calm her down by tying her up. But she keeps fighting, and she starts yelling. I thought someone might hear her and come rescue her, so I put the rope around her neck and started applying pressure to stop her from screaming. But, she won't quit. She's jerking and pulling and fighting. Then I realize she ain't fighting no more. So, I eased up and sat back figuring she's come to her senses and don't mind a little sex. After a couple of minutes, I put my hand up her dress, and she don't move a muscle. That's good, I think. But her leg feels funny. I take a good look at her face, and something is wrong. I mean, dude, there is something bad wrong. About then, I realize—I realize she's dead."

Marvin stopped talking, and Lucky could tell from his voice that he was emotionally drained.

"Damn her anyway," Marvin rasped through a tight throat. "Then, I panicked. I wanted to get her body out of town. Get it away from me. I got out and walked around my car. There was nobody around. I drove down to the party area there on Hangman's Creek. I was getting ready to dump her body there when I see ol' Art Tanderford drive in with his fancy high-clearance pickup, and he drives over and through the water gap and onto the site."

Marvin picked up the gun again and held it next to his leg. "Then I get to figuring that if I dump her body in the party area, someone will find it before morning. But, if I take it to the site and leave it there, they probably won't find it until Monday morning. So, I followed ol' Art's tracks and got through without too much problem, but it was scary. My tires weren't as big as ol' Art's."

"The day I was there to fix the dozer stuck in the gap," Lucky said, "the water through the gap was very deep. You're saying you both drove trucks through it?"

"Oh, yeah, well, the gap was kinda shallow that night. You see, the dozer you fixed was kind of smoothing the edges after they dredged the gap deeper with a bucket excavator. The dozer operator tried to swing around, and the gears stripped out and when he tried to back up out of the gap. But the dozer went forward into the deep water."

"The operator might have missed the right position for the lever," Lucky said.

"So, once I was through the gap," Marvin continued, "I drove around the edge of the site over to the office trailer area where he couldn't see me. I saw ol' Art fooling around, climbing the piles of dead wood, and all. I dumped—"

"Why couldn't he hear you?" Lucky wondered.

"Oh, man, he had the radio on that truck full blast, plus he got somethin' on his truck makes it louder. He had ta' leave it running to play his radio. He paid me no mind."

Marvin waved the gun at the windshield. Lucky could tell from his voice that Marvin was struggling to deal with what he was remembering.

"I ... I, uh, dumped Brit's body under that trailer and got out of there fast. Ol' Art had already left. I started to drive up the road back to the gap when I saw Brit's purse laying on the floor of my truck. I stopped at the edge of the culvert and threw it out. Then I went back out through the gap and drove home."

"So you didn't have sex with her?" Lucky asked.

"No. Hell no," Marvin said quickly. "Dude, she was like a nun. But everyone in town knew she put out—to that nerdy boyfriend of hers, at least."

"From what you just told me," Lucky said slowly, "This isn't first-degree murder. Probably more like manslaughter. Why not just turn yourself in to the law and take your chances?"

"So now you're a lawyer, huh?"

"God will take care of you," Lucky said. "Every minute you're on the run, you're in danger of the cops taking you down. There are so many things that don't go right with something like that, it's scary. Give it up, now."

"Oh, yeah, that's right, I heard the guys at site talking about you being a preacher."

Lucky realized Marvin was guiding him around the southwest quadrant of Masonville.

"Look, I'm not a lawyer or a preacher," Lucky said. "I'm just trying to talk some wisdom into your head, trying to keep you from ruining your life forever."

"I've already done that."

"There's still time."

"Just keep driving, dude. Get me to the river south of Kings Rapids. If your nickname is true to your life, Mr. Lucky, I might just jump out of this truck and disappear, and you live to tell the story. But, one screw up and you'll be as dead as ol' Brit."

"Marvin, I'm asking you to think this through, give it up. Go tell the sheriff what you've just got done telling me. You'll probably get a couple of years in the county jail and probation. But you get it behind you. It's not worth fighting anymore."

"Quit preaching and keep driving. I wouldn't be in this fix if Brit had just walked on past."

"Why did she pick you?"

"I have absolutely no idea. Like I said, five, six years ago we were an item in high school. And she's been back a couple of times since." Marvin laid the gun back in his lap and leaned his head back against the seat.

Maybe this is my chance.

But Marvin sat up straight again and moved the gun next to his thigh.

"How did you figure out who Angie was and all that?" Lucky asked.

"Pure luck," Marvin answered. "Bein' there at the right time. Not my best trait, but it worked this time. Last Wednesday, I had a dentist's appointment. Right across the street from Pleasant Valley Ford. I was leaving from that when I saw you drive into Ford. So I tailed you. I thought if you still had the rope you found in the back of your truck I could grab it and get rid of it."

"Last Wednesday?" Lucky asked.

I gave that rope to Weinberger a long time ago. This guy has been fuming over that rope all this time?

"Yup. Last Wednesday." Marvin bobbed his head. He moved the gun to his lap but did not let go of it. "I followed you over to Copperville and that restaurant there. I saw you meet up with that girl. I figured she was your girlfriend, or maybe a little extra on the side like my dad does. While you guys were in the restaurant, I snuck over and nosed around in the back of your truck. But, the rope wasn't there."

"How'd you know I had the rope?"

"I saw you pick it up that day you worked on the dozer that got stuck in the water gap."

That's right. This guy worked at Hangman's Creek Dam site.

"You followed me to Copperville and didn't find the rope. What did you do then?"

"When you got to Copperville, the girl in the Porsche next to you got out and ran to kiss you. Then you two went into the restaurant. Then I followed you up to that church. When you left the church, I decided to follow the girl. She led me to her house out in the country. Dude, that Porsche she drives is one classy car. How come you don't drive a Porsche like that?"

"The simple answer is, I can't afford one."

"I wish I could find a girlfriend like that. Hellfire, I'd marry her in a heartbeat," Marvin said. "Anyhow, she's got a really nice place there—something I'd like to have someday. That's when I decided to get the rope, I'd call you and threaten her and that little girl. I figured you'd do anything to save them."

Marvin laid the gun in his lap again and laid his head back.

If he goes to sleep, I'll make a move for the gun. He looks exhausted.

"Did you steal the license plates and the Jeep Wrangler I heard about?"

"Yup. I borrowed other people's plates or vehicles whenever I needed them. It's really pretty easy, you know."

"Did you shoot at me at the site?"

"Yup. I didn't try to hit you, though. If I wanted to hit you, I would've."

"What was the purpose of that?"

"I hoped you'd hightail it out of there and I could grab the rope out of your truck."

"How did you get from Pleasant Valley to Borsche's?"

"I figured the cops would be watching for my Ford Explorer. So, I remembered old Mrs. Bradford. She lives in the luxury apartments up above my house. She drives a Lincoln Continental, and she always leaves the keys in it. I've had that car in mind as a backup if I ever needed one. She also keeps a loaded gun in the glovebox. This one," Marvin said, as he waved the weapon in front of Lucky.

"Did you wreck her car?"

"No. No, I didn't hurt any of the vehicles I borrowed. I borrowed a big badass black Ram pickup when I went down to scare you. But, I left it in the same lot from where I took it—just a different location. I'm not sure the guy even missed it while I was using it. He didn't call the cops or anything. I didn't do anything to Mrs. Bradford's Lincoln. She can get in it and drive away like nothing ever happened."

"Do you know where we're at?"

"Yup. We're a couple of miles from the county line. The road jogs at the line. Somebody told me that the engineers from the two counties didn't like each other, so they never had a road meet in a straight line."

"I've never been out this way before," Lucky said.

"Me and my dad went huntin' all over this country," Marvin bragged. "In the good old days, we hunted deer along all the rivers around here."

As Lucky drove around a small curve in the road, he spotted the ess-curve ahead and noticed it was plugged with cop cars—an obvious roadblock. He eased up on the gas, and let the truck coast to slow down. Lucky glanced at Marvin, who was staring out the side window.

Lucky stopped the truck, leaped out, and ran, bent over, toward a nearby police car.

Marvin came alert and slid out of passenger door with the gun in his hand. He scurried under the truck and crawled between the two rear tires. A salvo of gunfire roared, echoing off the nearby trees. Lucky heard the thuds of bullets hitting his service truck and the shattering of glass.

Borsche's insurance company is going to hate repairing my truck a second time. Maybe they can get Marvin's dad to pay for it.

Marvin flattened himself out on the ground between the two tires and blindly fired two shots out toward the crowd of cops.

Lucky stood on the safe side of a cruiser and watched the standoff unfold. Then the shooting died down to nothing. An eerie silence settled over the area. Finally, Marvin yelled out, "I'm out of ammo!"

Lucky heard the discussion, and then one of the officers shouted out, "Marvin Lancombe, throw your gun out on the ground and show your hands!"

"No. You'll kill me. I know you will!"

Lucky turned to the officers near him, "He doesn't have any extra ammo. He said he stole that gun. Let me go to him."

"Man, where you been? I know you're ex-military, but geez, that's a hell of a risk."

"Something tells me 'dead' isn't what any of us want, including him."

The officers nodded. "Your risk. We'll try to cover you."

"Don't shoot back, Marvin," Lucky called, then stood up straight and walked back toward his truck.

From all sides, the cops yelled at Lucky to *Get down. Get back. Stay back. Get out of the line of fire.*

Lucky walked determinedly to the passenger side of his truck. He knelt, then went down on his knees. He looked Marvin directly in the eye.

"It's over Marvin. Give me your gun," Lucky said, through his constricted throat.

"Get the hell out of the way," Marvin yelled.

"It's over Marvin," Lucky said slowly. "There's more cops out there than anything you may have left in your pistol. If you keep fighting them, they'll kill you. Do you want to die?"

"Get out of my—"

Lucky caught the motion of the cops sneaking in closer while he had Marvin's attention. Lucky stood up and turned toward the cops. "Don't shoot him!" he yelled to the cops closing in. "Don't shoot him. Please. He's not a bad person." Lucky turned his back to the cops and got back on his knees. He reached under the truck. "Give me your weapon, Marvin."

Marvin looked beyond Lucky, looked at the gun in his hand. "I didn't bring any extra ammo," he said slowly. He lowered the gun. With shaky hands, he gave it to Lucky.

Lucky took the weapon and tossed it out into the open. He relaxed a little when he saw most of the cops standing down, lowering their weapons, some holstering them.

An officer walked up with another man. The man said, "Marvin, It's me; Hawkins, your probation officer. Come on out. We don't want to hurt you."

Marvin slowly crawled out from under the truck.

Lucky and Hawkins stayed between Marvin and the cops, making sure they didn't handle him roughly.

When they had Marvin safely handcuffed, Lucky walked back toward the police cruiser he had taken shelter behind.

My shoulders feel like I'm carrying a load of bricks.

Suddenly, Angie was beside Lucky. She embraced him—holding him steady. When he realized who it was, he leaned on her and let her lead him to the cruiser. Angie helped him sit down on the edge of the back seat.

"How did you get here?" Lucky asked.

"Sheriff Weinberger called me and told me what was happening—that Marvin had you hostage and you were heading for Kings Rapids on the old road. I just got in my car and came looking for a bunch of cars."

"Would you marry me?"

"God, I'm glad you finally asked." She pushed him over as she climbed onto him and kissed him hard. When she came up for air, she said, "I'm just glad you're still alive to ask me."

Then Lucky sat up straight, lifting Angie as he did. "Ollie. She's waiting for me at the library. I was going to pick her up at six-fifteen. What time is it? She's probably wondering where I am."

A uniformed officer walked up to the car. Lucky noted that she was a Masonville Police officer, and realized he was in a Masonville PD car. A bronze pin over the officer's left breast read *K. Lacy.* "Can you get someone to check on my daughter? She's probably sitting in front of the library downtown wondering where I am. I was supposed to pick her up at six-fifteen."

The officer sat down in the car and picked up her mike. Lucky and Angie listened as she radioed headquarters and told them about Olivia Maye O'Rourke waiting in front of the library.

"It's only six-forty," the officer said.

"Yes, ma'am, but she's as impatient as I am about things. I don't want her to start walking home. It's an hour walk, and it'll be dark by the time she gets there."

"If she's as tough as you are there's no one going to mess with her," Officer Lacy said.

"Yes, ma'am, but they probably don't know how tough she is just looking at her."

"Good point, Mr. O'Rourke."

"Just call me Lucky."

They sat silently for several minutes. Then the radio came alive. The officer grabbed the mike and told them to "go ahead."

"We've contacted the O'Rourke girl. She's worried about where her father is."

"Her father is safe," the officer said. "Can you guys take her home?"

"Sure. Be happy to."

Lucky stood up and looked toward his service truck. Angie stood beside him and put her arm around his waist. Lucky draped his arm over Angie's shoulder. Together they walked slowly over to the truck. Bullet holes had spider-webbed the windshield. Other bullets had gouged the hood and the cab.

"I feel guilty about making this truck suffer so much."

"This truck loves you as much as all the rest of us," Angie said. "So, it probably doesn't mind."

CHAPTER TWENTY-TWO
Masonville Oval: The Season Opening Race

Kurt Maxxon

In the rear-view mirror, Kurt watched Lucky come down the steps from the grandstand to the track, stop and look both ways, and then walk toward the pit. Lucky was wearing his blue denim pit coveralls he'd bought and customized with his name over the front pocket and KURT MAXXON RACING in an arc on the back with a stylized picture of the number 27 Ford Fusion in the center.

When Lucky realized that Kurt and Maurey were in the pre-start mode, he stopped and then waved, walking over to Kurt as he sat in Nikki's driver's seat. Kurt stuck his hand out through the window, and Lucky gripped it.

"How's Angie?" Kurt asked not taking his eyes off Maurey.

"She and Kyna are doing just fine," Lucky said. "Anything that needs doing?"

"No. Not right now. We've got it under control. Relax a bit, buddy. You're a new dad."

"Okay," Lucky said and moved back to watch Maurey. Each race day, he'd learned at least one thing new about taking care of a race car.

Maurey is going to be working on race cars when he's a hundred! He's got so much knowledge about cars under his cap.

Maurey moved around under the hood of the car and kept glancing at the monitoring panel of the roll-around test machine, reading gauges, flipping switches, and twisting dials.

Lucky was so focused on Maurey's actions that he didn't notice Christina Maxxon until she was standing next to him.

"How's momma and baby doing?" Christina asked. Lucky jumped a little.

"Both are just fine," Lucky said when he recovered. "That baby has a set of lungs on her. Wow, can she scream."

"That's so you'll know she's around and that she needs attention."

Maurey gave Kurt the signal and Kurt started Nikki's engine. The racket ended all conversation. Lucky and Christina fled across the track and stood next to the five-foot concrete wall that formed the foundation for the grandstand. They watched as two pickup trucks driven by track officials drove slowly around the oval, inspecting the track's condition. The Pace Car driver was driving a little faster, getting used to the banking.

Christina and Lucky saw Don Epperley come down the stairs of the grandstand and walk toward them. "Since you're here," Don said to Lucky, "I assume everything is going great with Angie and the baby."

"Everything is A-Okay," Lucky said, looking pleased as he accepted Don's congratulatory handshake.

Christina reached out to Don's arm and said, "Be careful, there's a car coming toward us the wrong way."

All three of them watched as the number 114 car come toward them, slowing as it neared. Eugenios Christofides steered his green and yellow Buick Lucerne sponsored by *Maplewood Transfer and Storage* close to the three people. His yellow and green helmet sat in the middle of the dash, reflecting the bright sun. "How Angie and Kyna doing?" he yelled over the racket of the engine.

"They're doing fine," Lucky yelled back, nodding and giving him a thumbs up.

"Why are you driving against the traffic?" Don Epperley growled. Lucky always admired Don's deep baritone voice. It seemed to carry over every other sound.

"I always do this," Christofides yelled over the noise of his engine. "I am in number two pit today. Right over there." He pointed with his right hand to the stall on the opposite side of the track. "You in my way from turning. If it just you standing there, I might have just run over you."

"Yeah, and you'd get a ticket for reckless driving. The first in the history of the SRVSCRA," Don shot back.

Christofides laughed and steered his car toward his pit.

A loud foghorn blared, and activity on the track started changing. Lucky pulled earplugs from his pocket and stuffed them into his ears, and he angled toward the number 16 pit where Kurt's number 27 Ford Fusion sat with Kurt and Maurey waiting quietly for the race. Kurt had qualified in the number sixteen position.

Lucky smiled. *It's all good. Christofides has a good starting position. He might win today. It would still be cool to see Nikki place in the top three, though.*

* * *

Christina Maxxon

Christina and Don Epperley walked to the stairs leading up into the grandstand and then walked along the broad concrete gangway until they were opposite the pit where Nikki was sitting. They walked down to the front-row seats.

Christina had dressed for the weather, wearing a sleeveless sundress, a wide brim hat and a sweater slung over her shoulders. She admired the rich green hue of the infield grass. The late-May sun was high in the sky. *The 72-degree weather promised a pleasant day for watching a race. In a few hours, the temperature will spike at about 80. By then, however, we'll be in the shadow of the grandstand roof, and the temperature will feel as comfortable as it does now.*

They watched silently as Kurt, Maurey, and Lucky pampered Nikki; checking tire pressures again, and eventually lowering the hood and locking the hood latches. Activity around the track picked up appreciably. The official pickup trucks came by occasionally, and several other drivers followed Christofides' maneuver of driving the wrong way, rather than drive a complete lap and some to get to their pit stalls.

Christina took out a folded race program and started scanning the names of the drivers. "This is the first race of the SRVSCRA season, so there are new drivers listed that I don't recognize," she said to Epperley.

"I never try to keep up with the driver's names," Don replied. "I hardly can remember my own name most of the time."

"Starting the new race season in style, Lieutenant?" a voice said behind them. They looked up simultaneously to see Sheriff Cletus Weinberger standing behind them. He was dressed in Dockers and a short-sleeved western-style shirt. He blended into the crowd as just another race fan. He was staring across the track.

"Hello Sheriff," Christina said. "How have you been?"

"Trucking along. I need to talk to Lucky," Weinberger said. "I figured I could catch him here today at the race. That doesn't look like Angie, though. Where's Angie?"

"Angie's home with their new baby girl," Christina said.

"New baby," Weinberger said. "When did that happen?"

"Night before last," Christina said. "About eleven fifteen."

"See, that's what I get for living out in the sticks. I didn't even know she was pregnant."

"You were at their wedding, weren't you?" Don Epperley asked.

"Well, yes I was. But I didn't realize—"

"She wasn't even two months along at the wedding," Christina growled. "Nobody does that math anymore."

Don Epperley straightened up and looked downtrodden. "Oh, hell, I didn't mean that I knew she was pregnant at the wedding. It doesn't matter to me. I just thought—well, it seemed like it's been nine months since the wedding. That's all."

"You're forgiven," Christina said, pulling her phone out. "I'll let Kurt know to tell Lucky come over after the race starts and talk to you." She texted Kurt the message. She watched as he pulled his phone from his jacket, glanced at it, looked toward her, and nodded. Then Kurt walked over to Lucky and pointed toward them. She saw Lucky look up, and wave recognition.

The group settled in, chatting with each other, until the race got underway.

* * *

Lucky O'Rourke

Soon after the race began, Lucky made his way to the tunnel under the racetrack at the center of the grandstand to the Winner's Circle and came up through the stairway from the tunnel. He walked straight to where Christina, Don Epperley and Sheriff Weinberger were sitting.

Weinberger stood up as Lucky approached and stuck out his hand. "You look awfully happy," Weinberger said.

"I have quite a few reasons to be happy," Lucky said.

"What's the new baby girl's name?"

"Kyna."

"I've not heard that name before. What's it mean?"

"Kyna is Irish for *intelligent*," Lucky said, laughing. "Right now, she could fool you, since all she does is scream at the top of her lungs. Her features, fortunately, favor her mother's."

"Angie's other little girl has golden blonde hair—"

"Kyna has my hair, coal black and straight as an arrow," Lucky said and chuckled. "Her bad luck."

"Lucky!" Christina spoke sharply. "Kyna doesn't need that kind of joking. She should grow knowing her Daddy is the most blessed man in the world and proud of the head of hair God gave her."

Lucky, bowed his head and pursed his smile to keep from laughing. "Yes, ma'am."

"Well, congratulations," Weinberger said. "What I need to talk to you about is—the DA is convinced he can't get a conviction for murder in the Garfield Homicide case. He's backed off and now is talking along the lines of Manslaughter One and would accept Manslaughter Two. He's very discouraged about the evidence, and then the Medical Examiners Report didn't help."

"What was wrong with the Medical Examiner's Report?"

"Only a lawyer can explain that," Weinberger said and looked off to the side. "From what I can gather, the rope around the neck *was not* the cause of death, as we would normally think of it, like in asphyxiation caused by lack of air. The cause of death was actually a fractured neck vertebra, which lacerated the windpipe, and then death being caused by strangulation on the blood that filled the windpipe. And, that probably resulted when the victim put up a struggle because of the clothesline rope around her neck."

Lucky leaned back and swung to look at Weinberger's face. "You're serious?"

"Unfortunately," Weinberger said. "Anyway, one of the questions still unresolved is the charge against Marvin Lacombe involving his Unlawful Detention—the fancy name for his abduction of you."

Lucky frowned deeply and said, "Well, yes, but I never—"

The sheriff interrupted him. "When the DA was riding high on a Murder charge, he pretty much downplayed your kidnapping by Lacombe. But, now that he's dealing with manslaughter, he's talking aloud about you and your abduction. I thought I'd give you a heads-up that he may be considering bringing that charge to the forefront again. The question will be how you feel about that."

Lucky wobbled his head. "I've forgiven Marvin for that. I told the DA that a long time ago."

"Well, yeah, maybe you've forgiven him, but, should society as a whole forgive Marvin for it?"

"If the only person actually hurt by the abduction says it's forgiven," Christina interjected, "Is it really that important to society?"

Sheriff Weinberger shrugged his shoulders. "We're on opposite sides of this forgiveness business," he said. "I respect both you and Lucky for being forgiving, given your Christian beliefs and all. But we also have to protect society in the future. The question has to be: Is Marvin Lacombe a threat to society? And, is—"

"Marvin Lacombe *is not a threat* to anyone," Lucky said emphatically.

"I understand you've forgiven him," Weinberger said.

"It isn't just that I've forgiven him," Lucky said. "Sheriff, the day we were out there, surrounded by cops pointing their guns at us, I went over to Marvin and said, 'Give me your gun. Even if you have a bullet left, there are two dozen guns with six bullets each out there aimed at your heart.' And you know what, I'm convinced that was not the reason he handed me his gun. As he held the gun out to me, I suddenly saw a young man—a young boy—who didn't understand why he got into this mess. And, he didn't want to stay in it."

"Okay," Weinberger said and scooted back in the seat and crossed his leg. "I'm sure the DA is going to invite you to come over and talk to him about the case. I needed to get out of the house, so I decided to come over and watch the first race of the year."

"Should I call the DA and offer to go over and talk to him?"

"No. Let him come to you. Just don't be surprised by what he says."

The group chatted as the race got underway. Each time the pack of race cars came by, the conversation had to be put on hold.

"Do you have an extra pair of earplugs?" Weinberger asked Lucky.

"I do," Christina volunteered and dug into the fanny pack around her waist. She handed the plastic envelope to Weinberger.

Weinberger quickly put the plugs into his ears. "Ah, I should never have left home without them. Thank you."

Just before the break between heat number one and heat number two, Lucky went back to the pit to help with Nikki. During the quiet of the twenty-minute rest period, Christina, Don Epperley, and Sheriff Weinberger watched Lucky help Maurey and Kurt check tires and fill the gas tank, while they chatted.

"Is Angie going to drive at all this year?" Weinberger asked.

"Kurt is going to drive the first five races," Christina said. "Today, Kings Rapids, Evandale, Maplewood and the first Centralia race. Angie says she'll be ready to take over after that."

"That's only two months and some? Won't that be hard on her?"

"She loves racing. She waited longer with Aurie and chaffed the whole time. We'll give her whatever she needs. She's a great driver. Plus, we've changed how we handle the car. Kurt and I won't be delivering Nikki to the tracks anymore. We've rented a garage here at this track. Angie will have the car down here. She's just bought a new Ford F-350 pickup to get Nikki to all the races. After each race, Maurey or Kurt will take Nikki to our shop in Centralia. Maurey will do his thing and get the car ready and placed in her carrier for the next track. Angie will drive up on the off weekend and bring Nikki back down here to Masonville. That way, Angie can go to the next track whenever she wants to practice."

"Sounds like a good plan," Weinberger said. "A win-win for everyone involved."

"Yes, well, except for Lucky. Angie gave him her Porsche Carrera. But he says it's too small for his six-foot-six frame. His knees bang against the dash. He's back to driving the new Borsche Excavating service truck all the time. Angie wants to keep the Porsche for running around town."

"They just need a three-car garage," Weinberger said with a grin.

"Actually, their place has a five-car garage," Christina said. "Their oldest child, Jason, turns sixteen next month, and they are already talking about getting him a car to drive. Then in just a couple of years, the two girls will be old enough to drive. So, before long, there will be no empty garage stalls."

"Yeah. I remember all that," Weinberger said. "I had three kids, each two years apart. They're all grown and gone now, but when they started turning sixteen, we had a struggle on our hands. We couldn't afford new cars, so we bought used ones. That meant we were buying someone else's headache. But we got through it."

"I'm sure what we remember most is worrying about our kids every minute after getting them their own cars," Don Epperley said.

Christina and Weinberger nodded.

"Is Angie's mother still living with them?" Weinberger asked. "I remember she was living with her and we were worried about her being home if Marvin went there for mischief."

"Angie's mother decided to buy into a retirement community in Masonville instead of live with the family," Christina answered. "Lucky already had his Granny Watson living with them. Angie and her mother didn't see eye to eye on many things," Christina said. "It was probably better for all that she went off on her own."

The group continued to watch the race and during the final heat, saw Kurt Maxxon move the number 27 Ford Fusion up to third place, and then finish in fourth place.

Dave Kellogg won the race and his sponsor, Lyle's True Value Hardware announced there would be a victory party at the newly completed Hilltop Motel Convention Center.

Lucky called Angie and told her that Dave Kellogg won the race and that there was a victory party. "You go to the party and then tell me what all happened," Angie told Lucky.

"Okay," Lucky said reluctantly. "I'd just as soon come home to you and the kids."

"You need the break," Angie said firmly. "Plus, I want to know what everyone's saying."

"About what?"

"About me. About you. About us. You know?"

"Uh. Okay."

Lucky drove to the new convention center and parked his service truck in the outer row. He walked to the ballroom door, wondering what he would see inside. He'd followed the news about the new convention center in the newspapers but had not been inside yet.

Inside there was a flurry of activity as white-clad wait staff finished setting places on several long tables. Several of the race drivers and their friends were milling around, close to the open bar. Lucky looked around but didn't see any people he knew. He walked to the bar and asked for a long-neck Budweiser.

At the same time, Don Epperley pushed through the door and stood to let his aging eyes adjust. Lucky thought about waving, but realized Epperley would soon discover the bar, and him. When Epperley oriented himself and walked toward the bar, he waved to Lucky.

"How'd you beat me to the bar?" Epperley asked.

"I have no idea," Lucky said.

Epperley ordered a tall Scotch and water and turned to look around the ballroom.

"Nobody I'm familiar with," he said quietly.

"They'll be along," Lucky said.

"Did you invite Angie to this party?"

"I called her and told her about it. She asked me to cover it for both of us."

Don held his glass up. "Yeah. Well, just having a baby two days ago, I doubt she's ready to go partying yet."

"Angie has never been a party animal to start with," Lucky said.

"Yeah, I know," Epperley said. "I can't tell you how many times I had to speak to the press about a new case, let alone how many times I had to say, 'no comment.' It's part of her job to show up for her fans."

Lucky nodded.

The door opened, and Christina Maxxon came through it followed by Kurt. They stood to survey the room. When they spotted Lucky and Epperley standing near the bar, they waved.

Susan Burpee came into the ballroom from the lobby and stepped up to the main table, right next to the doors. She looked around the room, waving to some people. She motioned to the Maxxons, inviting them to the main table.

Kurt and Christina walked to the raised platform and stood behind chairs. Christina waved at Lucky to join them.

Lucky felt bad for Don Epperley, not being invited to the main table. At that point, Christina frantically waved at Epperley to come up to the main table, pointing to a chair next to her.

David Kellogg and Peggy came through the lobby doors and walked up to Kurt and Christina and shook their hands.

"You did great," Dave Kellogg yelled to Kurt, as he gave him the thumbs up gesture.

"Thank you," Kurt yelled back. "Thanks for not running me off the track during the race."

"We'd never do that," Kellogg yelled back. "Especially to the grand old man of SRVSCRA racing."

"I hope that's not the only reason," Kurt yelled and grinned.

"Nah. It's not." Dave said emphatically.

Lucky stood watching the bantering play out. He thought about sitting in the seat next to Kurt Maxxon but thought there were probably others who merited that seat. He waited.

Eugenios Christofides came into the ballroom and walked straight to the bar. He waited a few minutes and then left the bar with a glass of Ouzo. Dave Kellogg watched Christofides and then waved him to a seat at the main table. Christofides sat down next to Kurt Maxxon.

Lucky decided to sit down next to Christofides. Don Epperley sat next to Peggy. Dave Kellogg's sponsors, Leonard Burpee and his wife Susan along with Leonard's brother Matt, had already seated themselves and were chatting with others. Suddenly, Lucky realized that between Susan Burpee and Matt Burpee, the lady at the table was Lucy Graystone, of Lucy's Diner. *How did they include Lucy's Diner when they built this addition? I'll have to ask Lucy when I get a chance.*

Lucky sat listening to the conversations swirling around him as the ballroom filled and people moved around the tables deciding where to sit. Christofides occasionally jumped into the talk. Then someone sat down next to Lucky. When he looked, he realized it was Sheriff Cletus Weinberger.

Christofides leaned toward Lucky and said. "The sheriff is here. We must be good now."

"Okay," Lucky said. "I can do that."

The party continued with frequent bursts of laughter and a cacophony of voices. At one point, Kurt Maxxon stood and clanged a knife against his glass for attention.

"Opening Day has always been one of our favorite days, and today, we have a special reason to congratulate today's winner. Dave Kellogg," He turned to raise his glass.

"Congratulations, Dave, on your first Opening Day win in the Swift River Valley Stock Car Racing Association! May you continue to see many milestones!"

The room roared approval as everyone stood to raise their glasses in a toast. Dave went around the room greeting people as the party continued in a monotonous din.

Lucky jerked to attention when Weinberger's cell phone rang. Weinberger answered it and listened. "Uh-huh. Uh-huh. No! Damn it! Okay. Uh-huh."

Lucky watched the sheriff put his phone away. He washed his face with his left hand. Then he stood. He motioned for Lucky to follow him. Weinberger led Lucky out through the lobby doors and then to a spot far away from other people. He stopped abruptly and looked around the lobby before he spoke.

"Marvin Lacombe is dead."

"What? No!" Lucky was shaken to his core.

"They found him hanging from bed sheets in his cell this morning."

Lucky walked to a chair and sat down. He held his face with both hands as his eyes filled with tears. "I was ... I was worried about this happening," Lucky looked off into space. "Dammit, I should have said something."

"Don't blame yourself," Weinberger said.

"I should have done more for that boy," Lucky said sharply.

"Maybe we all should have," Weinberger said.

"The last few months, Marvin was searching for Jesus," Lucky said. "I was trying to help him. Now, it's too late."

Weinberger put his hand on Lucky's shoulder. "If he was expressing a desire to know Him, you know that Jesus would have stopped him from going home—otherwise. We can't ever tell what happens at that last moment of life on this earth. Remember, Jesus told the thief on the cross that he would join Him in paradise. For that guy, it was the last moment. Maybe he's with Jesus right now."

Lucky twisted to look up at Weinberger.

"You know, I think you're right. Yes, sir, I think you're absolutely right."

The End

www.ingramcontent.com/pod-product-compliance
Lightning Source LLC
Chambersburg PA
CBHW051507260626
47162CB00008B/2860